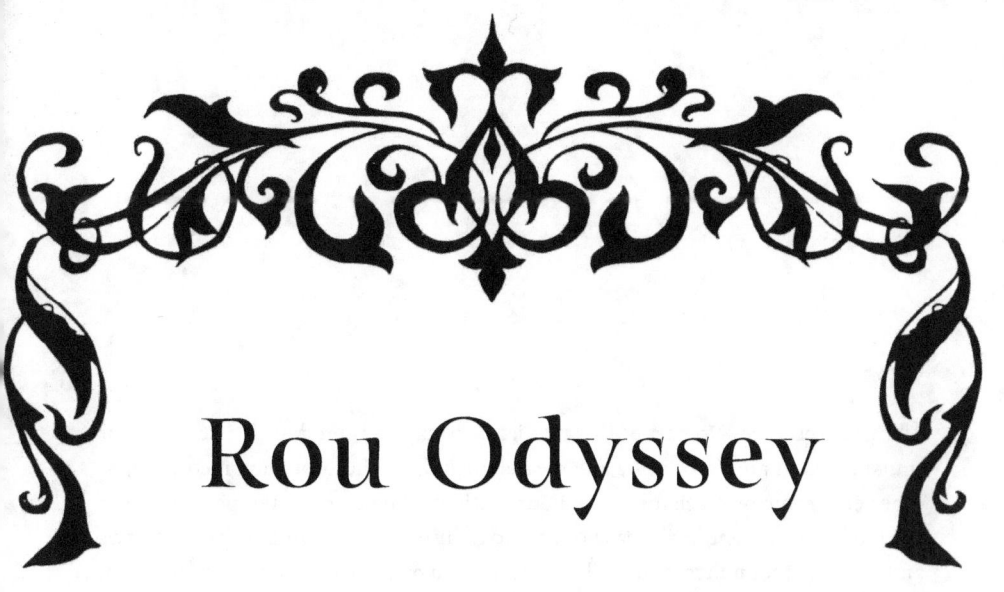

Rou Odyssey

BOOK I LOOK BEYOND

Kaiva Rose

MERCURY FALCON PRESS

Fargo, North Dakota

Kaiva Rose / Mercury Falcon Press
Printed in the United States of America 2019.
www.RouOdyssey.Com

Concept & Design by Kaiva Rose
Cover & Illustrations by Irina Kuzmina
Character Illustrations by Elizabeth Moore
Line Illustrations by Madelyn Kolenda
Layout Design by Taylor Montague & Douglas Williams

Rou Odyssey : Look Beyond / Kaiva Rose. -- 1st ed.
ISBN 978-1-7327911-0-7

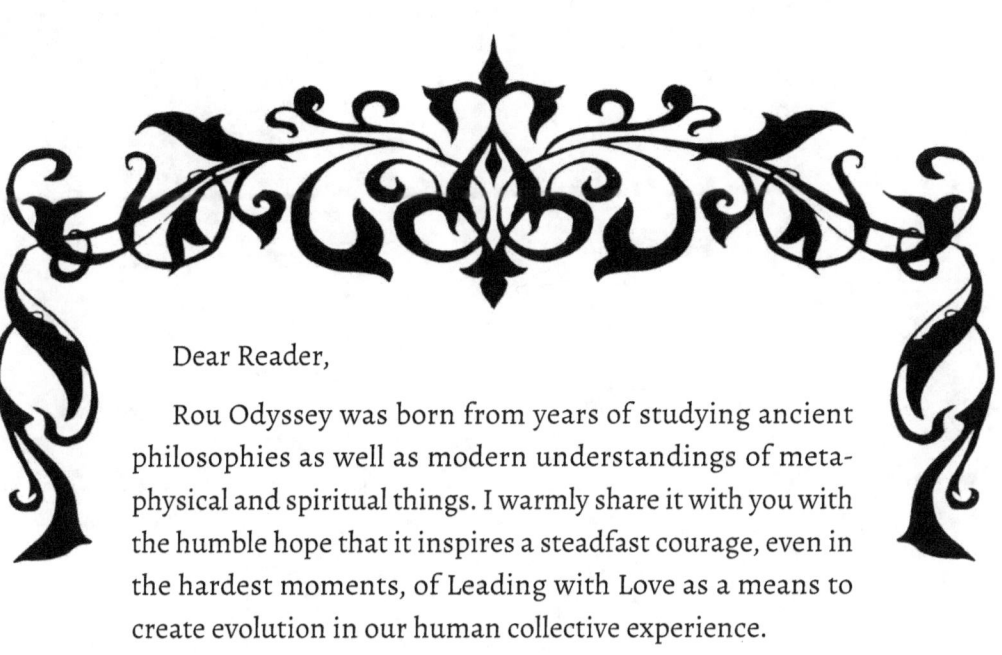

Dear Reader,

Rou Odyssey was born from years of studying ancient philosophies as well as modern understandings of metaphysical and spiritual things. I warmly share it with you with the humble hope that it inspires a steadfast courage, even in the hardest moments, of Leading with Love as a means to create evolution in our human collective experience.

Leading with Love means honoring yourself and others by offering compassion, understanding, and acceptance.

My hope for *Look Beyond*, the first book in the chronicles of Rou Odyssey, is to inspire people to lead from their heart's center and encourage those around them to do the same. In this way, one may feel inclined to embrace their own "specialness" as well as others'. For in truth, each individual has a divine essential purpose to the human collective, which deserves to be celebrated.

I invite you to enter a world where the pure-hearted lead the way and rise above the forces of evil in the most peculiar and magical ways.

Welcome to Rou.
Blessings,
Kaiva Rose

In dedication to all those who live love on the daily, may your compassion continue to transform the world and may you always feel the support and blessings all around you.

To my parents and my sister, I am honored to share this life journey with you. Your love and support is beyond this planet.

In loving memory of my grandmother Patricia, whose compassion continues to inspire me. For my family, friends and acquaintances, thank you for being you. Your eccentricities are truly inspiring. May today and all days meet you with love.

To all the people who have supported me on this journey with Rou Odyssey from screenplay to novel, I am sincerely grateful for your encouragement.

Blessings to the talented artists Irina Kuzmina, Madelyn Kolenda, and Elizabeth Moore for giving color and form to the elements of my vision. And to Kathrin Hutson at KLH CreateWorks for her keen eye in the editing process.

To the reader, may you experience the blessings and love all around you.

Contents

"Love all, trust a few, do wrong to none."

—WILLIAM SHAKESPEARE

Book I

DUST DEVILS DANCED upon the arid lands, spinning far into the horizon. The slithering cracks of dry ground spanned untold miles across the barren earth. Among spires decorating the landscape, steep hills of blowing sand shimmered with the reflective heat of a blazing-hot sun. All this was once colorful and flourishing but now drained of life. From the earth sprouted crooked skeleton trees like boney fingers, desperately reaching for rain that would never come— not here. Their long roots that had stretched far and wide were withered and shrunken away, dead upon the ground. Dry air rushed through the wasteland, carrying with it a howling wind that danced upon the earth, picking up clouds of sand to expose the contents buried beneath—piles of scrap and junk, cogs and screws and wheels galore laid bare by wind's chance. And beside them, ancient relics from long ago—golden trinkets and rusted weapons that never should have been forgotten. For but a moment, this collection of unearthed treasure glimmered in the sun's rays and basked in the warmth of the surface.

But soon, the wind howled again and carried the wasteland's drifting sands again to bury the past.

The wasteland ended only where it could not pass, at the foot of a great and distant mountain range. Craggy, jagged earth stood staunch and tall, as if it were a wall erected to hold off the desert's seemingly endless expansion. Standing below at the foot of the mountain range resided an iridescent dome, known as the Force Field, that nearly rivaled its stony neighbors. It was smooth on every side and emanated a softly glowing shimmer of vibrant blues and greens, violets and reds. Like a shield of prismatic mirrors, the Force Field reflected the blazing heat and light of the desert sun away from what lay within—secrets outsiders would never know or care to discover. The lawless, barren lands existing beyond the Force Field were sprinkled with rogues, ramblers, sorcerers, vagabonds, eccentric and lively people. But inside ... inside, they were of a different kind in a much safer place.

As it were, as it had come to be, the quaint village of Gangleton found its safety in the hands of the ever-respected Dignitaries. "We promise to protect Gangleton from all evils," they had recited so long ago. And with that single vow, the people of Gangleton never fathomed the idea of life beyond the dome. From wholesome to homogenous, the village and its people found safety under the glossy sheen of the Force Field created to keep out that evil. After setting up this high-tech form of protection, the Dignitaries tended to make their visits to Gangleton abrupt and short.

But as fate would have it, this visit had a different nature.

The howling wind of the wasteland blew louder, scattering sand and dirt into a surreptitious shroud that spread across the rolling, empty lands like a veil. From within it, the screech and clang of metal rang out from pumping apparatus. Dunes burst into billows of sand as surging treads thundered through the storm, smashing whatever artifacts and trinkets lay below their heavy, ceaseless advance. It was something like a tank and yet also unmistakably like an elephant—a mechanical elephant fashioned from ghostly-white iron and oily-black ingots. Every piece of the elephant-shaped contraption was an intricacy, forged with an uncanny and remarkable craftsmanship. Cogwheels and pistons hidden beneath the elephant's iron hide spun and pumped at vigorous speeds, creaking and whining with thrust and oil. Steam billowed from steel cylinders and copper columns running all along the contraption's back, leaving a long trail of thick smoke in its wake. Deep, treaded tracks bore into the desert as the apparatus moved with motorized efficiency, keeping to an expected and constant pace.

Upon the elephant machine's back rode a celebratory quintet—the Dignitaries themselves and their peculiar guest. Their eyes were set firmly ahead, their destination already decided. The five wore extravagant ensembles of waistcoats with tails and striped pants to match, each bearing their signature color, though purple was present on all to signify their status. Top hats and ornaments adorned their heads. They were an elegant view at first sight, a striking vision of the joy their visit would bring to this town. Onward they rode toward Gangleton and the Tower beneath the dome.

CHAPTER 1

Times Forgotten for Times Anew

INSIDE THE PRISMATIC dome surrounded by the endlessness of the barrens, below the protective shell of the Force Field, the quaint and rustic village of Gangleton resided. From one edge of the Force Field to the other stretched a verdant grassland studded with ample earthen greenery. A clear blue stream ran down from the neighboring mountains and along the village's edge. The stones filling its basin glistened with the sun's bright light. The water circled and spiraled all along the Force Field, reaching across the grassland and passing through a tall cherry orchard at the far end of the village.

Identical, half-timbered houses of various colors, each constructed with a doorway built into their slanted rooftops, filled the rest of the Force Field nearly to the brim. Every house was fitted with a painstakingly manicured and thoroughly trimmed front yard promising to impress even the most snobbish of onlookers. Brilliant flowerbeds bloomed in every color of the rainbow, each stem and petal raised with the utmost care. Vegetable gardens provided each family their own nourishment, different roots, stems, leaves, and seeds harvested for each season.

In front of one yellow house, the purple hue of cabbage heads stretched in long rows, while the neighboring pink house showed vibrant green carrot tops. Despite their differences, every yard had one identical trait—a pole firmly planted and proudly waving the Gangleton flag, which depicted a black raven holding a golden chain in its mouth against a dark-purple backdrop. Hundreds of these perfectly sized homes, fit for families of any number, were built in long, tiered circles spinning inward toward the center of the village. The colossal, circular township was connected by worn grass pathways weaving the village together into a revolving crossroads of flowers, bushes, trees, vegetables, and the fences connecting them all. At the center of it all, where every pathway in the village converged at a huge stone courtyard, a lone tower stood above all else within the Force Field.

The Cuckoo Clock Tower was by far the largest building in Gangleton, standing a full six stories tall amid the villagers' two-story houses. It was built from a special stone inaccessible by the villagers and unobtainable within the bounds of the Force Field. Decorative carvings and golden designs filled its frame with an ornate aesthetic. The Tower was a monolith of regal beauty, beaming brilliance in the otherwise quaint village. At its base, a large wooden stage had been built for presenting performances and making village announcements. The stage was fitted with a dark purple curtain suspended from the higher levels of the Tower and a spyglass with a megaphone attachment loud enough for the entire village to hear even from the farthest ends of the dome. Above the stage and halfway up the Tower, two doors were connected by a short rail track running through the Tower's shadowy interior. Above the rail track, the clock's giant glass face ticked with unceasing mechanical anticipation for the sound of the chime, its intermittent shifts sharp and audible from the stage below. Finally, above the clock face and at the highest point on the Tower was a small, elaborate balcony with a single, ominous doorway without a handle.

As the hands of the clock slid firmly into place, a mechanical whir emanated from within the Cuckoo Clock Tower but for a moment. The spinning of wheels, the turning of cogs, and the pumping of pistons all worked in unison without anyone to see. And as if each were a perfect reflection of the others, all the houses in Gangleton held within them a unison of actions occurring in perfect synchronicity and order.

—*Cuckoo*—

Every doorway built into the roofs of every Gangleton home sprang open dramatically, slamming against the wooden sides of the villagers' homes.

—*Dong*—

The Cuckoo Clock Tower's bells rang throughout Gangleton's conspicuously empty streets of the morning. Within their homes, at the sound of the bell and the opening of the roofs' doors, the villagers all set aside whatever activities had occupied them at the time and fell into a new routine.

—*Cuckoo*—

From the houses' open doors, groups of ravens emerged, nosily flapping their wings into the air. And with the ravens came the villagers, for the birds' tail feathers were long and bound to the black hair of every person in Gangleton. It was as if the villagers' hair had grown naturally from the flocks of birds above their heads, utterly indistinguishable from the silken feathers.

—*Dong*—

Just like the cogwheels guiding the hands of the clock to their inevitable destination, the ravens tirelessly flapped their wings and carried their attached villagers, one person at a time, down into their gardens.

—*Cuckoo*—

The men and older boys of each house came first, then the women and young ladies, and finally the children in order of age. Each member of every household wore mandarin-collared jackets with golden buttons. On every right breast pocket, a black raven pin connected a golden chain to a family emblem pin with three colored lines representing their chosen colors. Jackets too were dyed with the most important color of the three, creating a dazzling rainbow display floating out of windowed doorways and down into the dirt.

—*Dong*—

Once every member of every family had been set down in their front yards, the flocks of ravens curled up under their villager's long black hair for a well-deserved rest. Then the people of Gangleton set about their various jobs, as was their duty. The men moved throughout the garden, watering plants with measured dips of their hands, never sprinkling too much or too little. The women planted seeds in freshly dug holes and vacant spots in the garden, ensuring that every available space was being used to its utmost potential. The older boys and girls picked the vegetables ripe and ready to be eaten. And finally, when all else had been done, the children dug holes wherever they could, happily shoveling dirt with fitting abandon and youthful vigor.

But not all the villagers were so keen on their predetermined roles in Gangleton. While most of the cheery, bright-eyed citizens toiled away in their gardens, one young lady secretly covered the ravens atop her head with a raggedy old hat to block out the call of the clock and snuck her way through the spiraling cobblestone streets. Her name was Percilla, and her long, raven-black hair shone with a special shimmer uncommon among the dirt-covered, green-thumbed populace. She wore the standard Gangleton attire dyed with a magnificent maroon—her family's most specially chosen color.

The emblem pinned to her breast pocket was naturally maroon as well and superbly contrasted by a colorful combination of royal blue and ivory. Always carrying herself with a whimsical step, Percilla was a known rebel at the age of eighteen, often described unkindly by her elders as a hopeless troublemaker. She took to that title like a bee to a flower. And as such, it was no surprise she had a gift for not being found when it suited her—a talent she discovered was most useful when ignoring the call of the clock and the duties she did not care to perform. With graceful steps, she hid herself well, sneaking in and out of alleyways. Had anyone the inkling to look out past their gardens, they would have seen her; but of course, all the dedicated citizens of Gangleton were too focused on the work to be done inside their gardens to notice.

Percilla made her way across Gangleton, using all the short-cuts she'd learned, for this journey was one she'd taken more times than she could count. Though even with her most nimble movements, she was still later than she'd originally intended. She knew it wasn't suitable for anyone to be seen roaming Gangleton off schedule and attempted to reach her destination long before the Cuckoo Clock Tower's bell started its scheduled ringing, but circumstances had left her confined to her home longer than she would have liked. Regardless of it all, one last step out of another alleyway put Percilla squarely on the street of her grandmother's home.

Her grandmother Victoria was the reason she'd decided to skip today's routine schedule. As she entered the gates into her grandmother's yard, she took a full breath, and the smell of roses washed over her. This was the only routine she would ever entertain, for Victoria had the most abundant garden in all of Gangleton. Percilla admired the plots gracing the yard—beautiful flowers in full bloom with a perfect vegetable patch beside it. She always wondered how Victoria managed it when the woman swore she hardly spent that much time out there tending to the beds. After a brief moment of losing herself in the beauty, Percilla hurried up the ladder to the door on her grandmother's roof. As usual, the door was ajar, and she let herself inside.

"Percilla? You are late, my dear," Victoria hollered from out of sight.

"It was my garden. Had me all flown," Percilla said with a broad grin as she walked down the stairs to the main level of the house to join Victoria.

"As always," Victoria said, still out of Percilla's sight, though in this small room there wouldn't be anywhere to hide. Another might have questioned where Victoria was, but not Percilla. Without even a thought, she walked right into what appeared to be a broom closet. Stepping into the closet and beyond a hidden door at the back, Percilla found Victoria rustling around in her study.

Victoria was well into her nineties, making her one of the oldest living elders in Gangleton. She was an exceptionally classy woman who wore her royal-blue Gangleton attire with a refined elegance, rare even among the aristocratic community. It brilliantly bore all three colors of their family emblem—maroon, royal blue, and ivory. No matter where she went, she always wore an extraordinary hat. Among all the forbidden garments kept within her wardrobe, it was the only one she enjoyed publicly.

"You know, the people will talk if you continue to dig around in the dirt for anything other than planting," Victoria pointed out with a wink.

"As if you can talk," Percilla replied. "You're the one with all these... things." She motioned to all the relics filling the space.

Victoria's study was a large wooden room hidden behind a wall inside the broom closet underneath the staircase, with only a single entrance. If there was one thing Percilla could say for certain about her grandmother, it was that she knew how to keep things well hidden. The damask wallpaper interior of the study was dyed with a magnificent shade of green and dimly lit by the soft glow of a magical ivory light. Everywhere, tall bookshelves were filled to the brim with tomes both historical and magical in nature, detailing the vast history of Gangleton and what came before it. Old, dusty maps, photos, and newspaper clippings hung from every wall, most of them from or about places Percilla had never seen, been to, or heard of before. How her grandmother had collected so much contraband she didn't dare ask, for she knew the story could very well last longer than there were hours in the day.

At the far end of the room, a tiny wardrobe concealed clothing not anything like the Gangleton attire. From one curiosity to the next, her grandmother's desk was littered with magical and historical trinkets from times long ago, none of which Percilla could understand or even begin to describe. Next to the door, an ancient calendar hung from the wall. On its circular face, a red rune glowed, marking today's date.

Victoria chuckled lightly as Percilla followed her to the finely set table where two intricately painted teacups awaited.

"Victoria, why is Gangleton so stodgy? I swear, one second off routine would have them flown all day."

Victoria sighed heavily as she poured Percilla a cup of hibiscus tea from a considerably impressive height. "Oh, my dear, Gangleton wasn't always so dreary. It used to be genuine, innocent, joyful..." She paused, as if contemplating whether or not she should say anything else at all. "Just like in Rou."

"Rou?" Percilla asked.

"Yes. Rou. The home of our ancestors."

"You mean we're not from here? That's not surprising." Percilla let out a silent laugh. "We don't really fit in, do we?"

"This is true," Victoria replied. "None of us fit in here."

"Well, go on." Percilla found herself eagerly wanting to hear more, which was unlike her when Victoria usually prattled on about the olden days.

"It's time, Percilla. It's time you know."

Percilla leaned closer. "Time for what?"

"The truth. Let me tell you the tale my mother told me and would recite for all Gangleton as a reminder of our purpose." Victoria settled into her high-backed chair and wet her mouth with a sip of tea. "Do you remember the tale of the Dignitaries and their reasons for keeping Gangleton inside the Force Field?"

"No..." Percilla frowned. "Why do you keep giving me that look?"

"Percilla, you are my only grandchild," Victoria said solemnly. "The only limb left to hold the cherry of our history."

"Now you're flying," Percilla responded with a sarcastic wave of her hand.

Victoria's eyes narrowed, and she groaned. "If you weren't so unique, I would think what I'm about to tell you would be lost forever. Please, ready yourself for what I'm about to sound to you," she said, suddenly very serious as she smoothed her jacket and straightened in her chair to tell the tale of ancient times. "Our ancestors came from the mystical land called Rou, a utopian jungle metropolis. Hidden beneath the shield of the guardian deities, it was a pristine and luscious jungle. Rainbow mists filled the valleys where magnificent waterfalls kissed the rivers of pure, crystal-blue water. There thrived plants, flowers, and birds of all colors and forms only one's imagination could conceive. And in the skies, islands floated high above with the most breathtaking views of the Euphoria. Within the depths of this jungle, laced in vines, were the immaculate structures of Rou's civilization, as much a part of this place as if they had grown from the very soil. And our ancestors were not a sight to be overlooked, either. They decorated themselves in luxurious, flowing silk gowns adorned with golden jewelry and gemstones of all colors and styles, draping headpieces, pendants of pure essence, rings cut of the highest quality." She took a deep breath as she ran her hand down her own silk garment with a knowing smile.

"Were they like your gowns?" Percilla asked.

"Hardly. Theirs were much, much finer." She sipped her tea again and continued. "Their delicately crafted instruments played harmoniously with the sounds of nature. The people danced and sang. They lived in a true Euphoria."

Percilla sat entranced by her grandmother's tale, hanging on the edge of every word and barely sipping her tea. With each word, the passion built in Victoria's voice and surged through her lips. The old woman's eyes seemed to shimmer as the memories of their family's lineage were put into spoken word for Percilla alone.

"For many a growth cycle, the guardians' shield protected Rou from the evils of the outside world. It was the community's devotion to love, acting as many in body but one in mind, that provided the guardians their strength. The evils eventually made one final attempt to annihilate Rou but instead brought about their own demise. The dark times had finally come to an end, and as the golden dragons flew across the skies to release the shield, every one of our ancestors celebrated. The guardians believed it time for the people of Rou to once again recirculate into the world. A new growth cycle had begun, and the lifeless land was ready to live love once more."

"Wait, dragons?" Percilla could not help but interject. It was almost too fantastical to believe. "As in actual dragons?"

Victoria nodded. "Dragons. And that is only the beginning."

Outside Victoria's home, another found his time better spent not gardening like everyone else. Only nineteen, Vahn had become somewhat of a recluse in Gangleton. His lean physique, shaggy black hair, and light blue eyes accentuated by his emerald-green Gangleton attire made him ruggedly handsome. Unlike Percilla, Vahn's passion for rebellion was fueled by a fiery intensity and a core purpose within his being. He wore his attire with disdain and carried with him no trinkets or other articles of clothing. His uniform was never tidy, constantly spotted with dirt from what little time he spent in his garden. But he kept his family's emblem pin of emerald-green, purple, and a striking silver spotless and pristine. He always seemed to sport a dour frown, except when he could escape from the rest of Gangleton into the Cherry Orchard and the secret places many of the docile villagers dared not venture. In recent times, he had preferred the latter.

Like some sort of guardian, the young man watched with his eyes peeled wide, peering through a small, handheld spyglass into the wasteland beyond the Force Field. At this time in the morning, the rest of the villagers watered their plants, tended to their seeds, and dug their holes, contentedly performing their duties. But those were not Vahn's duties—not for as long as he alone understood the danger surrounding Gangleton. A danger threatening to end everything good still contained within the Force Field's barrier.

He moved the spyglass around, observing his neighbors close and far, so busy doing what they were told to do. As he watched them, he stepped graciously along the roof of his home until he reached its very edge. From his perch to the west of the town square, he could barely see anything in the Barrens beyond the dome. If he wanted to keep his eyes trained on the village's outskirts, he needed to be somewhere higher. Vahn dropped down from the slanted roof of his home into the garden below, the blow softened to a gentle jostle by the wings of his ravens. The birds made not even the slightest sound as Vahn's feet crunched rotten stems and fallen leaves littering the unkempt and messy front yard. Where vegetables and flowers were supposed to grow, weeds and moss and other wild plants sprouted in their place, climbing up the walls of Vahn's house and the fence at the edge of what could scarcely be called a garden.

"Rather quiet today, I see," he said to his flock as he pressed opened the gate leading into Gangleton's twisted streets. The birds remained still and silent perched atop his shoulders. It had been some time since Vahn had last gathered with his friends in the Cherry Orchard. And lately, he thought of his avian companions as perhaps his only friends. Some measure of autonomy remained within the birds even through their bond with him. Unlike the other ravens in Gangleton, they would not be as easily swayed away from his command.

Vahn cared little about being caught in the open during gardening hours. When he passed through the streets, he did so without any pretense of deception or stealth. He was bold and did not worry about what the rest of the villagers thought of him. Oftentimes, those who knew him, and even Vahn himself, pondered the idea of his rebelliousness having passed down his family line as a genetic trait. His grandfather had been the same way at his age, after all, always heading off to forbidden places and discovering things not meant for the simple folk of Gangleton. And because of that, most everyone in Gangleton had grown used to seeing Vahn walk about with a prideful, uncaring strut whenever it suited him. On this day, that same prideful, uncaring strut carried him to the Cuckoo Clock Tower at the center of the village. He passed into the large courtyard and approached the side of the tall structure, then lifted himself onto it.

Vahn climbed the Tower with a natural ease. His strong arms and fingers pulled him up to the next loose stone jutting out from the otherwise smooth surface. He ascended quickly and fearlessly, knowing his ravens would catch him if he fell. When he reached the middle of the Tower, he planted his feet aboard the rail track running along its edge and brought the antique spyglass once more to his eye. At the end rim of the glass, a magical rune had been carved into the metal grip from which a soft red glow emanated. At first, the lens showed him only a reflection of a blue sky in the Force Field's prismatic barrier. But as the magic rune on his spyglass lit with energy, the reflection in the Force Field faded, replaced by a view of the dry and decrepit wasteland beyond.

A child's voice rose from the center stage at the Cuckoo Clock Tower's base. "What are you doing up there?"

Vahn looked down at the boy Hect standing beneath him on the stage, gazing up at him in curiosity. At only ten years of age, this boy was the Dignitaries' chosen child. For his considerable loyalty and promised talent, he was afforded special privileges and duties exceedingly uncommon throughout Gangleton's long history. Vahn knew Hect well, though not because he wanted to; Hect approved of very few things Vahn did, and the child made sure Vahn knew as much.

"Sights are better up here," Vahn shouted down to the stage as he once again peered through his spyglass, trying to ignore the boy.

"You're not allowed up there," Hect hissed.

Vahn sneered, ignoring the petulant child. There were more important matters at hand.

Through the spyglass, Vahn could only see endless miles of sand and dead trees. The wasteland was empty. But still, he kept watch, for in his heart remained the anxiety he'd known since the day he was born. For a long moment in which time passed slowly, there was nothing at all. The wasteland lay still and undisturbed, like a painting bordering the Force Field's prismatic horizon. And then, stealthily, almost unnoticeable in the harsh winds, a thin pillar of steam rose from behind the gathering of hoodoos. Vahn felt his sneer fading, replaced by a heart-thumping fear as out of the canyon came a mechanical elephant, five riders and their companion aboard its back. The contraption pulled itself along at a steady pace, slowly but surely nearing Gangleton. They were close.

"Did you hear me?" Hect asked as he stomped his foot against the wooden flooring of the stage.

"You're not really doing your gig too well," Vahn shouted as he leapt from the stage, pointing at the Force Field with an extended arm. "Your masters are coming." His ravens floated him to the stage as the Cuckoo Clock Tower's doors sprang open.

The Cuckoo called across the valley, the Tower's bells tolled in response, and all of Gangleton rose in surprise.

Vahn noted the bafflement in young Hect's wide eyes and open mouth, then the boy ran for the spyglass at the front of the stage and peered through it. When he touched the rim of the instrument, a light glowed from the runes on its surface. Hect pulled away from the spyglass to meet Vahn's gaze, his mouth opening and closing, as if he couldn't find the words he wanted. Vahn knew the boy had seen the same thing—the Dignitaries were nearly at Gangleton's gates. Hect reached around the spyglass to grab the turning crank of the megaphone attached to the same polished wooden podium. His arm pumped furiously as he spun the crank's wheel, and a shrill, mechanical shriek filled the village.

If Percilla leaned any closer to Victoria, she would fall out of her chair. "Tell me more. What happened next? Where did the people of Rou go?"

"The elders were called to the Temple of the Timeless upon an island in the sky overlooking all of Rou. The Timeless Sages presented a large offering plate crafted of seashell and set it before them all. And on that plate were the most precious of all our artifacts. The Eyes of Rou. Seven gold-encased gemstones filled with Rou's very essence, one of every color in the rainbow. Our ancestors were divided into seven communities, each with a family designated to protect their own Eye of Rou, the only keys capable of returning them to their homeland in times of darkness."

"You're flown, right?" Percilla asked in amazement.

"Not in the slightest," Victoria replied before clearing her throat. "Our ancestors went beyond Rou's borders, celebrating the rebirth of our people. The seven elders had been chosen by the Timeless Sages to lead their communities forth, each of them responsible for twenty different families. All were brightly dressed, holding parasols, walking beside colorful, covered wagons, riding flying carpets or golden chariots. Some even took to the sky in colorful air balloons. The people sang, walked, danced, flipped, skipped, twirled, laughed, and smiled. Each of the seven took a different route across the Barrens. They left their lives within the thriving metropolis of Rou, bringing with them their joyful past and their hope to sow the seeds of love in a place where nothing lived. And yet the sky remained magnificently colored. Our ancestors sang this song as they departed their home and split into seven:

From the Gates of Rou into the open lands.
Fertile soil waits for us to plant the seeds of love.
From the Gates of Rou into the open lands, we part from
those we love to make a better world.
No matter where we are or how we sing our song, together
we are family, forever we are one.

From the Gates of Rou into the open lands.
Evil may beckon us to take another stand. Provoking fear
infects the soul to become a slave for them.
Look beyond their emptiness and we will carry on.
From the Gates of Rou into the open lands.
We spread our love to all the world."

Victoria settled back in her chair with a soft smile. The words of such a song hovered in the air between them. When a shrill shout echoed from outside, the old woman jumped to her feet.

"No," she gasped. "They're early."

"The Dignitaries?" Percilla asked. She'd never seen her grandmother so ruffled.

"Our time is much shorter than I first assumed," Victoria muttered. "It is most certainly your time, my dear. Most certainly indeed."

Vahn stepped off the edge of the stage, and his ravens lowered him gracefully to the ground as the quiet town of Gangleton burst into a bustling hub. "Thank you," he murmured to his ravens. "Take a rest." He peered around, watching the villagers scatter to and fro in confusion and panic. "Dignitaries. What do they want this time?"

He walked around the stage, stopping every few feet to raise his spyglass and track the great, mechanical beast drawing ever closer. Then he swung the instrument around to view the panicking town before Hect's shouting hurt his ears, and he rushed off into the streets.

"The Dignitaries are approaching!" Hect shouted into the spyglass' megaphone attachment with an excited desperation. His voice traveled throughout Gangleton and echoed off the walls of the dome. "The Dignitaries are coming! The Dignitaries are on their way!"

The Cuckoo cried again from the Tower's open doors, followed by the second deep gong of the bell.

Every man, woman, and child had frozen at once, then immediately burst back into action, dropping their shovels and baskets as their ravens took them into their homes. They moved in an urgent yet orderly fashion. Some of the children looked relieved to end their shoveling duties early, while others stared with wide eyes at the scattered movement all around them. The adults, however, smiled when they heard Hect's announcement over the megaphone and the chime of the Cuckoo Clock Tower.

Vahn walked through the streets as everyone else prepared themselves with perfect precision for the arrival of the honored quintet. He scoffed again, shaking his head.

A third cry and ringing bell rang from the Tower.

Inside their homes, every villager adorned themselves with striped sashes of their family's chosen colors and exchanged their casual footwear with pointed slippers of exaggerated length, which curled at the toes, meant just for this special occasion. Mothers rubbed a clear paste of mashed roots onto their children's teeth, the bitter taste proven to keep them smiling. Fathers and young men donned fancy hats distinguishing their status. Ladies blushed their cheeks with pollen harvested from the reddest and brightest flowers in their family gardens. Children of all ages gathered the most beautiful and richly scented flowers they could find in specially prepared baskets. If they had time, they washed as much dirt from their bodies as they could and brushed their Gangleton attire into as presentable a state of cleanliness as possible. When everything was ready, each family gathered by their front gate and waited with silent grins.

Vahn passed several of these yards. One mother leaned over her fence and scowled at him. "What are you doing? Get to your house, now. They're coming!"

Vahn gave a mocking bow before his ravens took flight and carried him away, but not to his house. "Always someone trying to tell me where to be. I go where I want."

His feet touched the roof of a house within an empty yard—Percilla's house. He knew well she would never be found outside at a time like this. Her house, however, sat just far enough from the gates of Gangleton, he could spy on the celebration without being seen. Vahn pulled his spyglass from inside his jacket pocket again to look.

"What's our countdown?" he whispered to the ravens.

He adjusted the spyglass and stared out across the Barrens. At first, he saw nothing, but then the rune glowed upon his instrument, and the Dignitaries appeared, right at the gates lending passage into the Force Field.

The red rune on the ancient calendar flared brighter, and Victoria frowned at it, cursing under her breath. "I was sure we had more time," she said. "Why have they come early?"

"The Dignitaries?" Percilla asked. "Did you know they were coming?"

"Yes, but that doesn't matter. You must know the whole tale before it's too late."

"Fly it at me, then."

Victoria sighed. "Love, I know you think what I say means nothing, but—"

"No, no," Percilla interrupted, eager to convince her grandmother. "Truly, I listen to every word."

Victoria fixed her granddaughter with a determined gaze tinged with concern. "Then please do not stop, because there is much you need to know."

Percilla nodded.

"Times were genuine," Victoria said. "Passionate. Grandmother said they danced the entire way to this valley. But even as strong as our ancestors were, the evils hadn't disappeared entirely. They lurked around the Barrens as black smoke, infecting our ancestors with their malevolent sting. It is said our healers used crystal wands to remove the black smoke pouring from the noses and ears of those infected by the darkness. The elders used these same crystal wands to raise a protective ward around their companions. To fend off the evils approaching in terrifying black clouds the best they could."

Percilla gulped, and a shiver raced down her spine. Dragons were one thing, but a wicked black smoke was something she'd rather not consider.

"Then one day, Gangelton appeared." Victoria walked around her study as she spoke, moving books and picking up boxes, as if it were impossible to keep still. "Our ancestors came upon the river leading to grasslands with a luscious cherry orchard filled with ravens. The people danced and ran toward the river to drink, to the Cherry Orchard to eat. Out of respect for the ravens who inhabited the land, the elders offered a golden chain from Rou to symbolize the strength that would come of their bond. In the days that followed, our ancestors cut the tall grass from Gangleton and erected colorful tents for homes, planters, gatherers, musicians, washers, cooks, tailors, magicians, and most importantly of all, historians. All of them no more than ten skips away from the Cherry Orchard. When they were hungry, they picked cherries, and when they were thirsty, they carried water from the river. In those times, people only had one purpose. To live in harmony. Their intuition was reason enough for everything they did, just as a cherry tree does not need to be told when to bloom or why. My grandmother used to recite the story of Rou in this Cherry Orchard, the very same place in which you and your friends lie about all day."

Victoria walked across the study toward her desk, more driven than Percilla had ever seen her. Then the old woman lifted an elegant hand and pressed her palm against the wall. "Fris-tah opren-tee." The words echoed around them.

And when they faded into the nether, a sky-blue glow emanated from within the wall above the desk. A prismatic rune formed over the place where Victoria's hand met the wall and circled left and right, as if it were a lock being picked. Then, much to Percilla's shock, the blue Eye of Rou emerged from the wall, shifting through the green damask wallpaper like it was water. The blue gemstone was even more beautiful than Victoria had described, its every surface glittering with the room's reflective light. The essence of Rou inside shone with the intensity of a star encased within what was purer than any light Percilla had ever seen. Her grandmother's words had been hard to believe, but this gemstone proved the truth of her tale.

Percilla gasped and nearly fell out of her chair. "What else digs in these walls?"

"Listen, Percilla," Victoria stated with solemn urgency. She clasped the Eye of Rou to her chest, allowing it to leave the safety of her grasp only so Percilla could see it with her own two eyes. "This is an Eye of Rou. It is our only connection to our true home."

"You *weren't* squawking."

"Of course I wasn't. Our family has been the trusted guardians of Gangleton's Eye of Rou for generations. My mother gave it to me when she passed, and—"

"Victoria!" The shout burst from Percilla's mouth only because she was too awed to say anything else. And more than that, she could only imagine what her grandmother had been about to say.

"Please, love. We haven't much time."

Percilla wanted to argue but restrained herself and nodded. "I'm listening."

"You'll have to do more than that soon enough."

Once the Dignitaries entered Gangleton, Vahn migrated from Percilla's roof to perch on his own. He looked through his spyglass once more to study the quintet.

"Still wearing the clown ensemble," he muttered. "My, Lyken, you're looking creepier than ever. How do you maintain such slimy hair? And you, Franc, still as staunch as usual. Drendle." He sighed, clicking his tongue. "Poor Drendle. The newest Dignitary and yet just as dim-looking as your first day. Oh, forgive me, Nylz." He shifted his gaze again. "I best not forget the fiercest of them all. You're just so cute and petite. How could I have missed you? Ons, you mysterious character. What are all those apparatuses for? Don't worry. I'll understand you soon enough. I know I'm close. For now, I must bid you all ado."

When he rose from another mocking bow, his ravens took flight and gently lowered him to his front yard.

While everyone else waited with forced glee and the coalesced perfume of hundreds of flowers hung strongly in the morning air, Hect remained on the Tower's stage, attended to by a younger companion holding an accordion. As his companion stretched a long, protracted note on the instrument, Hect took a deep breath and proudly sang into the megaphone. With a wistful harmony, he followed the rhythm of the younger boy's accordion and sang the song which beckoned the arrival of his masters and honored their esteemed presence.

"When the Dignitaries come, Gangleton's
quite a different place.
They come to check on us and see that we are safe.
They swore an oath to protect our village from anger and
from greed.
Their honor is their service to us and so abide their laws.
We raise up all our flags at once and polish all our flaws.
We dress ourselves with the colors of our tribe to remind
them where our history resides.
Even the children must put on a face. Everyone must smile.
The flowers are to show our grace and gratitude to them,
for the Dignitaries want it that way.
They want us at our best."

When Hect finished, parade music emanated from a wound-up gramophone atop the elephant contraption, and all the villagers whirled into a joyful dance. The Dignitaries passed through Gangleton, each one of them waving at their audience. The steam-powered elephant towered over the villagers, standing as tall as any of the identical houses in the village. Its treads rolled along the stones, loosing pebbles from cracks in the path and shaking the stems of nearby plants. Children tossed handfuls of flowers toward the machine and its riders, shouting, "Hooray! Hooray! The Dignitaries have arrived!" and grinning all the while.

The exalted group could now be seen from everywhere in the town—five and one, the Dignitaries and their traveling companion. The mere contrast in their clothing was enough to clearly divide them. Of the six, one wore little more than unkempt, soiled rags, barely passable as clothing. A shaggy beard obscured most of the man's face. The other five riders, however, boasted a proper wardrobe almost ceremonial in style. They all wore dark-purple pants with stripes of different colors and dark-purple waistcoats with tails, save for one in a floor-length jacket instead. Their lavish attire far outshone the quaint jackets of the Gangleton villagers, worn from daily use and stained with dirt from their gardens.

A handsome man with a derby hat stood at the front of the contraption, steering the elephant through the spiraling city streets. Behind him, a petite woman in a top hat sat with the group's gramophone between her legs, and two more men sat together at the rear of the mechanical elephant. The one boasting an eerie complexion was tall and thin, carefully pouring a pink liquid from a jar into the spout of a small cannon on the machine's back. His companion, refined and ornamented with a top hat upon which dark goggles perched, peered through a monocle with a magnifying lens attachment over his left eye and carried a fanciful wooden cane. Finally, at the center of the five Dignitaries stood a woman with a top hat taller than the rest. She stared straight ahead with a stern gaze, exuding an aura of absolute authority.

Then the mechanical elephant and its six riders passed by Vahn's front yard. His eyes met several of the quintet's gazes.

Others around Vahn smiled, but he did not—at least, not at first. When the moment was right, he burst through his front gate, whistling and calling, celebrating along with the other citizens but louder than anyone else. Several Dignitaries glanced at him sideways, but the procession did not stop. It wasn't really them Vahn wanted to see, anyway. No, it was their silent companion with them. And just before they continued too far out of his sight, the sixth rider locked eyes with him, and Vahn knew exactly what would become of this man.

As the others pressed on behind the procession to follow it to the stage, Vahn and his ravens returned to his rooftop, where he again brought the spyglass to his eye.

The whole of Gangleton followed the mechanical elephant's parade through the streets. The cannon atop the massive contraption rumbled with a mechanized whir. In a loud explosion, pink glitter shot from the cannon and scattered across the dancing villagers below. Children applauded and giggled, eyes sparkling against the wondrous sight.

Vahn lowered his spyglass, then raised it again, but he was too far away. "Take me closer," he requested, and his ravens carried him to another rooftop, then another and another, flying low enough not to be noticed by the Dignitaries. They moved through alleys and back roads and finally lowered him onto the ledge of a roof right at the edge of the square, with a perfect view of the stage.

The elephant had just come to a stop beside the Tower, from which a drawbridge descended to rest against the machine's metal back. As the crowd approached, fireworks burst from the sides of the stage, sending an explosion of color throughout the sky.

"Enough with the show," Vahn grumbled. "What is it you're here to do? What is our threat? Tell me." He strengthened his grip on the spyglass, waiting.

The Dignitaries had all walked into the Tower, but now they stepped out to the top balcony. To the villagers' surprise, a mechanical whir sounded from beneath the stage, and a trap door sprang open from the stage's wooden floor. Low and behold, the Dignitaries' ragged companion, sitting in a sparkling barber's chair, rose from beneath the stage on a lifting platform, still dressed in his filthy rags and buried beneath a mound of unwashed facial hair. A previously unseen crew of men burst from behind the stage's purple curtain. Barbers and tailors set about to wash, groom, measure, and finely tune the ragged man, who sat there in a daze, as if mesmerized by some hex. Scissors snipped, tape twirled, and razors shaved in a flurry of precise motion before the man was hidden behind another smaller curtain. Vahn rolled his eyes at the spectacle.

In mere moments, the curtain was removed, and the man stood there, hardly recognizable. His face was now clean-shaven and his skin cleansed of dirt and grime. What's more, his old and dirtied rags had been abandoned for Gangleton attire, which bore the colors of a brand new family crest. The man bowed to the villagers and leapt from the stage, joining them in their dance with a smile on his face.

"Just as I suspected," Vahn muttered. "And oh, what's this? A new family emblem? Never seen his kind in Gangleton."

From the sidelines, Vahn watched the stranger with a skeptical frown. The celebration would continue in earnest until the sun set over the prismatic horizon. When dark finally came and the sky grew black, the villagers would return to their homes, and the five riders would disappear into the shadows of the Cuckoo Clock Tower.

Vahn took it all in with an anxious wariness until he could stand the sight no longer. "Take me home, ravens. We haven't much time."

"Times are stranger now than they have ever been," Victoria said, breaking the silence. They had remained in her study as the hours of the day passed and evening finally fell, hardly saying a word to each other; the seriousness of the situation weighed heavily on them both. "There is no telling when I might go. I need you to promise me that you will protect this with your life."

"Victoria, I don't..." Percilla did not yet know how to process any of this. She never imagined she would have to take on such a responsibility or that one day, her beloved grandmother would no longer be with her. Or even that she could be any more than a rebel playing music with her confidantes in a homogenous little village beneath a force field.

"You must," Victoria insisted, taking a breath to clearly say more. Then a strange knock came at the front door of the old woman's home.

Both Percilla and Victoria jumped at the noise and swung their heads around toward the study door. "Visitors at this time of night?" Percilla wondered aloud.

"Quiet," Victoria whispered, studying her granddaughter's gaze. Another rap at the door spurred the old woman into action. "Quickly. You must get out of here and on home." She returned the Eye of Rou to its place within the wall with the whispered words that echoed through the study. "Hism loc-ton." With a flick of her wrist, the prismatic lock over the wall circled back into place and sealed shut. The runes brightened a little, then faded completely.

As soon as the Eye of Rou was secure, Victoria wasted no time pushing Percilla out of her study and up to the front door of her home. The careful old woman placed herself between Percilla and the door and quickly lifted a series of latched locks above the wooden handle. Slowly, Victoria pushed open the door, which screeched against its old hinges, then peered through the small crack. Then she opened it wider, and Percilla saw there was no one at the door at all.

"Go, love. *Go*," Victoria whispered into Percilla's ear, practically pushing her through the door opened just wide enough for the girl to exit.

Percilla climbed down the ladder and dropped into the shadow of her grandmother's garden. She opened the gate in the front yard and turned right onto the street.

Victoria watched her granddaughter unlock the gate, then looked around again to be sure all was as it should be. She did not expect the figure emerging around a bend in the road, who looked up to instantly meet the old woman's gaze. The Dignitary's eyes widened in surprise, then narrowed, and her pace slowed. Her features remained as stern and rigid as ever, the small spyglass strapped to her belt above aqua-striped pants swinging gently against her thigh. Franc, the leader of the Dignitaries, had found them.

"Good evening, Franc. Welcome back." Victoria forced the words through her lips as if they were sludge, feigning a smile through her shock. From the corner of her eye, she saw Percilla had paused just outside the gate, frozen now to see Franc coming their way.

"Evening, madam," Franc replied. Even that simple greeting hinted at some underlying purpose. The Dignitary's eyes wandered down the street toward Percilla, whose terrified gulp rose loud enough for even Victoria to hear.

The old woman lifted her arm and waved at her granddaughter. "Percilla, will you please join me for tea again tomorrow? I am so proud of your garden. You have a unique talent!"

Percilla turned slowly, looking up at Victoria with a frown until she seemed to realize what her grandmother hoped she would do. "Okay, Victoria. Love you!" Then the girl took off at a brisk pace down the street. Victoria kept waving until Percilla had completely disappeared from view.

Franc didn't seem particularly curious; she didn't say another word as she continued down the road past Victoria's home. So the old woman bid the Dignitary a good evening again and slowly closed her front door. Breathing a sigh of relief, she turned to see a raven perched atop the gramophone in the main room. The bird operated the device with just one of its feet, and the warbling first notes of the brass instrumental "Bella Ciao" filtered through the house.

Victoria's eyes widened at the lilting music now heard only by the raven and herself.

CHAPTER 2

Secrets for All

NIGHT SETTLED IN as Percilla weaved through darkened streets, the worn grass beneath her feet lit only
by the moon and starlight. Although Victoria had probably
thought Percilla would return home immediately, the girl had
different plans. She headed toward the Cherry Grove, where
the moon beckoned her to receive the messages of her ancestors. Tonight, it was full and bright for the first time in a long
while, just as her friend Sphan had predicted. This came as no
surprise to Percilla; Sphan had an excellent teacher, after all.

From her grandmother's home, the quickest way to the
Cherry Orchard was through the Gangleton Graveyard near the
center of town. And so Percilla found herself traveling down
one of the oldest and most worn grass paths in the village.
The moonlight cut through the thick fog guiding her through
the gates of the Graveyard. Long rows of colorful gravestones
marked by the emblems of their families studded the path
before her. On most graves, fresh flowers or the remains of old,
fallen petals had been left as signs of respect and remembrance.

Some graves, however, held no tokens from the living; not every person in Gangleton left behind a family to remember them.

An unnatural sadness seemed to permeate the Graveyard tonight. Most of those buried had been born in Gangleton and died in Gangleton. Almost all of them had never seen the world outside the Force Field for themselves or heard the tales of Rou and their ancestors. They had never known the possibility of a life beyond this quaint little grassland village. That was the saddest thought of all. Perhaps Victoria would die in this place as well, never knowing the majesty and beauty of Rou as she had described it.

Just as Victoria's grandmother had passed down the secrets of their family to her daughter Bianca, who in turn had given the knowledge to Victoria, Percilla's grandmother had kept the tales alive. Percilla wondered if, one day, she might pass them down to the next in her family. Her defiant spirit rejected that fate, but she had neither the courage nor the notion to defy the Dignitaries and pass through the Force Field. She plucked the anxious thoughts from her mind and hurried through the thick fog to the other side of the graveyard.

Right before she stepped back into the village streets, she noticed someone rummaging through the dirt in the Graveyard and realized it was Vahn. She quickly adjusted her course and headed toward him.

Vahn hunched over as far as he could beside the small gravestone, hoping that would help him remain unnoticed. He slowly passed his palms over the dirt, which lifted on its own to reveal what he'd come to retrieve—an ancient book hidden beneath the earth. Delicately, he brushed the dirt from the tome, which he placed in his coat pocket. Just as he lifted his hand again to return the dirt, a voice sounded behind him.

"What's good, Vahn?"

Vahn jumped but recognized Percilla's voice. Relieved that it was only her, he stood and turned swiftly around. "Didn't feel you coming. I'm just tending to my grandfather," he said, being sure to put himself between Percilla and the hole he had created.

"That's sweet," Percilla said. She peered around his legs, apparently trying to get a better look at the gravestone. "He was a great leader for us, wasn't he? I can't imagine what Gangleton would have been like without him and the other elders like him. I wish I could have been old enough to join them when they were around."

"Yeah, he was a special man," Vahn replied. "Tending his grave is the least I can do." He held his hand over his breast pocket. "I just have to place one last item." This gave him an excuse to kneel again, which he turned to do. He glanced over his shoulder to see Percilla respectfully looking away.

That was all he needed. With one hand, he dug in his pockets for the small silver button he'd found earlier. With the other, he returned the earth into the hole he'd dug, the dirt spilling back into place without Vahn ever touching it. Then he quickly brushed his hand on his pants and placed the silver button on the grave. "There," he announced. "All finished." He regained his feet, smiling to himself, knowing Percilla had not seen a thing. "What flies you here?"

"I was making my way to the Cherry Orchard."

"Still hanging out with the crew?"

"Of course," Percilla replied, eyes wide with what looked like surprise at the question. "They're the only ones I trust besides Victoria." She paused for a moment. "And you."

"Sure," Vahn said, offering a little shrug he hoped might hide his embarrassment. "I can relate to that."

"Vahn..." The girl hesitated only for a moment. "If you had a secret so powerful that even telling one person could put a whole culture at risk, even though you're not really sure what the thing at risk is because you've never seen it, would you tell anyone?"

Vahn blinked rapidly and cocked his head. He hadn't expected something so serious out of her so suddenly. "You have something you want to share?"

"I don't know," she replied, avoiding eye contact. "I mean, yes, but I don't think I'm allowed to."

Vahn chuckled. "You're funny." He looked Percilla in the eyes. "Share your secrets with me, and I may just do the same."

"You have secrets?" Percilla asked, eagerly searching his eyes for answers.

"Not for long," Vahn said with a smirk. "See you, Percilla." He started on his way but turned back toward her with a smirk.

"Oh, and if you haven't already started working with the ancestors beyond healing yourself, you probably need to put this concern of yours to them. There is more to the portal being open than just cleansing your energy. Just ask. They will hear you and respond. Trust me. What do you think happened to me? Ask them to show all of you more about your ancient lineage."

"You're still welcome to join us. I mean, you are the originator of the ritual."

"I am not the originator. I am merely the keeper of ancient traditions." He tipped his head to her and hummed as he walked past, heading toward the street. He had his own plans to see to this night—plans that took him far from this place.

Not too far from the graveyard, Sphan walked through the darkness of a secluded alleyway. At twenty-two, he was the oldest of his group of friends. Although no one paid much heed to age in Gangleton, he took a certain pride in his seniority. His taste was best described as funky, fitting well with his family's colors—fuchsia, black, and crimson. In addition to his Gangleton attire, Sphan didn't go anywhere without sporting his top hat and holster of crimson-dyed leather, which he had fashioned himself.

This night, he took special care with each step not to be seen by prying eyes—those of the Dignitaries most of all. It was his honored duty to retrieve the sacred resin and lead the ceremony for his fellow rebels. But what he hadn't planned for was the untimely arrival of the Dignitaries making his midnight plan a risky foray into almost certain danger. In truth, he really wasn't sure if the Dignitaries knew or even cared about the ceremony. All he knew was no Dig would keep him from doing whatever he wanted to do. Especially leading the one thing which seemed the most real in his entire life within Gangleton's prismatic walls.

Sphan followed the alleyway into a trash-heap junkyard bordering the dome of the Force Field, which in the dead of night had faded into an almost pitch-black reflection of the starry cosmos above. Wagon wheels laid broken, tent poles bent crooked, instruments with strings plucked in twain, apparatuses malfunctioned beyond repair, failures of contraptions, smashed and spilled alchemy things, and all manner of cluttered scrap were gathered here in this man-made hill of discarded refuse. The smell of rotting wood and rusted metal overwhelmed the senses. But despite its unwelcoming appearance, it was here that the Gangleton rebels gathered many of the materials they used to construct their various trinkets and accessories. For the villagers of Gangleton had many magical trinkets of old for which their simple minds no longer had use. Nor did the people still maintain the learning to use them. But the Gangleton rebels had many purposes for the discarded treasures within the junk pile. Setting straight to work, Sphan dug through the scrap with his bare hands for the required materials of tonight's ritual.

Once per lunar cycle, the portal to the ancient realms opened. In times past, this would have been a great celebration, where all the community came together in the center tent where the Cuckoo Clock Tower now stood. The elders would have lit coals, holding large metal pans filled with a heap of clear resin from the sacred trees of Rou. The coals would have burned the sacred resin and filled the dome with smoke, cleansing the people and returning them to their balanced state of living. Then they would set intensions and ask for guidance from the sacred guardians of Rou.

But now, in modern times, the ritual was a well-kept secret, known only to a select few. Sphan had been taught by Vahn, who had in turn been taught by his grandfather and his grandfather before him. To be a practitioner of the Moon Ritual was one of the highest honors one could receive, or so the most knowledgeable of the elders claimed. Sphan often wondered why Vahn had given up his role as the head of the ritual, but his friend's bouts of disappearances left little time for explanation. And Sphan wasn't one to complain about being granted a position of great importance. With the duty placed on his shoulders, he worked tirelessly to find even the smallest glimmer of resin—from the bark of fallen trees, from antique vessels holding trace amounts, and even from long-used pans within which the resin had been burnt in rituals past. The rebels' small group required only a clump of the sacred substance to fuel the messages of their ancestors. Sphan dug, and after some time, he had collected a satisfactory amount. The resin was clear and shimmered a little, reminding him of a diamond. Not wanting the sparkling clump to attract unwanted eyes, he quickly hid the resin in a leather pouch, then placed that in his coat pocket before silently hurrying out of the junkyard and running back into the shadows of the alley behind him.

But before the night was over, there was more to be done.

In Victoria's study, the raven who had snuck into her home perched upon the top of a bookshelf holding volumes of ancient knowledge from the world outside Gangleton. The old woman spoke with the raven in a hushed voice.

"What do you mean they know?" she asked. The raven simply tapped its feet against the bookshelf and cawed at her with a seemingly intended urgency.

A knock at the front door kept her from inquiring further. She held a sole finger to her lips as they both fell silent. Then she rushed out of the study and grabbed a broom from her closet, holding it out in front of her like a shield. Slowly, she pushed the front door's handle the tiniest bit, so the door opened just enough to peek outside. Unsurprisingly but unfortunately, Franc had again paid her a visit. This time, the Dignitary leader stood on the slanted roof of Victoria's home, waiting for the old woman with an impatient stare.

"Good evening," Victoria greeted her, wearing her smile as a mask.

"Doing some evening sweeping, Mrs. Bomqui?" Franc asked coldly.

"Yes," Victoria answered. "My granddaughter was over earlier showing me—"

"You know we find it suspicious when people don't stick to the schedule, Mrs. Bomqui."

"Forgive me. I do apologize. I shall not do it again. Good evening," Victoria stammered, attempting to shut the door and end the conversation.

Franc's arm caught the door before it could close completely. "That is not the only reason I have come." She forced open the door with a mighty shove and stepped inside Victoria's home, nearly pushing the poor woman out of her way with a giant stride. "I've come to warn you of an intruder in our community."

Victoria's eyes widened. She knew of whom Franc spoke, but she had no intention of revealing it.

"A raven was seen flying around at leisure," Franc continued.

"Oh, dear!" Victoria nearly shouted. "Do you think it means harm to Gangleton?"

Franc did not look at her. "You haven't seen this raven today, have you, Mrs. Bomqui?"

It took all Victoria's willpower to not allow a single bead of sweat to drop from her brow. "No. I've been indoors all day with my granddaughter." Her act would have been flawless for most, but not for Franc.

"Hmm. Right... yes. Well, if you hear of anything, do let us know straight away." The Dignitary commander turned to leave. "Times grow more precarious by the day. Good evening." She was nearly out the door when she spun around with a scowl half suspicion and half distaste. "And Mrs. Bomqui, stick to the schedule. It's for your own safety."

As soon as Franc was out the door, Victoria pulled it shut, latching its locks as quietly and quickly as she could before rushing down into her study. She swung the broom closet door open with such force, it nearly shook the very walls. The old woman scanned the room, desperately searching for any sign of the raven that had now disappeared.

"Symon," she said softly, turning about to look everywhere. "Symon? Symon!" A frightened shout loosed from her lips, but still, the raven did not return. Distressed, Victoria dropped to her knees and prayed in silence.

After the Cuckoo Clock sounded again that night, a crowd gathered at the Tower's stage. They'd been called there by the chiming of the bells while they slept—an odd occurrence, even with the Dignitaries in the village. Everyone knew how they so liked to keep to their schedules. But now, for a time that seemed to stretch too long, the Dignitaries had not appeared on the stage. The gathered villagers could only openly speculate as to the purpose of their summons to the Tower so late at night. Some of the younger men and women passed the time by singing, dancing, or playing music. Eventually, others joined in with them. But the moment trumpets sounded through the square from atop the Cuckoo Clock Tower, all members of the crowd fell silent and stood at attention.

The top balcony door sprang open as two Dignitaries took their places. Nylz was the shortest and most petite of the five.

She wore burgundy stripes on her pants, a top hat, and a curved sword at her side. Although her features were dainty and charming, she was the fiercest warrior among them. Lyken was arguably Nylz's absolute opposite. He was the tallest, his trousers boasting mustard-yellow stripes. His long, thin hair and eerie complexion were a ghastly reflection of his own cruel mind.

"Ladies and Gentlemen, be attentive," Nylz began.

"Your lives depend on it," Lyken continued theatrically, his body awkwardly slithering from side to side as he spoke; his boney fingers gesticulated, as if trying to speak a language all their own.

"We are in grave danger, my companions."

"A raven from another land has entered through the Force Field."

"We don't know how it entered or where it went, but we must warn you that you have reason to fear this creature. We believe it is a spy from the Frolly people." Nylz stared out over the crowd with a critical eye.

"For your safety, it is advised you stay inside your homes. Leaving only for Cuckoo Clock Tower meetings, yard manicuring, work, and school."

"Or you may find yourselves in deadly circumstances."

"That is all," Lyken finished with no further explanation.

When the two Dignitaries finished their speech, they immediately turned their backs to the crowd and disappeared inside the Tower's top balcony once more. The door behind them sprang shut with an echoing slam. Then a loud cry from the

Cuckoo bellowed out of the Tower, and the villagers' ravens uncurled themselves from their peoples' heads.

The crowd gasped, cried, whispered, and screamed. It had been some time since something this severe had threatened Gangleton's safety. The Force Field's barrier was supposedly impenetrable. The streets were no longer safe, they thought. Mothers and fathers gathered their families as they rose into the air with their ravens. A tidal wave of fear washed over the village, shaking them all to the core. Ravens flew everywhere, ferrying the chaos of what had once been the peaceful villagers and placing them safely inside their houses, where they attempted to settle for the night beneath their fears. A dark haze filled the streets as people vanished into their homes, leaving the village vacant and gloomy.

Inside the Tower, however, fear did not exist. Nylz and Lyken descended from the top balcony into a circling staircase of black stone leading to the bottom level. At the center hovered a large black orb, its deep, glowing blue light permeating its surroundings. The orb absorbed flying, colored energy seeping into the Tower through its dark walls, and with each passing moment, its glow grew brighter, sealing inside its depths every bit of energy it consumed.

Halfway up the Tower, the third Dignitary Ons sat at a control booth next to the orb. He wore a top hat and dark goggles strapped tightly against it, a monocle with a magnifying lens nestled in one eye. A cane leaned against his pants striped with olive-green. He pressed a series of buttons on the

control panel with malicious purpose, and a huge grin spread across his face.

"I think we've done well, Nylz," Lyken said as he descended to the bottom of the Tower's stairwell. His limbs moved like a spider's, legs and knees lifting unnaturally high as they extended into full, elongated steps.

"I expected no less, Lyken," Nylz replied happily, following close behind. "Your voice and appearance paired with my powerful nature are truly fearful."

"Do I scare you?" Lyken hissed, shoving his face into hers as his long, slender fingers crawled through the air toward her.

"No. I have no fear. But if I did, I would certainly turn in the opposite direction if I were to meet you on a path." She gave a wry smile, gripping her blade and nudging it toward Lyken. "Do you fear me?" she asked in turn, taking a fierce fighting stance.

"No," Lyken scoffed. "You are too petite."

"What about my threatening tone?" she asked, seemingly disappointed. "Am I not our most skilled fighter? Certainly, that must be a thing to fear."

Lyken gave a noncommittal hum but merely kept walking.

CHAPTER 3

Communion with the Ancient Ones

PERCILLA HAD ALREADY returned to the path toward the Cherry Orchard when the Tower's chimes sounded. She'd whirled around in confusion and tugged her hat down firmly over her head to block out the sound. Her ravens made their usual shuffling attempts to escape her hat, but her grip was solid, and she would not let herself be swayed. When the chimes finally fell silent, she picked up the pace and headed for the Orchard, hoping her friends had all managed to do as she had and avoided being dragged to the Tower.

When she finally reached the Cherry Orchard, she found Dant, Gahil, and Metia waiting there for her. Of the few places in Gangleton in which Percilla felt at home, this was her favorite. Rolling emerald hills encompassed the Orchard, making it an oasis of serenity, where large cherry trees sprang naturally at the foot of the mountains. The thousands of cherries hanging from the branches were ripe, filling buckets at their trunks as well as Percilla's nostrils with the intoxicating aroma of fresh harvests. She removed her shoes in excitement and let her toes sink softly into the loose soil beneath the grass, embracing the bare earth under her feet.

"Over here!" she heard Dant shout from across the Orchard.

Dant was the second-oldest of the group at twenty-two. Despite each of them rebelling against Gangelton's laws in some way, Dant had never minded working his hands in the gardens. He had a special connection to the earth—at least, that was what he'd told them. Always, he left his hands unwashed and walked around barefoot, letting his hands and feet touch the ground freely. His Gangleton attire was chestnut, amber, and moss-green with a few smudges of brown dirt for good measure. He wore a moss-green Fedora, always smeared with a tinge of dirt from the day's yardwork.

Metia was barely younger than Percilla at seventeen and the only other girl in their party. One could almost always hear her whistling a sweet tune for her avian companions. Unlike the rest, she felt she shared a special bond with them. Even when they were hidden under her raven-black bowler hat, she said she knew they appreciated her song. Her Gangleton attire fit her as perfectly as feathers fit a bird. Her family colors were sky-blue, raven-black, and white, and she particularly enjoyed adorning herself with more trinkets than any of her friends. She'd fashioned various bits of moldable metals and stone into studs and piercings on nearly every feature of her wardrobe without so much as a care for what others thought.

At twenty, Gahil fell in the middle of the group's various ages. Although many considered him as much of a bird-brain as the ravens in Gangleton, he was far from unintelligent. Rather, Gahil simply went with the flow, a constant source of positivity and happiness that often managed to turn any situation into a good time. His Gangleton attire popped with his family colors of sunburst-yellow, baby-blue, and cherry-red. While he didn't care so much for trinkets, Gahil always wore a floppy hat dyed with the same family colors.

Percilla dashed up the hill to meet her friends, where they stood beneath the tallest cherry tree, illuminated in a pale orange glow by the warm radiance of the fire they'd built. The usual ritual pyre had been lit upon a clay vessel and covered with an iron dish used specifically for nights like this. The fire warmed her, and the sweet melody of her friends' music filled her ears. Dant stretched the accordion in harmony with the sounds of Gahil plucking the strings of his violin and the brass tones of Metia's petite sousaphone.

"Today, I was stopped by a Dignitary for playing my accordion during yardwork hour," Dant sang. "Guess my music was a distraction to his simple mind. I think he was jealous of the new way I plant seeds." His accordion contracted and expanded in waves as he re-enacted the tale.

"Show us how you plant!" Percilla's voice rose with the tune, joining in the music with her own improvisation as she reached the ritual pyre and joined their circle.

A grin spread across Dant's face. With his foot, he pretended to dig a hole in the ground, using his toes as one might use a shovel. Then he reached deep into his pockets, the loose accordion sighing a prolonged tone as he tossed a handful of imaginary seeds into the hole. Without missing another beat, he quickly picked up the other end of his instrument and brought it back into a humorous harmony. To complete the verse, he mimed covering the imaginary hole with his foot and winked, bringing a round of laughter from the others.

Percilla picked up his song, loving the freedom of making it up with every breath, as she and her friends did together every time.

"Dignitaries beware.
Beware.
Beware.
Your games do not work here in the Cherry Orchard.
Oh, no!
You see we are a different kind of folk, not fools like the rest.
We live to be as our ancestors with music in our hearts and
love pumping through our veins."

Dant and Gahil joined in next with their own voices while Metia's sousaphone sustained their song. "Dignitaries beware. Beware. Beware."

The smooth burst of a clarinet joined the ensemble from the bottom of the hill. It rose quietly at first, barely audible over the other instruments but growing louder as its player climbed toward them. Finally, Sphan arrived to join his friends and lead the ritual, illuminated by the full moon kissing the sky behind him.

"The ancestors await us with love and blessings," he announced, lifting his hands.

The music came to a full stop. From within his coat, Sphan produced a clump of clear resin, held it up to the moon between his fingers, and let it cast its reflected light upon them. "I am honored to share with you, my companions, the sacred resin of our people. May this night beckon their loving touch and cleanse us of all that is not pure unto us."

With that said, he bowed to his friends, who each returned the gesture as he set the sacred, sparkling resin upon the metal dish at the center of their circle. The flames beneath it licked at the spiritual substance, the tamed heat releasing the resin's essence as a thin line of rising smoke. Together, the group took a deep inhale of the sweet, piney scent, opening their senses and their minds to its blessings. Next, Sphan removed the ceremonial raven feather from his hat and used it to fan the resin. A larger puff of thick white smoke filled their circle to become a wispy haze on the air. Everyone lowered themselves to the ground in a circle around Sphan and the resin's ritual pyre. The smoke only intensified, engulfing each welcome participant here in its otherworldly caress. An overwhelming sense of compassion washed over them, as if their very ancestors had come to join their circle and hold them in a warm embrace. Each of their minds cleared, willingly shedding the deceits and pressures put upon them by the mandates of their village, allowing them to feel once more their true spirits. Sphan guided them all through one more deep breath in and out.

"May you release all which does not serve your highest truth to the earth below you, so it may utilize this energy for purity and love to serve you and all the world. Now, please lay back and let the great Mother Earth hold you in her loving arms." The group lay back in the grass.

Feeling this was the right moment, Percilla took Vahn's advice and spoke aloud what none of her friends had said before. "Ancestors, if you can hear me, please give us the visions and messages of our ancient lineage." She was not certain what any of them would see, but in an instant, her wish was granted. In that moment, the ancestors replied in a way none of them had known was possible. For better or for worse, Percilla had activated something—some deeper connection—opening each of their minds to the voices of the past, the voices of all who came before them. One by one, words and visions filled their minds, each with their own message.

Sphan rested peacefully in the grass, his eyes fixed upon the glimmering stars so very far above them and yet so seemingly close. His mouth opened slowly before the words left him in almost a song. "Dragons... dragons used to be one among us..."

Beside him, Dant took a full breath as he closed his eyes and dug his fingers deep into the earth at his sides. His body swayed, and the tiniest smile bloomed upon his lips. "What is it I see in sparkling blue, deep beneath these trees?" he asked. "Tell me more of this radiant chamber."

Metia gracefully stood and walked to the edge of the hill to commune with the large, luminous full moon. She moved toward the celestial body, whistling a sweet melody inspired by the breeze and rustling trees fulfilling her tune's harmony. Showered by the lunar being's light and still humming, she caressed her ravens from their roosts beneath her hair, and in so doing, she moved them to float as gentle creatures in the breeze, the beams of moonlight shining upon their black feathers to display a sheen of colors.

Gahil sat up and rested his back against the foot of the huge cherry tree. He crossed his legs, pressed his palms gently together in front of his heart, and closed his eyes. "I am here to listen. I am here to receive. Please continue to lead." Then he lowered the backs of his hands to rest lightly on his knees, nodding sagely at the wisdom of it.

Percilla sat in the cool grass, letting the night breeze soothe her. She keenly observed a cherry dangling from the branch looming above her. The fruit's bright red skin shimmered in a thousand colors, then the countless images swirled within the cherry's new crystalline shell, like a mirror peering into the past, present, and future all at once. She saw Bianca, her great grandmother, walking through the Cherry Orchard. Her ethereal presence and poise were as beautiful as that of any woman Percilla had ever seen. The dourness in her eyes beckoned Percilla, but just before the girl could acknowledge why that was, the vision gave way to a dark presence. It shifted and jerked, crawling into the depths of some cavernous dungeon filled with black light and churning shadows. Within a cage of obsidian, Percilla saw Victoria held captive in chains.

A voice drew her out of the terrible vision and back into the Cherry Orchard. She let out a frightened gasp. What had she seen? Was it real? Was Victoria truly in trouble? But she did not have the time to ponder it further.

"Ravens, I honor you," Metia announced. Her avian companions swayed with the winds around her. "I am and have always been grateful for your companionship. I wish to release you from those who deceive you." The ravens' black feathers gleamed with subtle shades of blue and purple beneath the gentle beams of moonlight. "Please forgive us." She whistled her sweet song before offering the final piece of her command to the birds. "Fly me, ravens. Fly me as you wish. You are free."

Her ravens took flight into the sky, carrying her up into the moon-kissed horizon. The others watched in awe. None of them had ever controlled the ravens before. They were said to be bound only to the Dignitaries' word and the call of the Cuckoo Clock Tower. And yet here was Metia, willing her ravens to follow her words into the sky.

"Thank you, Ravens," Metia called. "Thank you, ancestors."

In utter amazement, Percilla watched Metia's ravens fly her farther and farther from the Cherry Orchard, their wings flapping freely by her command. "Metia!" she shouted. The rest of their group climbed to their feet to watch. "How are you doing that?"

"It's a message from the ancient ones," Metia called down from the sky. "I'll show you when we return."

"The ancestors are more present than usual," Gahil noted with nothing more than a hint of curiosity.

"How did she control her ravens?" Sphan asked.

"Metia is of the sky people, our ancient relatives," Dant explained, his body still attuned to the earth beneath him. He held dirt and grass in his hands, dropping it from one palm into the other. "There are secrets in the earth for all of us."

A strange breeze rushed over Percilla—the willful caress of the ancient ones, the voice of all her ancestors speaking at once. The scent of cherries vanished from the Orchard, and the huge cherry tree sheltering them suddenly seemed so very small and insignificant. There was so much more than Gangleton out there in the wide world. The Barrens, the infinite sky, and beyond even that, there was Rou. In that moment, Percilla alone understood what her grandmother had been trying to tell her. As long as the Dignitaries roamed Gangleton, none of them would ever be free, and they would never find Rou. Now she understood she had a duty, but she still did not entirely know what that duty was. One thing was certain—nothing would be the same.

Percilla looked out into the Cherry Orchard from the top of the hill. A ghostly figure wandered the grounds—an elegant, glowing lady in white. When Percilla focused a little more, she realized it was Bianca, the same woman from her vision. Their gazes met, and within the eyes of Bianca's spirit, she saw a terrible sadness welling in the earthly soul. Then the next moment, the woman vanished, wispy tendrils spreading through the Cherry Orchard from where she'd just stood, the last of the sacred resin dissipating into the moonlit night.

Gahil played his violin, composing beautiful strings into a symphonic hymn for his friends. Sphan joined in with his clarinet and Dant with his accordion, coming together seamlessly into a three-man orchestra of divine harmony. Together, they played with a defiant passion inspired by this night. Gahil plucked the strings of his violin fervidly, Sphan's clarinet stoked blusterous notes in the air with sharp precision, and Dant stretched his accordion with a master's hand, bending the musical contraption from side to side as if it were a pendulum.

Percilla, however, did not take part in the performance. The sight of Bianca's distressed spirit wandering the Orchard had dampened her mood, and she could not help but wonder whether all she'd seen was really true. She felt the wind change again in the darkness of the night. The sweet scent of fresh cherries still eluded her senses. Visions of her grandmother in the dungeon haunted her sight. Again, the unknown breeze rushed down her spine. A cold shiver took hold, and she stepped closer to the massive cherry tree, wrapping her arms around herself for warmth.

Leaves rustled above them, this new wind inflicting a cruel chill upon Percilla and her friends. Disturbed, Percilla could not help but glance nervously over her shoulder. Fear hung all around her—fear of ravens, fear of the Dignitaries, fear of her ancestry, her duty, and her life. The wind rushed toward her again, nearly knocking the poor girl off her feet. She resisted the strength of its assault, but for how long could she stop its advance? Her whole body shivered as if to bring her into motion. Bound by her anxiety, there was nothing she felt she could do.

With no other option, she took off down the hill, out of the Orchard, and back toward her grandmother's house. Even as her friends called out for her to return, she dared not go back. In her heart, she knew the only place she would feel safe now was with Victoria.

Dark shadows gathered in the streets of Gangleton. From within the Cuckoo Clock Tower, the Dignitaries emerged, cloaked in darkness. The five nodded to each other and stalked through the spiraling city streets, their minds set to a single purpose. The moonlight cast their shadows over the dimly lit houses of sleeping villagers. Before long, they gathered in Victoria's front yard—Franc, Nylz, Lyken, Ons, and Drendle. Their very presence seemed to wilt the leaves and petals growing in the garden. Franc snapped her fingers, and a conspiracy of ravens swooped down to, by her command, lift each Dignitary and fly them one by one to the roof.

Victoria still prayed silently in her study. The foreign raven had not yet returned to her, and time had finally run out. She heard a door creaking open beyond the study, followed by the sound of footsteps bending the floorboards above her head, so many of them moving in unison. Without delay, she left her study and closed the door behind her. Taking a deep breath and mustering all her courage, she exited the broom closet and stepped into the main room, where the Dignitaries waited for her.

Back across houses and streets, darkened gardens and yards, Percilla ran through Gangleton with tears streaming down her cheeks. She rounded corners and hopped fences out in the open, for once not caring who saw her. There was a fear in her, too—a fear stricken by a cold wind and the duty of her family, the duty she alone must receive and accept. Her ancestors' visions had only granted her more questions and no answers. But most of all, the sight of Victoria in the dungeon tormented her tired mind. She resolved to see her grandmother at once, if only to put the vision to rest and replace it with the tender sight of Victoria's smile.

Taking the circling shortcut around the edge of the Force Field, Percilla bumped into someone she didn't expect to meet at all. Much to her great surprise, Vahn entered Gangleton from outside the Force Field, stepping straight through the barrier as if it were nothing. She struck him hard and stumbled, but he steadied her with a grip on both her arms. She could only stare at him, confused and alarmed and unable to believe what she'd just witnessed. Vahn blinked back at her, obviously at a loss for how to explain himself. When the strange breeze that had followed her from the Orchard now sent another chill down her spine, she banished the questions brimming behind her lips and set off once more toward Victoria's home. She could not ignore the sense that something terrible was about to happen, and she didn't want to spend another second exposed to the darkness of the night.

"Percilla!" Vahn called. He sounded worried and a little urgent, and despite the soft echo of his footsteps flying after her, she did not turn around.

The minute they stopped and stood side by side at the garden gate into Victoria's yard, Percilla knew something was terribly wrong. An unusual darkness permeated her grandmother's home and tainted it with unease. On the street corner at the other end of the garden, Lyken closed the door to a long black trailer pulled by a motorized bicycle, which Drendle then started. Nylz, Franc, and Ons exited Victoria's house, and the unbound ravens flew them down to the yard. The warm kindness Percilla had always felt standing at this gate had gone cold and dark. Even here, the strange breeze blew through the night, and a dark cloud hung above the starry dome.

"What's going on?" Percilla asked, refusing to acknowledge what she had just seen. "Where's Victoria?"

The Dignitaries ignored her, exiting her grandmother's yard in the dark.

"Answer me! What are you doing here? Where's my grandmother?" None of them looked her way, and her heart plummeted. She shuffled after the Dignitaries, repeating her questions again and again but forced to endure their silence. Each one of them walked by her without even a glance. Percilla's fear, driven by her vision of Victoria in that dungeon, threw her into a rage. She charged Nylz with raised fists. "What have you done to her?" she cried. "Tell me!"

"We have had an intruder in our community," Nylz replied, unfazed by Percilla's advance. She nudged her away. "Victoria was its first victim. We were too late to save her."

"Sorry," Lyken remarked with no emotion at all as he paused beside Nylz.

He didn't care. None of them did.

"Dead?" she whispered in disbelief. "She's... she's dead?" All the strength left her body, even as she told herself they were lying to her. "That can't be true," she whispered, dropping to her knees in the warn, grassy path. Her tears stained the earth. She couldn't understand why this was happening, nor could she bear to watch them take her grandmother from her. Victoria's body must have already been in the wagon. She had to see it— had to know for certain. She charged, but Ons stepped into her path. The force of her urgency nearly toppled him to the ground when they collided, knocking his cane from his grip. But even so, she wasn't strong enough to get around him.

Ons grunted and tried to push Percilla off him. "Will someone help this poor girl?"

Vahn ran toward her and tore Percilla away from the Dignitary. "Hold on, Percilla," he whispered.

"Stop," she cried. "I have to *see* her." She wasn't strong enough to break away from Vahn, either. "I have to say goodbye!" She wasn't strong enough to save Victoria.

The Dignitaries set off without another word, quickly disappearing into the night. They rode for the Cuckoo Clock Tower—the shadow at the center of Gangleton.

Percilla did not resist Vahn's arms drawing around her, pulling her close to comfort her with his warmth. She buried her face against his chest and let her tears run dry as the full moon's light blinked out beneath the spreading shadow.

CHAPTER 4

Rebel with a Cause

THE FOLLOWING MORNING, a rapid, jarring announcement to the villagers declared Victoria dead. Despite the devastating surprise, each family fell back into their routine and crept across their yards, brandishing gardening tools as weapons and shields in case the alleged Frolly folk disguised as ravens attacked again. They went to work as always but kept their eyes peeled for signs of danger, watching their children with vigilant wariness. The stale air of fear hung over Gangleton as the villagers toiled away in their gardens that day. One of their number had already been taken. How long before another was claimed?

Vahn stood atop his roof, spyglass lifted to his eye, and watched the Dignitaries exit the Tower before taking their leave of Gangleton. As usual, they made no announcement as to where they were headed or why or even if they were to return. But

the moment they had cleared the town, he bade his ravens take
him closer to the Force Field. They flew him over Gangleton
and high up to the Cuckoo Clock Tower's top balcony. There,
he surveyed the Barrens beyond the Force Field through his
spyglass. When the instrument's rune glowed, the elephant
contraption came into view, bursts of steam signaling its position through the storm of dust and sand. For but a moment, its
levers and cogwheels pumped and turned, moving its powerful,

rolling treads toward the mountains. In the next instant, it disappeared into the abyss.

"The mountains?" Vahn wondered how long they'd be gone this time. The Dignitaries were ever unpredictable in their presence here. Sometimes, they didn't appear for months. Other times, they left and returned again with day- or even hour-long absences. If he wanted to do this, he needed to do it now.

Vahn sprang into action. He jumped down to the stage below, letting his trusted ravens soften his landing. With a powerful, impassioned stride, he moved straight for the megaphone. It was still morning in Gangleton, and most of the villagers still worked within the safety of their gardens, heeding the Dignitaries' words and warnings.

"Excuse me," Vahn shouted into the megaphone, his voice amplified loud enough for all the town to hear. "Let my words be heard!"

Many villagers stopped what they were doing; some even left their yards to investigate. This was not a part of the schedule, and that was reason enough to be concerned with the goings on outside. Others, though, still feared the threat of Frolly attack too much, instead pretending they did not hear a thing. Parents covered their children's ears; some villagers waved Vahn away from their places within their gardens.

"We are being deceived by our Dignitaries," Vahn continued, his voice lifting in confidence. A crowd gathered now at the Tower's stage. He glanced past the houses, over fences and yards, and his gaze fell on Percilla. She looked tired and confused, and he wished he'd had a chance to explain himself to her before he'd decided to reveal what he knew to all of Gangleton. A frantic mother, holding her child to her breast and running back toward her home, nearly knocked Percilla over in her haste to escape his words. Vahn wanted to make sure Percilla was all right, but he had to finish what he'd started.

"Please hear me out," he shouted desperately, then forged ahead despite knowing only too well the consequences. "For some time, now, I have been stepping beyond Gangleton's boundaries in search of the truth."

A wave of terrified gasps and murmurs of disbelief rose from the crowd. "That is against our agreement with the Dignitaries," a woman shouted from the front of the crowd. "They must know of this at once!"

"Cage it, Demi!" Percilla's sharp voice rang out from amid the crowd, and she pushed her way toward the stage where both her friend and the woman who opposed him could see her clearly. "Let him fly."

Vahn smiled and nodded at Percilla in appreciation. "I have been searching for answers about the mysterious threats we receive every time the Dignitaries return from their travels," he continued. He scanned the crowd, looking for signs of any more resistance his claims might bring. "Frolly, Krinkton, Dawookrunk. None are true."

"You can't prove that," Demi yelled, her face blooming into a dark shade of red. "How do we know you speak the truth? Your grandfather was exactly the same. Strange, always lurking around in the evenings, speaking ancient tongues."

"Unless you can prove otherwise, keep quiet," Percilla snapped, and the woman glared at her.

Although they had at first been of seemingly two minds, the crowd seemed swayed by the strength of Percilla's conviction in Vahn. Hushed whispers filled the air as the villagers discussed these claims among themselves, though a consensus had not yet been reached.

"Let him speak!" a sharp voice rose above the crowd.

"Vahn's grandfather was a loyal companion of ours."

Eyes turned to study Tig and Asa, both respected members of Gangleton. Tig was an honest and humble man, who always spoke the truth; Asa was known as a strong, nurturing woman upon whom the villagers had always been able to depend. Their support alone made a world of difference. More voices of approval followed from there, and it seemed most of the crowd had decided to accept the truth behind Vahn's claims.

The encouragement bolstered Vahn's own confidence as well. Percilla shot him another reassuring grin.

"That man threatened the very safety of our village," said the well-manicured, abiding Devin, who'd naturally floated his way to the front of the crowd. His reputation meant his words carried as much weight against Vahn as Tig's and Asa's had worked to support him. "The boy's actions put us all in danger. Who knows what may follow him through the Force Field on his trips in and out of Gangleton? Most likely, that's what allowed the Frollian spy here in the first place!" Half the crowd fell into an agreeing rabble, and it seemed any really progress as to a communal decision would be impossible.

Tig charged Devin, glaring at the man and clearly on the verge of raising his fist, if it came to that. "If it wasn't for Vahn's grandfather," he said, "we wouldn't have the few freedoms we do today. Let Vahn speak."

His words struck true, silencing Devin's nonsense and bringing the eyes of nearly every villager eagerly back to settle upon Vahn.

"I have visited each location to see for myself if their threats were true," Vahn continued, speaking with a calm, rational voice he hoped would keep things from escalating any further. "And in every place, I found the same thing—"

The doorway atop the Cuckoo Clock Tower sprang open, as did every door atop every home in Gangleton. The Tower's bells sounded the end of Gardening Hour, overpowering Vahn's words before he could say anything else. The villagers' ravens uncurled from their hair, moving in sequence with each chime of the Cuckoo Clock.

They lifted the villagers off their feet. With the next chime, they took flight as one. Every villager—except for Vahn—was flown to their rooftops and deposited exactly where they were supposed to be. As if the act had erased the last few minutes, everyone disappeared inside their houses, and the town fell silent.

Vahn gazed at the empty space in front of the stage, crushed by the result of all his careful planning. He fell to his knees, silently cursing the Dignitaries and their damnable Cuckoo Clock Tower.

Percilla twisted in the air as her ravens flew her back to her house. She could not stand to see Vahn broken like this. If he'd had just a little bit more time, perhaps he could have convinced them all to fight back against the Dignitaries. If she had spoken up and shared what the Dignitaries had done the night before— that they had murdered her grandmother—perhaps the crowd would have believed Vahn. A sharp guilt struck Percilla's heart. There was no doubt in her mind; she *had* to help him.

"Ravens," she called, "please return me to the Tower."

It was only the vain struggle of a rebellious girl. She hadn't expected anything to come of her shouting, and nothing did. She shut her eyes in frustration, but she could not give up—not yet. "Ravens, I beg of you." Still, they drew closer and closer to her home. She clenched her fists and called upon all the strength of her ancestors to help her understand what to do, to aid her in this time of need. "Ravens, if you do as I ask, I promise I will set you free. Please, listen to my request. Take me back to the Tower."

She held her breath and dared not open her eyes. To her surprise, her ravens' wings turned on the wind, and her stomach fluttered when she felt their course change. Percilla opened her eyes and found herself headed now toward the Cuckoo Clock Tower with avian haste. Swiftly and gently, her ravens flew her back down to the Tower's stage. Vahn stared at her with wide eyes, then rose from his knees with the light of hope renewed in his features.

"Percilla. How did you—"

"No time to talk." She grabbed his hands. "Will you meet me in the Cherry Orchard at sunset?"

"Yes." Vahn grinned.

Percilla released his hands. "Ravens, take me to Grandmother's."

She flew, free of the Dignitaries' control over her for the first time in her life — not just physically free but mentally and spiritually liberated. The Force Field could contain her no longer. In her heart, she knew what she must do. Her family's duty would be fulfilled, and she would be the one to do it. Victoria's death would not be in vain—not as long as the Eye of Rou remained safely locked away within the walls of her study. Percilla would meet with Vahn in the Cherry Orchard and hear him out.

For now, she decided to have her ravens set her down in Victoria's front yard. Flowers of every kind and color grew freely in the well-maintained plots. How many times had Percilla been in this same yard with her, helping her dig holes and plant? Or listening to Victoria tell her one story after another? Percilla brushed her fingers over the soft rose petals with a sharp pang of loss. As she wandered around the yard, she found herself humming the song Victoria had sung to her about the people of Rou. She did her best to remember the words, summoning every moment spent with her grandmother right here. Victoria had always been so kind, so welcoming, wise, elegant. It made Percilla proud to be her granddaughter.

"I'm going to miss you," she whispered and sat on the lawn. "I don't know what to do now," she told the wind and the sun shining down on her. "Who to really talk to. What do I do?"

But there were no answers, no more visions from her ancestors to guide her—nothing at all. She stared around the garden, knowing there wasn't a chance she could preserve it the way it deserved. She was no gardener. The flowers would never be as vibrant as they were now, the vegetables never as bountiful again; all the plants Victoria had cared for since she was a child would wither away without her. That thought brought tears springing to Percilla's eyes. She would do her best, but even when she tried to get up, her heart wasn't in it. An unknown weight bound her to softness of the grass. It seemed nothing could move her, not even the abrasive screech and clang of the mechanical elephant heralding the Dignitaries' return after their short leave of absence from Gangleton.

After a while, she finally found the strength to stand and brushed grass and dirt from her pants. She turned her back to the road, debating if she should go into Victoria's house or return to her own, not sure she could handle the immense sorrow that would most likely hit her the moment she stepped inside.

Something hard and cold pressed into her back, and she gasped. When she turned around to see all five Dignitaries standing behind her in her grandmother's yard—without her ever having noticed their approach—she dared not gasp a second time. Ons still pointed the end of his cane at her back, and he adjusted his monocle with a gruff clearing of his throat.

"Good day, Percilla," Franc said. "We wanted to see how you were doing. We are ever sorry about your grandmother."

"Victoria was a dear member of our community," Ons added.

"Which is why we have come to extend our hands to you," Drendle said, reaching his open palm toward Percilla and bowing his head in offering.

Franc pushed Drendle's hand back down to his side before Percilla even had a chance to respond, shooting her overeager companion an assertive glare.

"There is no telling what the intruder sought," Nylz said, keeping one hand on the hilt of her blade. "May have been something in your family's possession."

"We want you safe," Lyken assured Percilla.

Percilla's hands shook with fright as the quintet surrounded her in the garden, their shadows casting over her in the sun's light. Their voices were poisonous, masked, and filled with lies, yet they remained so captivating despite it all—every word chosen with care, every annunciation spoken with purpose. Percilla thought the true danger of the Dignitaries lay in their tongues.

"I would like to offer you a position on our team," Franc stated.

"Huh?" Percilla blinked at them a few times, unable to say anything else. She feared these people, yes, but she was also smart enough to know what they really wanted from her. She forced herself not to glance nervously toward Victoria's home.

"Yes, we know. It's a great honor," Nylz said.

"We can be your family from now on," Lyken added.

Percilla remained silent, unsure if it was better to tell them yes or no or if she even had the courage to give an answer. Did they suspect her? When would they get rid of her too? Surely they would need more proof. She had hardly known one full day about the Eye of Rou or even Rou itself; there was no way they could already know.

The awkward pause continued for some time, then Ons cleared his throat once more and took the initiative. "We will give you one night to prepare your answer."

Franc eyed Percilla's head, taking note of the hat covering her ravens. She scoffed and reached over to pluck it like a feather from Percilla's head. "You won't be needing this raggedy thing any longer," she said with a dark chuckle.

All five Dignitaries walked out of her grandmother's garden and back into the streets of Gangleton. She watched them stroll down the path leading toward the Cuckoo Clock Tower until at last they had vanished out of sight. At sunset, she would talk to Vahn, and she prayed he could help her decide what to do.

CHAPTER 5

Intentions Set

AT SUNSET, THE golden tones of the day lit the Cherry Orchard. The Gangleton rebels sat atop the hill, playing music to pass the time. Together, they crafted sweet melodies, bringing the Cherry Orchard to life with their own blooming creations. But on the opposite end of the Orchard, Percilla sat alone, her legs swinging beneath the branch of the tree she'd climbed. She did not normally distance herself like this from the others, but her friends understood she needed some time alone after what had happened to Victoria. Her grandmother's murder weighed heavily on her mind, especially with no certain answers as to how it had come to pass. Still, none of her friends could have imagined Percilla's true purpose in the Orchard this evening. Nervously tapping her feet against each other, she waited for Vahn and watched the sun's last rays fade to give rise to the almost imperceptibly waning moon on the distant horizon.

The caw of familiar ravens sounded in the sky. Percilla looked up and caught sight of Vahn flying toward her from the village. Smirking, she plucked a handful of fresh cherries from the branch above her and launched them toward him.

"Flisp ta-pow," she said, concentrating on the spell her grandmother had taught her many long years ago.

The cherries pulsed with a flickering orange light, then exploded in a rain of multi-colored sparks. An uproar of applause rose from Percilla's friends at the other end of the Orchard. Vahn clapped while his ravens flew him down to the ground below Percilla's tree with their usual elegant landing. Percilla jumped down from her branch just before the cherries' sparkling lights sifted down around both her and Vahn. The dancing sparks reflected brilliantly in his eyes, which stared directly into hers, and they grinned at each other.

"Thank you," Percilla said anxiously. "For meeting me. I don't know who else to trust. Nothing makes sense anymore. Or maybe it makes perfect sense. I just... I don't know." She glanced down at the ground, trying to sort through the words she wanted. "Victoria's gone, and now the Dignitaries want to be my family." Vahn's eyes widened at this. "Yes. They made me an offer to join them. Either I'm missing something, or... Well, I'm really not sure I want to think about the other options."

"There *isn't* anyone else to trust," Vahn said. "Not anymore." He searched her gaze in earnest, then took her hands in his. "I need you to listen to me, Percilla. Victoria wasn't the only one."

"What do you mean?" Her heart thundered in her chest.

"The Dignitaries murdered my grandfather too. For the same reasons they murdered Victoria."

Percilla gasped as her disjointed thoughts wove into consciousness the one fact she had hoped was false. "The Dignitaries..." she whispered. "Vahn, I knew there was something they weren't telling me. I didn't want to believe they were capable of such horrible things. I just... I'm sorry, Vahn."

Vahn's eyebrows drew together with a pain she'd never seen on him before. "No one else in Gangleton ever knew," he said. "They tried to manipulate me with fear. Tried to convince me my grandfather's murderer was still after my family. But I knew... I *knew* they were the ones who took him from me. They made me the same offer, too."

"Vahn... I..." Percilla did not know what to say. Vahn was the strongest boy she'd ever met. This side of him was fragile and wounded, and it caught her completely off guard.

"It's in the past," he said and took a deep breath.

"What am I supposed to do now? I don't want to accept, but I can't even imagine what might happen if I tell them no. I know things, Vahn. Things that have to be kept secret. The idea of them finding out that I—" A chill slithered down her spine at the thought of it, and she stepped backward to be closer to the cherry tree, as if it would keep her safe from their grasp.

"You can't join them. But if they're after whatever it is you know, we don't have much time." He reached into his coat pocket and pulled out a black leather book, the symbol of Rou burned into its cover. "When my grandfather passed, he left me this book. It's a book of spells. Of the wisdom that all our people used to know. My family have been the Guardians of the original book for generations."

Percilla's eyes widened. "Victoria told me that my family are the Guardians of the Eye of Rou."

"The Eye of Rou?" Vahn exclaimed with urgent delight. "Where is it?" He grabbed her shoulders and stared at her with wide eyes. "Do you have it?"

"No. Not here."

His smile disappeared. "Is it safe?"

"Yes. It's... it'll be fine." Percilla would have liked to explain everything to him, but she was more interested at the moment in hearing everything Vahn had to say first.

"It must be kept hidden from—"

"I know.

"The Eye of Rou." A chuckle of disbelief escaped him. "You've actually seen it? In person?"

"Yes."

"I should have known Victoria would be a Guardian. I thought for sure the Digs had it."

"They don't. Please, finish what you were flying at me."

"I hope wherever she hid it, it's well out of the minds and eyes of—"

"It is, Vahn. Tell me more about what you know."

He took a deep breath and nodded. "We are a lot more powerful than any one of us could imagine."

"What do you mean?"

"Your ravens used to fly free." Vahn looked at the ravens on his own shoulders like they were animals in a cage and frowned.

"The Dignitaries somehow managed to ensure our ravens control us, now. Most respond only to the Cuckoo Clock Tower."

"They're murdering people, Vahn. And they know. I swear they know what I have. They just don't know where it is. What do we do?"

"The only thing that makes sense," he declared. He stared at her so intently, he didn't have to tell her what her heart already knew.

"We have to get out of here," Percilla said with a nod, now truly beginning to realize the extent to which the Dignitaries controlled everything in Gangleton and how far they would go to keep its people in the dark.

"Yes," Vahn replied. "But we can't just leave the rest of our people. Not knowing what we know. The descendants of Rou cannot live in fear."

Percilla looked away from him, recognizing now how much her own life was in danger. When the Dignitaries came for her, who would protect her? Then the lilting words of her grandmother's stories fluttered across her mind, and she thought she had the answer. At this point, it was up to her—and Vahn, if he even agreed after this to go with her—to protect herself, her friends, and the rest of Gangelton. But not without aid from those much more powerful than the Dignitaries. "We should go to Rou," she said. "Ask the guardian deities for their help."

Vahn blinked in surprise. "You want to go to Rou?"

Percilla shrugged. What other option was there? That was the only place she knew capable of defending her and releasing

Gangleton from the captors they'd always thought were their protectors. After all, Rou had dragon guardians.

They stared at each other, debating this huge decision. The music rose from the instruments in her friends' hands and drifted across the Cherry Orchard.

The people of Gangleton gathered in front of the Cuckoo Clock Tower for a late-evening meeting and watched the moon rise. On the balcony halfway up the tower, wooden figurines glided across a rail track to perform an imitated celebration of old-time Gangleton. Seven figurines proceeded as the cogwheels inside their carved bodies forced them to march and play music, their constructed instruments striking the blissful cadence of a full brass brand. The crowd below the stage erupted in applause.

At the end of the rail track, the figurines returned one by one into the Tower until the final drummer remained. As it neared the doorway, it stopped in its procession, firmly lodged in place. The exit door attempted to close but only slapped flimsily against the figurine. The door opened and closed over and over, and each time it swung ajar again, the drummer's ceaseless beat rang out from the Tower only to be cut off completely when the door closed once more.

Many of those in the confused crowd danced while the drummer's music played and ceased when it disappeared, not knowing what else to do. Such an accident was exceedingly uncommon. Finally, as if someone inside the Tower had taken notice of the issue, an unseen controller switched off the contraption running the figurines, and the drummer's wooden mallets froze above the drum.

A loud click echoed from the Tower, then all five Dignitaries stepped out onto the uppermost balcony. The entire village fell silent in their presence, save for the still constant slap of the lower exit door opening and closing against the drummer figurine. Nylz peered down over the edge of the balcony to inspect the issue and saw the malfunctioning door. She leaned toward Franc and whispered something in the other woman's ear. Franc frowned in annoyance, then mumbled something to Drendle beside her before leading the Dignitaries back inside the Tower.

After a short, highly awkward pause, the faulty door opened and stayed open. Drendle's form loomed behind the wooden drummer, and with a grunt, he pressed his weight against the figurine's back and gave it a curt shove. When he realized that wasn't working, he backed away and paused for breath. Then he charged full-speed at the figurine, ramming into it and wrapping his arms around its wooden body. His face reddened with extreme exertion until finally, the drummer moved—though not as the Dignitary had hoped. The drummer spun rapidly around and with its mallets slapped Drendle square in the face. Then, as if following a new routine, it pushed itself back the way it had come, charging toward Drendle and nearly toppling him to the ground. As if under some hex, the figurine abruptly stopped, Drendle's face positioned perfectly between the mallets, then bashed him in the face with both of them.

Drendle let out a surprised moan, desperately struggling not to lose his balance and fall from the Tower while the figurine's drumsticks smacked him over and over. The crowd could not help but chuckle at the sight of one of their great leaders being slapped around by little more than a wooden doll.

Then Nylz burst through the rail track entry door, axe in hand. With a series of swift chops and slices, she sent the drummer figurine flying from the balcony, where it collapsed as a heap of scrap on the stage below. The crowd fell silent again, and Nylz bowed to them before returning through the entry door. Drendle picked himself up, shook his head, and stepped back inside the Tower without acknowledging his audience.

Shortly thereafter, all five Dignitaries appeared once more upon the top balcony and gazed down at the villagers, as if waiting for the appropriate reaction. The villagers looked to each other, then slowly applauded their leaders' exploits. This seemed satisfactory enough for the five.

"As you all know," Franc announced, her voice echoing from the tower and cutting off the applause instantly, "we lost a dear member of our community last night."

"We have proof that the Frollian spy was the murderer," Nylz added, shouting loud enough to ensure everyone heard her.

"We also have proof someone within our community let it into Gangleton," Lyken interjected, abruptly leaning out over the balcony to scan the crowd with a condemning eye.

"The proof lies in the missing person of this evening's meeting," Ons said and adjusted his monocle.

"Vahn Blunderworth, are you in the crowd?" Lyken roared.

The five Dignitaries and all villagers present searched those gathered for Vahn, waiting for him to make his presence known. But there was no answer.

"Vahn is missing," Lyken said with a sadistic smile.

"Then let's summon this traitor forth, shall we?" Nylz looked more than ready to draw her blade.

"Ravens of Vahn Blunderworth, take flight," Franc shouted. "We summon you to the Cuckoo Clock Tower!"

"No fight be made. We mean no harm. Come at once," Nylz said.

"Or he loses an arm," Lyken whispered.

And with that, Ons pushed a button on a handheld apparatus.

Back in the Cherry Orchard, Vahn finally found himself agreeing with Percilla's suggestion when she said it was truly their only option. He was all for leaving, but a trip to Rou was no small feat. He rubbed his temples, taking a few more moments to weigh the consequences and the dangers of doing such a thing. "What else do we have to lose?" he remarked, opening his eyes and readying himself for the journey ahead. "To Rou we go, then."

A burst of light shot down from the Force Field, focusing on Vahn's ravens and making them shiver atop his shoulders. The birds flapped their wings and took flight, lifting Vahn off the ground with much more speed than usual, as if their strength had been somehow amplified.

"Where are you going?" Percilla called after him, reaching for his hand already too far from her grasp.

"Ravens, I ask you to halt," Vahn instructed. "Halt, ravens. Halt!" But the ravens would not listen. The light shone brighter and brighter, captivating the ravens in a trance beyond Vahn's control. He reached into his coat pocket for the spell book of Rou and hurled it toward Percilla. It landed in the soft grass at her feet, and she scooped it up immediately to place it inside her jacket. "Go," Vahn shouted, rising higher and farther away from her. "Find Rou. Read that after you've crossed the Force Field." He hoped she could still hear him when he shouted as loud as he could, "And cover your ravens!"

Percilla scoured the Orchard for any object she might use to cover her head. A tin bucket meant for harvesting cherries rested against the base of the tree. With nothing else to use, she stuck the bucket over her ravens and ran as fast as she could for the Force Field. When the foreign winds she'd felt the night before rushed up her spine, she stilled.

Percilla looked up again at the full moon rising and saw the silhouette of a single free raven flying against the inky sky. Something in the sight calmed her, and she took a second to think. In that moment of clarity, she realized she couldn't leave

Gangleton yet. If the Eye of Rou remained here, all would be lost.

Circling back, she made her way toward Victoria's house. "Percilla!" Sphan shouted from where her friends had gathered. "What's going on?"

Although it pained her, she had no time to answer. And even if there had been time, she couldn't involve her other friends in what she was about to do—not now that she knew full well what the Dignitaries did to people who knew too much. Entering an alleyway, she slipped through the growing darkness of the streets, evening giving way to the full blackness of night. The worn paths of Gangleton had emptied with every villager now gathered at the Cuckoo Clock Tower. Percilla saw the bright lights emanating at the base of the Tower and caught the echoes of a shouting voice she recognized as Franc's. She feared for Vahn's safety, but she had to remain hidden at all costs. So she stayed as far away from the Tower's stone courtyard as she could until she reached her grandmother's house. Seeing it again at night brought the memory of what the Dignitaries had done to Victoria flaring up inside her. Not some intruder—oh, no. The people Gangleton trusted had murdered her grandmother. It felt as if a darkness now gathered in the home that had once meant so much to her but was now empty.

With the shadows of Gangleton's streets creeping up on her, Percilla climbed the ladder to the roof, where she snuck into the darkened house through the spring doorway. When she dropped down onto the floor, the wooden slats creaked beneath her, amplifying the pounding of her heart. But she collected herself, ran down the stairs, and burst into the broom closet then again into the study. She had never been in this room before with no magical light to brighten her surroundings, and it was indeed dark. But she did not know the spell to produce such a light. Luckily, all she needed here was the Eye of Rou, and she knew exactly where to find it.

Percilla approached the far end of the room with an extended hand, searching for the wall cloaked in shadow. The floor groaned beneath her feet with each long, slow step. Stretching into the void, her fingers pressed into the wall and reached for the same spot Victoria had touched before. A hesitant whisper escaped her. "Fris-tah opren-tee."

The spot glowed as her spell unlocked the prismatic safeguard, filling the room with a sky-blue light illuminating the entire study. The Eye of Rou presented itself to its new Guardian. But this time, the gemstone passed through the wall not just by itself, but with a note.

"Fly back," Percilla muttered in awe. She grasped the Eye of Rou in one hand and the note in the other. Once she'd unfolded the note, she held the Eye of Rou up to it, using its brilliant light to see the paper. At first, the page was blank, but as the Eye's light spread across its surface, words filled the page in a heavy, cursive font she knew all too well.

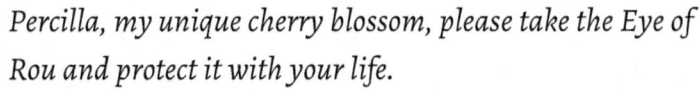

Percilla, my unique cherry blossom, please take the Eye of Rou and protect it with your life.

Forgive me, for if times aren't hard enough, I must ask you to take the Eye of Rou back to its home.

I fear the Dignitaries have caught word it still exists.

I have faith in you, my love.

Remember, compassion is always the strongest power and the quietest voice from within.

To exit the Force Field, recite this spell...

One last tear fell from Percilla's eye as she finished reading the note. She held the Eye of Rou above her head and let its golden chain fall around her neck. What remained visible of the precious gemstone she hid beneath her jacket so no one would see its bright light in the dark.

Percilla's eyes had now adapted to the darkness of Victoria's study, and through it, she made out the most basic of shapes around her. Only one stood out to her above the others. Victoria's stunning hat sat atop the tea table in the center of the room. Percilla flung the bucket from her head, where it clanged against the floor. Victoria's hat fit Percilla as well as it had fit her grandmother. Now, she could truly call herself a Guardian, just as Victoria had been. She looked at herself in the mirror beside Victoria's secret wardrobe, straightened her hat, and rushed out the door.

CHAPTER 6

Trusting Fools

COLD RAYS OF moonlight guided Percilla's path through the tall, dew-soaked hedges of glittering grass on the outer rings of Gangleton. She hid herself skillfully behind bushes and beneath the shadows of tall trees, avoiding the ever-watchful eyes of the Dignitaries and the villagers loyal to them. The night air bent beneath the howling, furiously sweeping winds, masking the crunch of fallen leaves and the snap of wayward twigs beneath her feet. Distant, muffled voices projected from the Cuckoo Clock Tower to fill the night, free to roam the empty streets within the darkness reaching into every corner of the village.

Percilla had nearly come upon the outskirts of the village and quickly approached the Force Field. The satchel she carried contained barely more than Vahn's spell book and her grandmother's last batch of cherry tarts. She would have retrieved more if she had the time, but the gravity of protecting the object around her neck pressed her into fulfilling her filial oath. One hand pressed firmly atop her grandmother's hat tipped downward to conceal her face. The blue hat and maroon jacket faded into black under the moonlit sky, blending into the tall grass surrounding her. Moving quickly, she climbed with brisk ease up the tall hill coated in uncut grass—the last obstacle between her and the Force Field. But when she'd almost crested the hill, something tugged at her from behind. It was not a physical grasp but an emotional weakness she could not possibly overcome. Gangleton, the village she had known from the day she was born, called to her. Time seemed to slow as the howling wind subsided and Percilla's past pulled her away from the Force Field. She turned back toward Gangleton to gaze at the village from atop the hill.

Even after all that had happened, Gangleton was still dear to her. The hues of orange-yellow candlelight dimly lit the village streets and illuminated the colorful homes. The river running through the village shimmered in the moonlight, and the soft babbling of its currents was just barely audible now that the wind had calmed. The ground beneath Percilla's feet seemed warm even in the cool night air. She always felt Gangleton was such a dull place. But now that she had to leave it behind, she recognized the truth of her grandmother's words. Gangleton had not always been so lifeless. It was a quaint place with kind people. If it were not for the Dignitaries, perhaps she would have noticed that sooner.

Struggling against herself, Percilla forced her eyes shut, and the wind picked up its howling, as if urging her to decide. Just as she thought she'd found the strength to tear herself away from her home, her eyes drifted toward the Cuckoo Clock Tower. She could not ignore what she saw there now atop the stage.

Although their features were not as sharp from so far away, the Dignitaries were unmistakable. And at the center of their circle stood Vahn, his arms bound behind his back and his ravens curled at his feet. A crowd had gathered around the stage to watch. Lyken's relentless voice carried toward her as he gesticulated wildly at Vahn, though Percilla could not hear the words. Nylz stood guard with her hand wrapped tightly around the hilt of her sword. Franc and Ons waited patiently, watching the interaction as if it were a performance. At the side of the stage, Drendle spoke with Demi, the village woman who had so fiercely protested Vahn's speech. Despite only catching the cadence of their voices, Percilla could guess easily enough what they were saying. Vahn's secret had surely been discovered somehow, and now the interrogations had begun. The fact that her ravens remained so calm made it highly likely her involvement had not yet been discovered despite the Dignitaries' suspicions of her.

"I will come back for you," Percilla whispered to Vahn, willing him to hear her words. "I promise."

Then she tore herself away from the village and turned back toward the Force Field. She had not expected to come face to face with Tig, and the man's sudden appearance made her stop short. She clenched her satchel tightly in both fists.

He glanced down at her satchel, then back up at her face. "I suggest you stay clear of the Digs," he whispered.

Relieved he did not try to stop her, Percilla whispered back, "Yes. Thank you." Then she rushed past him and down the hill toward the Force Field. With the Dignitaries all gathered at the Tower's stage, no one could stop her now. Freer than ever, she nearly flew to the bottom of the hill until she faced the Force Field—the sole barrier to the world outside she had never seen before.

Up close, the familiar dome now seemed strange. The stars and moonlight bent unnaturally against the prismatic shield. From afar, these oddities had not been visible, but now the imperfections in the sphere were plain to see. Percilla realized just how naïve she had been to believe for even a moment the shield surrounding her home was meant to protect her. She had always felt in her heart the Dignitaries were corrupt. But only recently had she understood why. All it took to see the truth was one misstep for the Dignitaries. And now their lies were exposed.

Percilla recited the words her grandmother had left her at the end of her hidden note. "Clis-tin opren-tee."

Each word slid from her mouth with an uncertain hesitation. And yet the words themselves filled her with pride, for they were the words of her family and her freedom. The spell took effect, and her hand passed through the dome, followed by her foot and finally the rest of her body. With a brave leap, Percilla emerged into the Barrens with the prismatic curve of the Force Field at her back. Its multi-colored light lit only a little of what lay ahead, revealing a forest of crooked, skeletal trees. Hundreds of leafless branches formed a hollow canopy overhead, through which so much of the pale moonlight passed. Only denser gatherings of the same dead trees blocked her path on either side; the only way through the forest of wooden bone lay right in front of her, shrouded in a thick darkness that seemed to tempt her into its depths.

A cold and distant wind shuddered through the forest, but Percilla would not be thwarted by dead trees and shadows. If Vahn had braved his way through this place, she too would find her way. She stepped forward into the shadowy threshold, and with each step, the shimmering light of the dome behind her faded farther away until it vanished from sight completely. Without the unnatural light, the full moon shone its brightest. For a moment, the spilled light illuminating the path comforted her. But as she scanned the surrounding darkness, finding nothing beyond the black veil hiding whatever existed out here, she found that comfort fading.

The silence of the forest filled now with the creaking trees swaying in the wind and the crunch of twigs. But whether those sounds came from the wind and her feet alone or something else within the forest, she could not tell. Percilla quickened her pace, imagining shapes moving alongside her, things darker than the forest and lurking just out of sight. Her breath came rapid and uneasy now, and she was sure she'd caught movement in the shadows and heard the footsteps of some unknown thing following close behind. Something lurked in these woods—something that would catch her if she stopped. Percilla's feet moved faster than they ever had in her life, slapping against the path beneath the dead trees and away from the darkness at her heels.

She ran deeper into the forest, only to find herself without warning in a large clearing. Turning, Percilla studied the hollow trees, searching for what had been following her and now surely waited for the perfect moment to attack. In her fear, she did not see the obstacles beneath her feet before she tripped and sprawled with a grunt across the ground. Then she saw what she'd failed to notice before—the ground littered with fragments of old, splintered wagons, fallen tent poles, and torn canvases. Dusty books, muddied clothing, and all manner of aged and indiscernible items from early Gangleton rested here. Still unsettled by the pervading darkness, Percilla slowly pushed herself up, gazing at the remnants around her, and made her way carefully through the heaps of scrap. She did not wish to fall like that again.

The farther Percilla traveled, the older the junk scattered throughout the forest became, until finally she reached another clearing completely open to the night sky and the freely falling moonlight. Tired from her late journey and the spikes of anxiety through the darkness, she knelt beside a broken wagon to rest. It was impossible to tell just how far she had come from Gangleton, but she thought the Dignitaries would surely be unable to track her this deep into the forest. With a heavy breath, she took a look around her now and ran a hand along the side of the broken-down wagon. The rough exterior of the wagon crumbled beneath her fingers, coating them with a fine powder. She inspected her hand to find that powder was old, charred ash. Then she realized the entire wagon was burned to a pitch black; everything around her, in fact, had been scorched by fires long since dwindled out.

Percilla nervously wiped her hands on her pants, her mind racing with what might have occurred here. With that thought, she reached for the one source which might provide answers. The spell book had given Vahn all he knew, so she began her first lesson as she opened to the first page. Before her eyes had even settled on a single word, a rope dropped from the sky in front of her, and Percilla yelped in alarm. But nothing else happened, and after a few moments, she found herself wondering just how it had gotten here in the first place. She reached out to touch the rope and flinched away again when she realized it was indeed real and not her imagination. The rope appeared to be the same as any other, except it had fallen from the sky in the middle of this open clearing. This had to be more magic.

She looked up, wanting to see from where the rope had fallen, and found something even stranger approaching her from above. A man dressed in clothing that might have once been considered dapper slid his way down the rope and plopped to the ground in front of her. Startled, she stared at her reflection in black-rimmed goggles worn over the man's eyes. Quickly looking him up and down, she thought the worn countenance of his attire suggested it had been some time since the man had changed his wardrobe.

"Greetings. Kinda hard ta see down here, ain't it, sweets?" the man said in an oddly suggestive manner. He reminded Percilla of a weasel, his short scruff, perhaps shaved but not recently, covering his chin and upper lip.

"What?" Percilla asked, not entirely convinced this wasn't merely a dream.

"The name's Shru," the man replied. "Who are you, my fair lady?" His eyebrows wiggled as he spoke.

Percilla slid the spell book deeper into her satchel, hoping Shru hadn't noticed her holding it or worse yet perceived its true value. But unfortunately, her hands had not been quick enough. The man was already staring at the book. "Percilla!" she shouted, hoping to bring his attention back to her. "That's my name."

"You can read in this dark?"

"Read? What? You're flown. Why would I read in the dark?"

"Want ta use my light?" Shru asked, sidling closer to her.

"I don't know what I would use it for," Percilla replied curtly and inched away from him.

"Where ya headin'?"

"Nowhere at the moment."

"Ya lost?"

"No, I just don't... Why do you care so much?" She frowned at him, no longer startled but now reaching the limits of her patience.

"Well, well, naw. No need ta get all kerfunkled." Shru lifted his goggles onto his red fedora and shoved his face toward hers, stopping mere inches away. Startled yet enticed by the blackness of his eyes, she felt beckoned to find something deep within the abyss. He imparted an odd sense of familiarity, and her anxiety slipped away. "I was just goin' ta offer ya a hand in the matter," he continued. "The Barrens can be a dangerous place this time of night."

"What's up there?" Percilla asked, pointing to Shru's rope.

"You'll have ta see. Join me for a stroll?"

"I don't—"

"How do ya plan ta find what ya lookin' for down here? It's a bit dark."

"I'm not sure."

"If it ain't outta ya way, I can take ya to meet a sorceress who can help ya."

"Help me how?"

"Trust me. Now, up we go. Yes?"

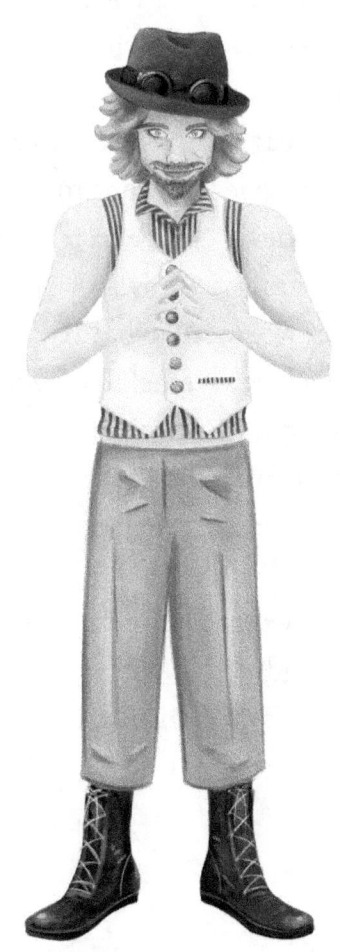

Shru gazed sternly into Percilla's eyes again, as if he expected her to do something she couldn't fathom. But then she felt the most peculiar lightness. Whatever hesitation she'd held toward the odd stranger melted away, drifting into the open air around her. She could go with him up that rope. Of course she could. "Yes," she replied, surprised by how flat her own voice sounded.

"Let me take ya bag for ya. The first time up can be a little tricky."

Percilla handed him the satchel, spell book and all, wondering briefly why she would do such a thing before that confusion also disappeared.

"After you, my dear," Shru said with a smirk.

She stood, approached the rope to grasp it with both hands, and climbed. She'd never climbed a rope before in her life, especially not one hanging soundly from the sky. But apparently, her body now knew exactly what to do. The sounds of Shru rummaging through her satchel rose below her, and while some tiny voice screamed in the back of her mind that he shouldn't be allowed to do so, her hands and feet inched her skillfully up the rope. It all seemed perfectly normal and so very wrong at the same time.

"Ya doin' okay, sweets?" Shru called up to her.

"Yes," Percilla said.

"Peaches." She heard him offer a short chuckle. "Just peaches."

CHAPTER 7

Eccentricities

WITH RELATIVE EASE, both Shru and Percilla climbed all the way to the top of the rope. Much to her surprise, the rope hung, as if levitating, off the edge of a transparent walkway in the sky. Through this, she saw the blurred reflections of the clouds, which were the only reason she could see the structure at all. In a dazed state, Percilla hesitated to step foot onto the mirror-like surface for fear of falling straight through it. She looked down to Shru for guidance with wide eyes.

"Keep going," Shru shouted from below. "Nothin' gonna hurt ya. It's only the Sky Way."

Obeying his orders, Percilla leapt and steadied herself on the Sky Way, finding it to be remarkably stable despite its fragile appearance. Shru followed close behind and joined her among the clouds, leaping onto the platform and patting the dust from his clothes.

Percilla's legs wobbled as her vision got the better of her senses and filled her with a queasy discomfort. But after a short moment and a few more steps, her feet grew used to the invisible floor beneath them. Filled with wonder, her eyes surveyed her new surroundings. When she looked up from her feet, however, the waning full moon's bright light blinded her. Up close, the lunar sphere glowed far more intensely than it had when viewed from the ground. She shielded her eyes with both hands, crouching down to keep herself from tumbling over the edge of the walkway.

But Shru, with his jet-black goggles now back over his eyes, was seemingly immune to the blinding luminescence and simply went about his business pulling his magic rope back up to the Sky Way. He hurried onward, taking no interest in Percilla or her discomfort.

"No time ta waste," Shru called back to her without turning around. When he received no reply, he whirled toward her to finally notice she had made little progress on the Sky Way. With an annoyed groan, he approached her again and produced a sparkling pair of glasses from his pockets, which he handed to her. "Moonglasses. You'll be needin' these. And this, I suppose." Also from his jacket, his pulled her satchel and pressed it toward her. "Come."

Percilla did as she was told, too distracted by the light to do much more than accept the return of her satchel, then put the Moonglasses on her face. She hesitantly lifted her head toward the moonlight for an unsure peek, half expecting the light to still blind her. But instead, it was now dim and pleasant to look upon, providing only as much light as was needed to illuminate her surroundings. She admired the moon's beauty for a moment, and when it became clear the sparkling spectacles had permanently tamed the moon's brightness to a soft glow, she let herself fully take in her surroundings.

The night was filled with clouds shimmering in the moon's brilliance. Behind the wispy puffs, an empty canvas of black sky had been studded with millions of dazzling stars more colorful than Percilla had ever noticed from her vantage point in Gangleton. In the far-off distance, groups of neon-colored, glowing air balloons floated through the midnight skyline with rhythmic gasps of flickering flames. Beside them, people gathered atop flying carpets, holding parasols illuminated in a variety of colors, painting the sky wherever they went with vibrant hues. Elegant, long-tailed night birds flew from cloud to cloud with absolute freedom. Fluorescent lunar butterflies fluttered, spreading softly glowing pollen over the Sky Way with each flap of their wings. And the night itself joined the travelers in their frolic, the stars twinkling and the full moon beaming down upon it all.

Shru walked briskly along the Sky Way, too accustomed to the marvelous sights around him to care for their beauty. Percilla by comparison walked leisurely, taking her sweet time to fully take in the experience that so enchanted her and filled her with wonder. By the time she had finally caught up to Shru, he was smoking a pipe and gestured to a rope at his feet when she arrived.

"Bout time," he said with obvious impatience. "Here's our departure. Now, ya won't be wantin' ta wake her. She's got a horrible temper. So just find a tree and rest for a bit, and we'll talk with her in the mornin'. Got it?"

"Flyin' on it," Percilla replied, thinking she had perhaps misjudged Shru. She took to the rope and traveled down through cloud and moon and starlight. Shru followed her closely, constantly looking about as if preparing for something to attack.

At the bottom of the rope, Percilla dropped down to a patch of soft grass. The cool air, now thick with moisture, caressed her face, carrying with it a pungent smell she'd certainly never recognized. At first, she couldn't see a thing, and she didn't hear much more than water pouring and crashing, creating a liveliness of its own. Her eyes settled on the dimly lit patch of grass where they'd landed, and Percilla saw an old, tall tree, its scent and the pattern of its bark reminding her of Gangleton. Tired from her journey so far, she sat with her back against the tree and allowed herself to rest while Shru wandered away into the darkness.

Percilla felt the weight of her body finally releasing into the ground below her. It had been some time since she'd had the opportunity to sit and do nothing. A glare of light pulled her eyes up toward Shru's dark silhouette; he stood just beyond her with his sight fixed on a metal object dangling from one of the tree's branches. Scanning the rest of the tree, Percilla was shocked to see an array of oddities dangling from nearly every section of every branch. These things were more like a collection Percilla's grandmother might very well have kept hidden in her study. Once more coaxed by the moonlight's charm, her gaze drifted out toward the luminary glimmering upon a vast expanse of water all around the sandy shores of this land. Its ebb and flow washed over her with a sound very much like deep breathing. The soothing rhythm dissolved her anxious thoughts

and gave way to the emptiness awaiting dreams. Just before her eyelids closed, one final spectacle caught her attention. The moonlight danced upon a formation of sparkling gemstones rising from the ground, filling her mind with wonder—a curiosity she knew would be better satisfied in the daylight.

Percilla slept under the grand cherry tree until the waning moon had long fallen over the horizon and the glorious seaside sun had risen from beyond the coastline. She was awakened by a cherry hitting her head, jolting her from a peaceful slumber. Startled, she wiggled against the tree in a daze. And then another cherry hit her head. Aggravated and fully awake now, she looked up to see a third cherry falling toward her but was too slow to escape it. The fruit hit her smack-dab between the eyes.

Frowning, she peered up toward the top of the tree to find what caused so many cherries to fall from the sturdy limbs. There she saw a woman lounging above her on the tree's upper branches, snacking on a handful of its fruit, seemingly unaware of Percilla's presence below her.

The enigmatic woman had a poised eccentricity about her and wore a royal-blue, full-length jacket with lace cuffs. Beneath the jacket peeked a silk maroon dress with a lace hem, shorter in the front and draped in the back. Long, lace stockings covered her legs, tucked neatly into short boots. The woman gazed through glasses without lenses at a peculiar painting of extremely long-legged elephants in some sort of procession. This artwork was mounted on the thick bark of the grand cherry tree's trunk where the woman sat, and she closely admired its fine brush strokes where a ray of sunlight perfectly struck the artwork.

Percilla figured this woman was surely the sorceress of which Shru had spoken. Remembering his warning about her temper, she attempted to sneak away from the tree until Shru could properly introduce them. She had barely taken a step before the woman above her loudly cleared her throat, stopping Percilla dead in her tracks.

"I've already seen you," the woman said, more than loud enough for Percilla to hear and never looking away from the painting.

"Oh," Percilla said, surprised she'd failed to slip away unnoticed despite her impressive record of stealing through Gangleton's spiraling streets. If she could evade the Dignitaries but not this woman, this stranger sitting in the tree was surely just as Shru had made her out to be.

The woman retrieved a pair of petite, ornate binoculars from her jacket to peer through at Percilla and stated very matter-of-factly, "You were sleeping under my tree."

"Did you just drop cherries on me?" Percilla asked.

"Welcome to Fridanda!" the woman shouted whimsically and stood upon the branch. Then she disappeared in an explosive cloud of maroon smoke.

Five little musician figurines carrying a tuba, a trombone, a clarinet, drums, and an accordion suddenly sprang up from the base of the tree. In an instant, they grew to human size and came to life, playing a spirited marching-band show with the magic of melody. The woman in the royal-blue jacket appeared at the center of the enchanted figurines, slipping right into the band. With a playful rhythm, she sang as the figurines danced and played around her, putting on a show with lifelike shaking and spinning for Percilla—their sole audience member.

"Welcome to Fridanda.
Welcome to Fridanda.
I have potions, wands, and shoes.
Crystals, books, and bikes for two.
Welcome to Fridanda.
Welcome to Fridanda.
Where travelers come to find their way or dealers seek to make a
trade.
Welcome to Fridanda.
Welcome to Fridanda.
There's only one thing I can't do.
I really can't change your fate for you.
Welcome to Fridanda.
Welcome to Fridanda."

The performance ended, and the figurines collapsed back into their original sizes and places on the ground. Just as the woman finished her song, a coconut flew right into her waiting hand. She picked a sprig of mint from a hanging basket on the tree to go with her tropical fruit and completed her performance by boasting again, "Welcome to Fridanda."

"Who are you?" Percilla asked in amazement.

"Frida," the woman replied. "And you?"

"Percilla."

"Now that the formality is out of the way, what do you want, love?" Frida cracked the top off the coconut and dropped the mint inside.

"I'm going to... well, I need—"

"To have some clothing made?" Frida interrupted, replacing the top on her coconut and staring curiously at Percilla's hat. "Give up the hat, and we'll call it a fair trade." She tossed the coconut to Percilla and walked to one of the extremely worn-out chests lying around the grand cherry tree's trunk.

"Fair trade?" Percilla shouted as she stumbled to catch Frida's coconut. "Give up my hat? No!"

"You'll have to speak up, love," Frida replied, her head half buried inside the chest. "My head's in a trunk. Oh, and do shake the coconut please." She pulled out a tape measure, pins, and a pincushion. "Lift up your arms so I can get your measurements."

Amused by Frida's performance and unusual nature, Percilla shook the coconut while Frida approached with her tailoring tools. "I don't want any clothing made."

"What do you mean?" Frida asked, feigning shock. "At least let me put you in something with a little more... zazz."

"Why?"

"Well, wherever you're going, you ought to look nice." Frida cocked her head. "Where are you going?"

"To Rou," Percilla replied.

"Rou?" Frida asked in an obvious mockery of amazement. "Really? And how do you suppose you'll get there?"

"That's what I need to know. Where is—"

"Splendid!" Frida shouted. "Everyone seems to find me when they need me. How do you think I got all these things?" She grabbed the coconut from Percilla.

"I don't know," Percilla said, half curious and half peeved.

Frida stabbed a straw into the coconut and handed it back to the girl. "I help people, people help me. Drink up." A chime rang out from the tree. Frida whisked her head toward the sound, and the chime repeated. "Oh, seems we have movement up there." The woman hurried toward the foreign sound.

"Up where?" Percilla asked, following close behind.

Frida retrieved the noisy apparatus from a hanging basket, and when she tapped it, a light appeared on the device.

"What is that?" Percilla could only peer in wonderment for a better look.

"My planetary apparatus, though I believe it was called an *I phoney*," Frida replied, as if it were obvious. "Bit beat up and old, but it works quite nicely."

"What does it do?"

"All sorts. The alchemist who gave it to me went on and on about its purpose in ancient times. Really, I couldn't care less for the lot. Though its extremely accurate location of the planets and notification of the astrological happenings, that... *that* I could not turn down."

"Interesting," Percilla replied.

"Seems Pluto is squaring Mars, Uranus trine Pluto, and Venus square Jupiter," Frida said, scrolling through the screen just out of Percilla's sight. "No wonder."

"What?"

"You showing up here all determined for something you're so unsure of."

"I am not unsure," Percilla corrected. "I know where I'm going. I just don't know how to get there."

"Yes... so... uh-huh." Frida filled a golden chalice with water from a tiny waterfall cascading from a cloud in the sky. "I've got it. The perfect jacket for you." The woman took a quick sip of water, then dashed up the tree and retrieved a box from one of its branches. Just as quickly as she had grabbed it, she swung back down to the ground and opened the box in front of Percilla. From within this, she revealed a teal, knee-length, form-fitting jacket with a large hood and gold detailing. "Extraordinary piece. I was saving it for when this marvelous number burst out, but you look like you need it now. Yes?"

"Okay," Percilla replied, impressed by the jacket. "But I don't have anything to trade. I only have this..." She looked inside her satchel and found Vahn's spell book missing. "It's gone. That worm!" she shouted, remembering Shru and realizing he wasn't anywhere to be found.

"Excuse me?" Frida asked.

"Shru. The weasel who brought me here," Percilla replied, looking around for any sign of him.

"What? *Shru* was in Fridanda?" Not waiting for Percilla to answer, Frida darted about, stooping to rifle through trunks and boxes scattered in and around the cherry tree. She stopped at the tree, where one barren nail lay next to an empty hook. "Blah! He's always taking, taking, taking. Never trading, just taking. I hope that watch turns him back in time to the apocalypse. That'll teach him." Her dubious chuckle seemed highly uncharacteristic, for as little as Percilla knew of her. Seeing Percilla near frightened by her outburst, Frida straightened herself out, dusted her cuffs, and regained her composure.

"Apoca—what?" Percilla asked, beyond confused by this point. "He took my spell book. I need it back."

"Yes," Frida replied succinctly. "You can't trust that man. Hmm, what about the hat? I'll take the hat instead. It's all right."

"I can't give you the hat. It... it was my grandmother's. It means a lot to me."

"Right. No worries." Frida gave a tight smile, but her voice was laced with agitation. "Today is free day at Fridanda. Have the jacket. You need it." She flopped the jacket into Percilla's arms. "Dressed like that, people are bound to know you're from Gangleton. And then you're just asking for trouble."

"What do you mean?"

"Gangleton folk are the perfect example of what happens when you believe everything you hear. Targets for the evils that lurk. What brings you to Rou?"

"I'm returning the Eye—" Percilla realized her mistake and forced a cough in an attempt to cover it up. "Oh, excuse me. I'm returning to the home of my ancestors."

"Were you about to say..." Frida leaned in to whisper, "Eye of Rou?"

"No. Maybe." Percilla leaned in as well to whisper, "What does it mean to you?"

"What does it mean to me?" Frida shouted, as if she had been personally insulted. "Excuse me, but you are talking to an *original* member of Gangleton. My family was the sworn guardian of Gangleton's Eye of Rou. Mother must have passed it to another family when she died."

"No, it's been in my family since Gangleton's beginning."

"Impossible." Frida huffed. "Who gave it to you?"

"My grandmother Vic—"

"Victoria! But she... you're her granddaughter?"

"Yes."

"So you're my grandniece?"

"What?" Percilla stared at the woman. "How? You're like a hundred years younger than she was."

"No, I'm eighty-eight." Frida seemed to take great pleasure in making the correction. "Three years younger than she. Time is a lot different beyond the Force Field of Gangleton."

Percilla perked up at the thought of more revealing tales of the village she called home. "How's that?"

"Well, that's a whole history. Let's just put it this way. Any place where people are constantly in fear and don't know their purpose causes one to age twice as quick. Not to mention the Force Field holding in old, stagnant air. That's why we left."

"Who?"

"Victoria and myself, but let's save that for another time, shall we? Tell me, how is my sister? I thought for sure they had done something horrible to her."

"They did," Percilla muttered, her head sinking down until she stared at the grass beneath her. "If by *they* you mean the Dignitaries."

"You just said she was alive." Frida tipped her head and stared at the girl.

"Until yesterday or the day before." Percilla sighed. "Time is weird."

"You mean they murdered her?"

She nodded slowly, trying as hard as she could to keep her composure. Percilla would always love her grandmother, but she wished to leave the pain of Victoria's death behind her in Gangleton. "That's why I'm going to Rou."

"All by yourself!" Frida shouted.

"Didn't really have time to invite anyone. *You're* going to come with, right?"

"Come with?"

"Yeah. I mean, you are part of the family."

"I am," Frida replied with one eye open. "Let me just sit with it for a moment. Ta-nan." Her right hand whisked in a circle, fingers twirling together then pulling downward, and a sparkling amethyst sphere manifested from the ether, upon which she now sat. Eyes closed, she fell silent for but a moment before she nodded. "No time to lose."

"You'll come?" Percilla asked.

"Yes. You obviously need my help."

"Obviously."

"Put on that jacket. Aw... Victoria always had good taste in hats." Frida sighed, eyeing the hat atop Percilla's head. "Such a fine hat."

"Would you like to wear it?"

"No, it looks lovely on you. Plus, it hides your ravens quite nicely."

Percilla's eyes grew wide. "How did you know about my—"

"Darling, I have been on this island for many moons. I have experienced it all. From secret motives to intellectual brawls debating where we come from to dragons to flying carpets. I can tell a fish hook when I see one. Okay. Now, let me just pack a little bag." Frida opened a petite, embellished bag hanging from one of the tree's branches. "Tin-sin tin-sin ahn. Prim-sin prim-sin. Fip-sin fip-sin ahn. Krim tra mana."

Every object in Fridanda at once levitated from its place and shrank down to a tiny size, pulled by Frida's spell toward her little bag. There, each thing proceeded to pack itself. For only a few seconds, it seemed as if a blissful tornado had blown through to rhythmically sort through the island, gently whisking Frida's vast collection of trinkets into a show of splendor, only for the whole island to be left completely empty of her things.

"All right, that ought to do it," Frida said, apparently quite pleased with herself. "And this is for you." She handed Percilla a black raven pin and golden chain upon which was strung a pointed crystal wrapped in gold wire.

"How did you do... *What?*" Percilla barely managed to get the words out through her shock.

"A story for another time. And that is your very own pendulum made from your old jacket materials."

"What?" she repeated.

"It's a pendulum already programmed for your personal use." Frida produced a small contraption from her bag and set it on the ground at her feet.

"Okay," Percilla said, still staring at the pendulum, "and what do I do with it?"

"Ask it questions, of course. Kry-sm hip-sna." The contraption swelled to full size, startling Percilla, who was still not used to Frida's miraculous sorcery or the appearance of such sleek contraptions.

"Why would I ask it questions?" Percilla asked.

"Many reasons," Frida replied. "Perhaps to find Rou. Shall we?"

Percilla thought about what else she'd ask, and her eyes drifted from the pendulum toward the now rather large machine. "What is *that*?"

"An automobile, or so I've been told. A much finer contraption than any of our modern machines. The ancient ones truly had such fine craftsmanship." Frida pointed to a T on the front of the vehicle. "Called it a T... Teeshla? Something like that. I've been waiting for the day I could use this treasure. Hop in."

Frida opened the car's passenger door, and Percilla cautiously slid inside. She stared at her pendulum, still not quite sure what she was supposed to do with it. With a fluid wave of her hand, Frida split the aqua-blue water of the coastline into walls on either side of them, clearing it from the bottom of the sea to create a sandy path to the distant blur of the mainland miles away. When Percilla looked up at the sound of rushing water, her mouth dropped open at the sight of the sea parted in front of them.

"How did you do that?" she whispered.

Frida closed her own door and settled behind the wheel. "Magic. Hang on. I've never done this before. To Rou!"

CHAPTER 8

Vengeance

NYLZ AND LYKEN followed close behind Franc, who led them into the chamber room of a secret cavern within what was known as the Caves of Seoj. The caves were well hidden in the steep mountains neighboring Gangleton. Smooth obsidian stone paved the path through twisting subterranean tunnels and darkened depths carved out long ago by magic of a kind no longer used or known. An eerie white light from some unseen source lit the walls just enough for the Dignitaries to see their way through the caves. Inside the chamber, Vahn, now the Dignitaries' prisoner, sat in a wooden chair at the center of the cavern.

Franc slowly approached the boy with Nylz and Lyken flanking her. She dominated the room, her shadow cast across the obsidian walls slowly closing in on its prey. She tried to lock her eyes with his, but the strong-willed lad resisted her gaze with a fiery glint of defiance. He had not said anything useful to them since his capture, and he would not be broken as easily as the Dignitaries' other prisoners.

"What have you done with the Eye of Rou?" Lyken asked, skulking behind Vahn with prowling steps, spindly fingers reaching for his head.

Vahn gave an irritated sigh. "I told you, I have nothing to do with the Eye of Rou." He wondered how many times he had already repeated himself. "That was not my family's duty. We were the—"

Lyken wound his fingers through Vahn's hair, then yanked back, cutting off the boy's words. The pale man loomed over him, his piercing eyes stabbing directly into Vahn's. "I can sense falsities." Vahn knew Lyken would not tolerate any lies, yet he also knew the Dignitary was quite aware he'd spoken nothing but the truth. "Vahn, it is quite necessary for the safety of Gangleton that we have the Eye of Rou."

Vahn sighed again, his aggravation growing. "I don't—"

"Don't lie," Franc warned. "Just tell us where it is!" She hadn't been this curt and abruptly impatient with him before now.

Lyken offered a toothy grin and leaned toward Vahn's face. "Or we will pull the information from your mind," he said with grotesque excitement.

"You can't. None of you have that power," Vahn argued. Lyken only cackled. "You can laugh, but you've already tried to break into my mind. Look, I'm still me, free of your evils." The Dignitary's laughter grew louder. No one had such power; Vahn had to believe it wasn't true.

But then Drendle came lumbering down the corridor from beyond the chamber with a man walking closely behind him and dressed far differently than the Dignitaries. Beneath his long black cloak, he wore a belt of artifacts, bones, feathers, pouches, and other curiosities. His face remained concealed under the shadow of his wide-brimmed hat adorned with the same types of bizarre objects, his lips stretched into a mischievous grin. As he came to a stop, leaning on his intricately carved staff, he peered out into the room, unfocused and seemingly unimpressed by any of it.

"I heard you are in need of my services," the man said in a raspy voice.

Only able to hear the voice and see the shadow of the man against the wall, Vahn wondered who this tall, hatted figure was towering behind him. As the shadow shrank, its source drawing closer, Vahn turned his head and was met with the stranger's milky-white eyes. He gasped, never having seen an oracle in person before. He'd only heard tales of their power of prophecy. His blood ran cold, and he grabbed a tighter hold of the chair's arms. Could this man really do what the stories said? Vahn did his best to hide his fear, but Lyken's sneer told him he was failing miserably at it.

"Vincent," Franc said as she approached the man. "We need answers from him."

"And I am here to help. For the right price, of course."

"Don't help them!" Vahn yelled, unable to stop himself.

Lyken darted his pointed finger at the boy with a sinister smile, warning him to keep quiet without having to speak a word.

Vincent blinked but paid no attention to the exchange. "Price, Dignitary. Make it good. I know where you've been."

Franc ground her teeth and reached for a small leather pouch at her hip. She tossed it to him. Vahn expected it to hit the ground, but Vincent caught it and hefted it in his hand.

"I expect more next time," he said, digging into the bag to pull out a handful of blue gemstones. Satisfied, he dropped them back in the bag and slipped it beneath his robes. "Can an old man get a chair?"

Drendle dragged over a second chair and placed it before Vahn. The oracle found his way to it without any help and sat down. He rested his staff against the back of the chair, then placed the backs of hands on his thighs. In a muted voice, he recited incantations Vahn had never heard. The words spilling from his lips became blue fumes flowing from his mouth, lifting through the air between them to encompass Vahn. A new wave of terror ran through Vahn when the man's white eyes blinked into black tunnels pulling his gaze. There was no way to escape the oracle. Eyes locked firmly, Vahn trembled at the sight of the swirling clouds within the old man's eyes. The oracle continued his incantation, stealing from Vahn every memory, every thought he'd ever had or known.

"Ask your questions." The oracle's voice droned, completely flat.

Vahn feared the worst; this man possessed magic far beyond anything he had ever heard mentioned.

"He'll leave you with no memories of your life if you don't cooperate," Lyken crooned.

"Let's begin," Franc insisted. "Vahn, how long has your family held the Eye of Rou?"

"My family was the keeper of the spell book," Vahn reluctantly divulged, preferring to cooperate rather than have the answers ripped from his mind.

"A lie will not slip from a tongue so pure," Vincent said. "A girl overlooked as weak is the one with whom you need to speak."

"Is that so?" Franc asked. Her eyes widened, and a slow, intrigued smile curled her lips. "Which girl?"

Vahn struggled to think of anything but the girl in question. He forced himself to remember his grandfather, the gardens, his ravens, anything at all, but then her face flared to life in his mind, and he sagged against the chair.

Vincent's eyes narrowed with his stolen knowledge. "Percilla."

"Percilla?" Nylz asked, her jaw hanging open below wide eyes.

Though Vahn heard the fury in Franc's voice, her lack of expressed emotion did not change in its delivery. "Bring in Percilla," she commanded, swiveling her head toward Nylz. Nylz instantly reached for a rotary phone built onto the chamber wall and hastily phoned Gangleton.

The Dignitaries watched her intently, as Vincent remained deep in a trance, holding Vahn's gaze. Then a flash of light flared into Vahn's eyes, releasing him from the forced contact with the oracle. He looked in the direction from where the light had come and saw it just barely discernible against the far wall of the chamber. It grew, almost seeping through the stone wall, and Vahn thought he saw it take on a blueish tinge.

"Percilla should be here shortly," Nylz announced, slamming the phone back onto its cradle.

"Let's hope she's ready to accept our offer," Franc said with a devious grin.

Vahn glanced from one Dignitary to the next, all of whom seemed completely unaware of the blue shimmer now making its way toward them and where Vahn sat strapped in the chair. It didn't seem dangerous, as far as he could tell, and the curious fact that he saw something the Dignitaries did not made him hold his tongue.

Almost instantly, the rotary phone rang again, its cradle rattling against the stone wall. Nylz shot a confused, hesitant glance at the phone, then answered it. Her brows lifted, then she scowled. "What do you mean she's not there?" she shouted.

Franc silently turned to Nylz with a stare bordering on murderous.

"In the Barrens?" Nylz shouted again.

Something warm fluttered against his shoulder, and Vahn turned his head to see the blue shimmer had now made it across the chamber. He thought he would have flinched away from it, but the brief contact had filled him with an undeniable peace and comfort in the presence of this unknown thing. He watched it float past him and come to a stop behind the oracle, still apparently unseen and unfelt by anyone else.

Highly intrigued now, Vahn stared at the wavering presence, which surprised him by taking on the general shape of a man, though its features were still mostly blurred. In two seconds, the shimmering blue solidified just enough for the man's face to take on detail. Eyes glowing in an unearthly blue aura opened from within the vague form to catch Vahn in their ethereal gaze. A wide grin spread across the figure's face, and it lifted a blurred, spectral finger to its lips, warning Vahn to be quiet. It wasn't a harsh warning at all—more like a child planning to sneak up on its parent—and Vahn pressed his lips together to keep from inadvertently alerting the Dignitaries to this foreign presence. Then the details of the figure's face blended again into more ethereal blue, and the figure placed both hands against the oracle's temples. The old man did not respond to the contact.

Nylz hung up the rotary phone once more, then turned to Franc and reluctantly reported, "Percilla is in the Barrens."

"Of course she is," Franc snapped. "Perhaps we have underestimated this one. Track her down immediately."

To hear that Percilla had escaped Gangleton and was now out in the Barrens made Vahn's heart soar right before it sank to the very bottom of his chest. He was glad she was far away, maybe even out of the Dignitaries' reach. At the same time, he'd meant to go with her, and he would probably never know whether she had help now on her way to Rou or not. But she did have his grandfather's spell book, so that was something.

Franc and Nylz dove into some new conversation Vahn did not hear; he was too focused on the blue, spirit-like form turning its head toward Franc. When the shimmering man opened his mouth, he perfectly mimicked Vincent's voice, which echoed throughout the chamber, as though the figure were a ventriloquist and the oracle his new dummy. "Be still. The girl is clever, for she hath never left Gangleton."

Franc turned toward Vincent with a momentary flash of rage, which subsided instantly when she saw him. Vincent was still lost in his trance, eyes focused on Vahn. "What?" she replied. But the blind seer had nothing to give her, for he had not spoken at all. "Oracles," she grunted, then turned away from Vincent to continue her orders to Nylz. "Send the message to Gangleton that Percilla has turned against us."

Nylz opened her mouth to respond, but the shimmering presence behind the oracle spoke first, louder this time and still perfectly mimicking Vincent's voice. "Beware. Anger is your downfall and will come back to bite your ass-ets off."

Vahn fought to contain his smirk. Watching Franc's face turn three shades of red was well worth the effort.

Franc turned again to Vincent, seething. "What do you mean my assets?" Again, the oracle gave her no reply. Franc let out a sharp growl of irritation, then turned back to Nylz. "Let it be known Percilla was the one who betrayed Gangleton."

"You have been warned," the spirit continued. "The next full moon shall strike vengeance on thee."

"We do not fear vengeance!" Franc shouted, no longer able to conceal her rage when she whipped back around toward Vincent. "We *are* vengeance. Drendle," she barked, pointing at the seemingly calm Dignitary and then swinging her finger back toward Vincent, "take him out of here."

Drendle lumbered toward Vincent as the spirit moaned, "Beware! Beware! For as a raven is fare, you shall find your despair."

An eerie laugh bellowed from Vincent himself this time, and the second voice mimicked him. Louder and louder the eerily hollow tone and the echo of itself grew, filling the chamber entirely. Drendle hesitantly approached the oracle, pausing with a look of alarm aimed toward Franc.

"Now!" she shouted. "Don't look at me with fear in your eyes. Take him away, or I'll have you washed again to remind you why we don't fear."

Drendle snapped into action, tapping the oracle on the shoulder. Vincent slowly exited the chamber, still laughing, his staff clicking against the obsidian stone at his feet. Franc groaned in frustration and slowly rubbed her face.

With the oracle gone from the chair in front of him, Vahn had a full view of the still hazy form that had spoken with the old seer's voice. Again, the eerily blue eyes that apparently only he could see materialized just long enough to offer Vahn a quick wink. Then the entire spirit-like form dispersed into a cloudy blue mist, its presence Vahn had been able to feel no longer with him in the chamber. But the peace it had given him remained.

CHAPTER 9

Art of Sorcery

RIDA'S CAR STOPPED just before it would have emerged from the pathway leading them effortlessly across the ocean floor to the mainland leading into the Barrens. The watery walls raised by Frida's spell remained standing, shielding Frida and Percilla from the crashing of waves and the cold embrace of the sea, along with the creatures swimming through its depths. Heat poured down onto the earth from a sizzling mid-day sun looming over the wasteland. The coastline was a long stretch of ashen sand touching the shore where Frida had parked the car. As the sand was pulled further inland, it gave way to a sparse and scattered web of cracked, dry earth strewn about with long-worn, ancient trinkets and skeleton trees jutting from wherever life had once grown. Farther in the distance, Percilla saw the outline of mountain ranges. All across this landscape, rising towers of weathered rock jutted from the baked earth. This was no land for the living.

"Here's our exit," Frida announced. "Don't forget anything."

"What?" Percilla asked with some discomfort. "Why don't we just go all the way to Rou?"

"Don't be absurd. This thing is a show in and of itself," Frida said, gesturing toward the car. "Best to go subtly across these lawless lands."

Percilla found a wise truth to Frida's words. If any more devious characters like the Dignitaries or Shru wandered the Barrens, it would certainly be best to keep hidden and out of sight. And this car would without a doubt attract unwanted attention.

Frida and Percilla both stepped out of the car and onto the wet shore. But as the pair set foot onto the solid ground, a gurgling slurp alerted them to a third figure looming at their backs. When they looked over their shoulders, they found themselves staring at a giant sea creature, which had suctioned itself to the back of the car. The slimy beast was three times the size of a man, its five massive tentacles latched onto the car's rear bumper. A rather slippery-looking, neon-pink slime coated its glowing green skin, and its two huge, intimidating eyes—as large as dinner plates—stared at Frida.

"Oh, goodness." Frida gasped. "See what I mean?" Despite the creature's appearance, the sorceress remained remarkably calm.

Percilla, on the other hand, leapt back from the car at first sight of the brute, her arms shooting up in defense.

"I didn't even realize he was aboard," Frida said with a chuckle, then turned away from the sea creature to face Percilla. As she did, the slimy beast raised its tentacled body off the car. Apparently threatened by the sorceress' sudden movement, it lifted one of its slippery appendages to reveal what could best have been described as a mouth. Pointing itself directly toward Frida, the creature froze, and its maw snapped open.

"Come to think of it, I did feel a little tug at one point," Frida mused, oblivious to the rising beast behind her.

Percilla pointed at the creature. "Look out!"

The creature shot a thick spray of jet-black ink from its mouth with incredible accuracy. At the same moment, Frida spun around and calmly chanted, "Cap-tru-num!"

The ink stopped mid-air, frozen on its course amid the multi-colored specks twinkling throughout the black mass now at Frida's command. The woman pulled a miniature jar from her bag and added, "Instra-ma-naen." The ink poured itself straight into the jar. "Thank you," she said happily to the creature. "Your ink is not easy to acquire. Good day." The beastly thing shook itself, rose from the back of the car, and lumbered back into the sea. Frida stored the ink-filled jar within her bag and raised a hand toward the standing walls of the ocean's water. "Ya-bis Eer-ita," she said, and with a flick of her wrist, the water crashed back into place. Nodding in apparent satisfaction, she hastened her steps toward the Barrens, leaving the beach behind her.

Percilla quickly followed her in absolute awe of her skill and composure. "How did you learn all this?"

"Marvelous teachers," Frida replied.

They left the beach and strolled into the Barrens at a brisk pace, casually chatting about anything and nothing. A thin sheen of sweat built on their foreheads and cheeks, intensifying with every step. Once they had lost sight of the coastline behind them, their environment did not change no matter how far they traveled. Everywhere, it was the same—cracked earth and dead trees bursting through it, the ground studded by the occasional cliff of hard, jagged rock. Soon, even the desert sands had vanished completely into the flat plateau.

When the sun had reached its apex, the pair came upon a strangely shaped silhouette in the distance. Percilla stopped and looked to Frida for guidance, who simply strolled toward the unknown thing without the slightest worry or word of warning. Percilla followed close behind her, and when they'd approached enough to make out what they'd seen, both were surprised to find a force field similar to Gangleton's. Only this was much smaller, and it contained a person instead of a town. The force field hummed, and the prismatic light emitting from it flickered across the ground. Far too curious for caution, Percilla stepped toward it.

"Get away from that," Frida scolded. "There's no telling when they'll come for it."

Percilla stopped in her tracks. "That force field trapped someone on purpose?"

"Exactly," Frida replied, "and the people coming for him or her or whatever's in that cage would be overjoyed to see you again..." The woman peered at the small force field again, and her eyes narrowed. "Is that..."

"That's Shru," Percilla confirmed. "We need to get him out. I want my spell book."

"No," Frida said. "He deserves a good manipulation hex. I can get you another spell book. Why don't you have it memorized?"

"First off, Gangleton doesn't teach magic or wisdom or whatever is in that book anymore. Second, that is *the* original spell book."

"Original?" Frida's eyes widened, and a slow smile bloomed along her lips. "That's a good trade."

They further approached the force field, still unsure as to whether this was only a shrewd scheme and hesitant to be tricked yet again. Shru had to have seen them, but he did not try to meet their gazes or call out. Percilla found a certain satisfaction in what seemed the thief's moderate embarrassment at now being discovered caught in this trap. Frida waved at him, and when they were close enough that the man couldn't pretend not to notice, he offered a sheepish smile instead.

"You finally got caught," Frida gloated. "How did they do it?"

Shru gave a defeated shrug.

Percilla stormed past Frida and added, "We will let you out if you give back the things you stole."

Shru's eyes widened, but he shrugged again, like he had absolutely no idea what she was talking about, and didn't say a word.

Frida frowned, studying the trapped thief, then glanced behind him and shouted, "Look!" She pointed toward the empty red horizon in the distance. "A white elephant contraption heading this way. Who could it *possibly* be?"

Shru twisted around within his prismatic cage, searching as if the mere thought of the Dignitaries' approach on their elephant terrified him.

"I imagine it's quite difficult to see anything from where you're sitting," Frida added.

This seemed to spark the thief's decision, and he hastily pulled from his jacket the spell book he'd stolen from Percilla and a gold-framed mirror he'd taken from Frida's cherry tree.

"That's nice," Frida said. "You're giving back half of what you took." She looked out into the Barrens again. "Splendid. It's the Dignitaries. They must be coming to throw you a welcoming party."

Shru cringed and rifled through his pockets, shamefully pulling out an antique pocket watch on a gold chain, which shone with the effects of proper care. It jingled in his hand, swaying and glinting in the sun as he gazed at it in reluctance.

"How kind of you." Frida's sarcasm could not be overlooked, and she placed her open palms above the force-field cage. "Havana-keet-sen."

The force field disappeared, and Shru sat there dumbfounded, both hands extended toward Frida and Percilla. In them, he held all the things he'd stolen from them, offering the return of his saviors' belongings.

"Thank ya, sweets," the sly thief said. "How did ya do that?"

"It's a secret you'll never know if you keep stealing," Frida scolded, as if speaking to a child. She quickly scooped up the pocket watch, mirror, and spell book, then passed the man and kept walking. "Come, Percilla."

"What about me?" Shru asked.

"You stole from me," Percilla replied. She couldn't believe how anyone could be so incorrigible and shameless.

"I won't—" Shru said, cutting himself off in an attempt at honesty. "I can help. Ya need a man around."

"We most certainly do not," Frida said, lifting her brow. Then she blinked and studied the expanse of sunbaked earth on the horizon. She leaned forward and lifted a hand to shield her eyes, squinting to make out the foreign shape Percilla now noticed as well. Frida seemed surprised—and Percilla definitely was—to see the Dignitaries' mechanical elephant actually approaching this time. "The party has arrived," the woman said. "Act natural.

Put this on and march to my lead." Frida reached into her bag and pulled out a furry brown mask with comically large ears.

Not knowing what else to do and finding she trusted her great aunt, Percilla took the mask and put it on without question or complaint. Instantly, a tingling surge shot from her head to the tips of her toes, making her rather itchy.

Shru looked her up and down with a smirk, then chortled and said, "Well, hello, Percilla monkey."

"Don't call me a monkey," Percilla protested, and Shru's eyes widened in amusement.

"Can't understand you, dear," Frida said, turning around with a wry smile of her own. "This illusion extends to your voice as well. All I heard was a screech."

In that moment, Percilla realized the mask had indeed made her look and sound like a monkey—at least to everyone else. Not wanting to give Shru more ammunition for teasing her, she could only reply by stomping a foot down on the dry earth and folding her arms.

"Running from the Dignitaries, are you?" Shru asked with a smirk. "Maybe *they* will need my assistance, seeing as you don't."

"Fine. You can come," Frida replied, waving her hand in reluctant acceptance. "Now march."

Frida raised one foot in front of the other and took a big, long step forward. Percilla and Shru followed her lead, copying her movements for an exaggerated and tiresome march across the Barrens.

"Now to your left!" Frida ordered. The group veered to the left. "Lift your arm. Spin around. To your right. Lift your arm and spin around." Her orders came fast and loud, giving Percilla a bit of a panic as she struggled to march in unison with her aunt. "No, no," Frida said. "You're doing it all wrong. Let me show you."

Drendle and Nylz rode toward the three-member marching band, gazing around from atop their elephant machine as if they'd just woken up in a new and strange place. When they neared the trio of strangers, their eyes narrowed in confusion. Drendle produced a handheld rotary phone from his pouch.

Percilla couldn't hear his words, but he sounded anxious and hushed. She felt his eyes on her and the little ruse of their three-figure band. It made her nearly certain the Dignitaries were out here looking for her—maybe even for Shru, after the thief had been caught in their force field. With each passing moment, Percilla's skin crawled with wave after tingling wave, as if she had a physical reaction to how wrong everything felt.

Drendle spoke something into the phone, lifted a piece of paper to gaze at it, then glared toward her party. Percilla's heart pounded in her chest, and her legs wobbled. The Dignitary stared at her just long enough that she wondered if the monkey disguise had worn off. But she had to reassure herself with the fact that Frida would have said something if that were the case.

Nylz snatched the phone from Drendle and scowled at the three-person marching band. "Vagabonds," she uttered just loud enough for Percilla to hear. And with that, the Dignitaries rode away on their elephant, looking back every so often to convince themselves they hadn't missed a thing. Finally, they disappeared behind the closest butte.

With danger flown out of the way, Frida's enchantment wore off, and Percilla's appearance reversed itself entirely before the monkey mask fell at her feet. "*What* was that?" Percilla asked in disbelief. "Honestly, Frida? A monkey disguise was the best you had in your bag?"

"I was rushed, and it was all I could find. Plus, I've never seen it on anyone. You do make a cute monkey." Frida smirked. "What you just witnessed, my darling, was an almost certain attempt at what I call Dignitary deception."

"I've experienced that firsthand." Percilla shook her head to release the memory. "I thought for sure they'd discovered where I was."

"The force field in which we found this imbecile is most likely what led them here," Frida said, nodding with disdain toward Shru. "The Dignitaries use false compassion to inject fear into their captured prey, then carry them away under their oppressive conditioning."

"Where do they take them?"

"Have you ever noticed the population of Gangleton growing?"

"No. I kept to my friends," Percilla replied.

"And you all rebelliously lounged around in the Cherry Orchard without a care in mind as to what the Dignitaries were actually doing?" Frida asked.

"What else were we to do? Just agree to be puppets like all the rest?" Percilla tried not to shout in her own defense.

"Things just aren't as they used to be."

"Victoria said the same thing."

A loud, crunching footstep rose from behind them, and Frida whirled around to see Shru trying to sneak across the Barrens with the gilded mirror he'd now stolen from her for the second time. She took after him, snatched the trinket out of his hands, then removed his hat and flung it as far as she could. Without a word, she returned to Percilla's side and urged the girl to keep moving.

Shru quickly retrieved his hat, placed it back on his head, and walked after Frida. "Oh, come on. Ya said I could join," he whined.

"I saved your life," Frida shot back without turning to look at him. "We're even."

"I don't suppose you have the newest map of the Barrens, then?"

"Newest edition?" Frida stopped, then spun around to face him. "Let me see it."

Shru produced a rolled-up map from within his jacket and held it just out of arm's reach, pulling it back again when Frida made to grab it. "Ah, ah, ah. No touch till ya let me join."

For a minute, Percilla wasn't sure whether Frida would agree to let Shru join them or simply magic the thief out of existence. But then her great aunt smirked and caught the man's gaze. She leaned toward him, and Percilla saw without a doubt the man's pupils dilating into huge black pools. "Fine. You can come," Frida said with a smirk. "Under a few conditions."

"Lay it on me, sweetcakes."

"Keep your hands to yourself."

A cloudy haze swirled in Shru's dilated pupils. A bit thrown off by the sight, Percilla glanced at her great aunt to see the woman's gaze growing in concentrated intensity. "Yes," Shru replied, all emotion plucked from his voice.

"And you wear these." Frida removed from her bag a set of anklets draped with small, tinkling bells.

"Yes." Shru took them from her and slipped them onto his ankles.

"And these." She handed Shru a pair of donkey ears next. "Let me help you." With a beam of light emitted from a pendant around her neck, she cut two holes into Shru's hat before slipping the ears through the holes and placing both on his head. "Oh, and this," she added through a half chuckle, grabbing a beaked mask as well.

Shru took it without a hint of hesitation.

Frida dug around even more in her bag before slipping out a woman's tutu meant for a circus performance.

"Frida," Percilla said, partly annoyed by these shenanigans interrupting their journey and partly amused by Shru's fitting punishment.

"And this," Frida continued.

"Yes." Shru obeyed, of course, and now donned the tutu.

"And..." Frida pulled an entire parasol from her bag, which Shru seemed to gladly accept.

"Um... Frida?" Percilla tried again, realizing now that her great aunt hadn't heard her the first time.

"This," Frida said. "And..."

"*Frida.*"

"Yes?" The woman turned to Percilla and blinked rapidly, as if jerked out of a highly entertaining daydream.

"I think we should focus on where we're headed."

"Right." Frida dipped her head in acknowledgment, then turned back to Shru. "One last thing. You must give me the map."

"Yes." Shru did as he was told.

Frida unrolled the parchment and scanned every inch of its surface, turning it around and looking it over from top to bottom. "I believe this can help you find what you're looking for," she told Percilla, then rolled the map back up and handed it to her grandniece. "Not for your ears," she scolded Shru, who still stood perfectly still and stared straight ahead in a daze. Frida pulled out a small photograph of a white lotus flower and lily pad floating on a pond, which she set on the ground in front of her and recited her spell. "Kan-tem."

The photo sank into the dirt, seeping through the cracked earth like water, and the image floated there like the very lily pad within it. Frida took Percilla's hand and guided her to step together onto the photo. "Na-mae na-kan." The women's feet slipped into the photo before the rest of their bodies followed.

Percilla blinked, finding herself standing beside Frida on a white lotus flower and lily pad floating on calm waters. Green algae formed a thick ring of vegetation in the water around them, which remained perfectly still despite their sudden appearance atop the lily pad. Trees and plants and flowers grew in harmony with the wetland forest at the edge of the pond, removed from any signs of civilization.

"Amazing!" Percilla shouted. "How did—"

"You have plenty of time later to inquire all you want," Frida interrupted. "Now, if you would please find Rou on the map."

"How?" Percilla asked, unrolling what was nothing more than a blank piece of parchment. "There's nothing on here."

"Look again."

The minute she did, thin lines of black ink appeared in highly accurate and lifelike representations of their surrounding environments, including villages and nomadic communities and remarkably detailed topography. Gangleton nestled beside a river running from a mountain range in which Frolly was located. Krinkton lay in a forest lush with vegetation. Evanstide existed in the middle of a grand ocean. Dawookrunk moved through the center of the Barrens, its position shifting every few seconds despite its portrayal in ink on parchment. Wonkt traveled away from a mountain range at high speeds, and Panya drifted slowly over a particularly large, dense forest. Finally, an ornate arrow glowed inconspicuously with a soft blue outline.

"Whoa," Percilla murmured.

"You are the glowing arrow," Frida said, pointing to its position on the map between Gangleton and Dawookrunk.

"Right," Percilla said. "But I still don't see Rou."

"That's because it's hidden. Only the one with the Eye of Rou can locate it. Why don't you ask your pendulum for help?"

Percilla took the pendulum from her pocket and nervously held the golden-wrapped trinket in her hand, having no idea exactly what she was supposed to do.

"Put down the map," Frida explained, "lift the pendulum over it, and ask away."

Percilla laid the map on the lily pad and hung her pendulum above it by the fine gold chain. "Find Rou," she said in a firm, loud voice.

The pendulum moved all on its own in a large circle over the map, guiding Percilla's hand with it. Then, as if drawn to some unseen magnet on the map, the crystal stopped over a barren expanse quite a long distance from Gangleton.

"Flown! Is this real?" Percilla asked.

"Indeed," Frida replied, nodding at her grandniece with a contented smile. "Remember that spot. Kim-ta-la."

They vanished from the lily pad and returned to the Barrens, now stepping over the photograph where Frida had placed it. Shru remained in his dazed state, staring at nothing but empty desert and awaiting Frida's next order.

Frida chuckled and turned to Percilla with a grin. "Which way, Captain?"

Percilla looked at the map, then pointed in the direction of Rou over the faraway horizon, past the endless sands and rock.

CHAPTER 10

Wits of the Witness

"WHAT HAPPENED TO Gangleton?" Percilla asked. After hours of travel, the sun still beat down upon the threesome with a nearly unbearable heat. By the afternoon, the shadows cast by the buttes scattered about the wasteland had grown long and dark, providing the occasional spot of cool shade.

"Well, that's a whole story," Frida replied, looking up to gauge the sun's position. "And I think we have the time. Our community came from a place called Rou. Which, aft—"

"Oh, Victoria already told me that part," Percilla said.

Frida sighed. "All right. Where would you like me to begin?"

Percilla pondered it for a few seconds, remembering the end of Victoria's last tale. "Right after Gangleton was built in a day."

"A very long day. The community didn't stop until Gangleton was complete," Frida said, her words lifting with pride.

"Right, and then everything was complete. Now fly." With the heat and the hours of travel, Percilla had grown particularly impatient.

"Fly? No, I let my ravens go. I can't fly. Why don't you just let me tell the story?"

Percilla reined in her zeal and forced herself to remain silent.

"As I was saying... What exactly did you want to know? There's a rather large snippet of time between the beginning and the deception of Gangleton."

"What made—"

"It was the evening of Gangleton's thirty-fifth anniversary," Frida interrupted with a grand sweep of her arm across the wasteland before them. Percilla stifled a laugh. "A brass marching band paraded through the settlement into the largest tent at Gangleton's center. Acrobats flew across trapezes in the circus performance put on for all those gathered. Yenz and Nudel, the most talented and comedic clowns in all of Gangleton, juggled sticks of fire with deftness of hand, reaching a most dangerous point... only to be doused with water enchanted to hose them down from offstage. We all laughed as the clowns exited the tent. But when the tent's lights went out and the entrance fell shut, the gathering hushed into tense whispers. When the lights sparked back on and my mother Bianca stepped into the center ring, she told the history of Rou to all of Gangleton. Mother was in her sixties then, and what a dainty woman she was, always wearing only the classiest things. She wore her favorite outfit that night. A long maroon jacket over a charming dress of ivory lace. And, of course, a fabulous hat."

"She wore that when I saw her in the Cherry Orchard."

"You saw her? Well, she must be one of your guardians. Splendid. Hello, Mother!" Frida called, throwing her head back toward the sky. "Lovely, now back to the story. Mother's tale did not last very long. She had barely begun before the tent flaps flew open again. Yenz and Nudel came running into the tent, shouting, 'Fire! Fire! They're burning everything. We must get out.' At first, we didn't know what to do. They were clowns, after all. But their fevered shouts did not give way to the normal grins and reveal of their clownish pranks. Even then, the rest of us could not decide how to respond. Just then, the top of the tent was ripped off. We were exposed to the night sky and what lay within, looming over us beneath darkened clouds that hid even the moon."

Percilla stared at Frida, wondering if she should never have asked. Her great aunt took a deep breath and continued.

"Frolly people levitated above us, looking down into the tent with disgust and rage. Their foreign spells set everything to flame, and the tent filled with panicked screams and the struggling rush of so many people surging toward an exit. Most of us escaped, but outside, it was no better. Tents and wagons and gardens burned to cinders all around us. The Frollians' wrath was a brutal, ruthless attack entirely without warning, for we had never had enemies before. And these enemies were also from Rou.

"And the battle went on through the night until Gangleton's elders could summon enough magic to push the Frolly people out of the village. Afterwards, we mourned our losses within the destruction of our village, but our elders had kept us safe. At least for the moment. We turned to consoling each other, and when the elders gathered to speak of what we might do next, they spotted a massive contraption shaped like an elephant approaching in the distance. It hauled a wagon beneath the rising sun, and riding atop that mechanical elephant was the first Council of Dignitaries, the original, wicked quintet that struck fear into our people. That is when the evils found a home in Gangleton and changed it forever."

"What do you mean, evils?" Percilla asked.

"Evils. The energy which disturbs harmony. It instigates anger, feeds on fear, loves greed, and thrives on stupidity."

"How did—"

"Shh. Do you hear that?" Frida whispered.

For a second, Percilla did not. Then the distant, pleasant echo of a song drifted toward her on the wind. The brass instrumental "Bella Ciao" played faintly, sounding in and out of perception as it gently grew.

"I think so," Percilla whispered back.

"That song. It's... it's..."

A thick, blue orb of a new force field unlike any Percilla had ever seen before erupted around Frida, stopping the woman from saying anything else. With Frida imprisoned behind its shimmering walls, her hold on Shru broke instantly. The man stumbled forward as if pushed and vigorously shook his head.

"Frida!" Percilla cried, rushing toward the force-field cage and pressing her hand against its blue-tinted exterior. "No, no, no. How do I get you out?"

"Too bad ya didn't tell me how ta do it," Shru said. Percilla turned back to glare at him, and his smugness melted away when he glanced down to see the parasol in his hand and the tutu and anklets he'd donned. Then he seemed to notice the donkey ears and the beaked mask, which he ripped off with his free hand and spent a few seconds studying in confusion.

Frida remained strangely calm inside the force field, slowly examining her surroundings as Percilla flipped through the pages of her spell book, looking for anything that might help. Frida turned to look her grandniece in the eyes, put her hand against the prismatic wall, and vanished.

"No!" Percilla reached out to grasp her great aunt, then cried out when her fingers smashed against the wall of the force field. "No." She whirled around, searching across the open expanse of cracked earth for any sign of the woman. "I need you. Please. Don't leave me." No answer came, and Frida did not reappear.

Realizing this was real, Percilla collapsed to her knees and hung her head, holding back the tears ready to escape. Her only remaining family had been swept up and taken away, and Percilla felt that overwhelming sense of weakness and hopelessness settling upon her once more. Would she ever manage to be useful to anyone? How could she expect to survive on her own? Without Frida, she had neither protection nor guide through the Barrens.

Shru dusted off his hanky before offering it to her. "Dry your eyes, sweetcakes. Everything's going to be fine."

"Go away," she said, pressing her hands to her eyes that were, in fact, still dry. "You're the last person I want to see." When he didn't move, she lifted her head to look at him. Metal chimes dangled from his ankles, sequins sparkled on the tutu, lace adorned the parasol, and the donkey ears peeked out from behind the beaked mask in his hand. Despite herself, the sight brought a small smile and a smaller chuckle from Percilla's lips. "She really did a number on you."

Not wanting to spend a second longer alone with Shru, she regained her strength and decided there was only one way to go—toward the distant music. Praying whoever played the song could help her find Frida, she set off in that direction.

Behind her, she heard what had to be the parasol, donkey ears, and mask hitting the dry ground before the rhythmic jingling of the bells around Shru's ankles making a whole lot of racket in the otherwise silent desert. Then the man was walking beside her.

"Why don't ya tell me what it is we're looking for?"

"Go away," Percilla said again, a little more gruffly than the last time, and walked faster.

"Ya obviously can't do it alone. Especially with those Digs lookin' for ya and Lady Frida no longer around."

"It's really none of your b—"

Another force field erupted around Shru for the second time that day, delivered with a flash of green light and then Shru's satisfying gasp when he struck the wall of his new cage.

Percilla stopped for a moment to peer at him. "Serves you right," she said. "I hope I never see you again, you no-good, irredeemable, selfish weasel." Now that she'd started, she couldn't stop the barrage of scolding words spilling out with all the pent-up emotion she'd bottled since her journey had begun. "With any luck, the Dignitaries will strip you of your wickedness so maybe, just *maybe*, you'll be able to enjoy a life of usefulness and common decency. Right now, you're nobody's friend, and nobody's to blame for that but you." With that, she spun on her heels, listened a moment for the distant music, and set off toward it again, leaving Shru for the Dignitaries to find.

The farther she walked, the hotter the sun shone down on her, pressing against her and the pale, scalded ground like a hammer against an anvil. Heat also rose from the parched earth, bringing more and more to Percilla's mind the fact that there was no water to be found here at all, and she had none of her own. The blurred horizon shimmered, and her tired eyes could no longer discern any distance around her. More than once, she swore she heard things where nothing existed—imaginary sounds to match the frequently shifting illusions in the haze of emptiness.

'Percilla... Percilla...'

She slowed when the entrancing voice, both familiar and unknown, whispered in her own mind. Then she stopped, turning to search for the source of such a voice. There remained nothing but the simmering-hot stone and sand at her feet.

'Percilla,' the voice whispered again. 'Tra-nas maka...'

A burst of hot air churned behind her, and she spun around only to see a quick blur and a puff of disturbed sand filtering back toward the ground. Then the same sensation struck behind her once more, and she whipped around again in circle after tight circle, pushing herself to be fast enough and find the cause of such an oddity. Finally, she spun in the opposite direction and saw in her periphery the distorted but entirely recognizable shape of a man.

Startled, she leapt back, entirely forgetting the voice that had entered her head. The man zoomed by her once more, and he must have tripped; he flew forward at a much slower rate to end up sprawled across the ground in front of her. Percilla stared at him for a few moments, more concerned than anything else, and the man lifted his pinky in the air with a high-pitched moan.

Cautiously, she approached the odd stranger. "Are you okay?"

"The pain," he wailed, the sound muffled by his face in the dirt. "Oh, it hurts. It *hurts*! I can't go on."

"What hurts? Your finger?"

The man only moaned and wiggled around on the hot ground in a highly exaggerated display of agony.

Percilla sighed. "Let me see." She knelt beside him and reached for his hand. "Here... stop flailing. That won't make anything better."

"Oh. Oh. It's dead. I can't feel it." The man pushed himself up to sit in front of her, tears welling in his eyes. Then he held his pinky toward her and stared at it.

"If you can't feel it, how can it hurt?" Percilla asked, feeling like she spoke to a child. The man just moaned again like a pitiful dog. "Do you want me to fix it?"

The man stopped and finally looked her in the eye. "You can find her?"

"I thought you hurt your finger..."

"Barna, my love. My love. *Barna*!" The man threw his head back to shout at the sky.

"Okay," Percilla said, keeping her composure with a deep breath. "What happened to her?"

"She was dancing to my song, then a force field swept her up, and she disappeared!"

Percilla frowned, but she spoke kindly. "The same thing happened to my great aunt." She could sympathize with the poor man now despite his overly dramatic tantrum.

'Percilla...' The alluring voice had returned. 'Tra-nas maka dis-en...'

The man on the ground wailed again in heartbreak or physical pain or both, drowning out the new whispers in her mind. "Did you hear that?" Percilla asked, searching cautiously around with wide eyes.

"Oh, it hurts!"

"I guess not," Percilla mumbled. She looked back at the poor man in front of her, pitying his situation and concerned for what might become of him. Her own journey was certainly important—most likely far more important than his—but nonetheless, she couldn't help the urge to aid him however she could. After all, another traveling companion might be just what she needed. "Why don't we look for them together?"

The man's wailing ceased, and his tear-filled eyes drifted from the ground to her face in surprise. "You'll help me find Barna?"

"Yes. We can go together."

"There's no time to lose!" The man jumped to his feet.

Her new companion's urgent zeal struck a refreshing new excitement in her, and she rose quickly beside him, eager to begin. Then she recognized their dilemma. "Um... well, I'm heading this way. I suppose they could all be in that direction, right?"

"I thought you knew where they went." A whimper escaped the man. "You mean you're not even certain?"

"No... I am. I just wanted to make sure you didn't have a better way to go. I think it's best we follow the music."

The man hopped toward her with a grin. "Oh, thank you, thank you, *thank* you!" he cried. "My name's Zyne. What's yours?"

Percilla smiled back at him as the pair set out toward the distant music. "Percilla."

CHAPTER 11

Fleeting Friends

"WHERE ARE YOU from?" Percilla asked as they walked steadily toward the source of the music. She squinted in an attempt to glimpse what lay ahead, but nothing came to her, only the faint melody carried on the wind.

"Nowhere, really," Zyne replied. "At least until I met Barna." He frowned at the mention of her name, and with a zippy wave of his hand, he produced a concertina from nowhere and played a quick song with a happy rhythm. "Allow me to imitate my memory for you." He cleared his throat and spoke above his own music, spinning a melodic tale for Percilla. "It was many moons ago by a dazzling river in Frolly country. I was playing my concertina, much like I am now, when a flock of spellbound ravens came to peck and pull at me. 'Enough,' I told them. 'Leave me be,' I shouted, swatting left and right. Suddenly, the most beautiful woman appeared. She raced toward me and lifted her hands to those awful birds. 'Klist-ka fromp-ta,' she said, and like magic, the ravens flew right off. I was mesmerized by her and needed to know her name. And that's when I heard the sweetest sounds I've ever known. 'My name is Barna of Frolly,' she said."

"She sounds lovely," Percilla said, admiring the woman's supposed skill, bravery, and appearance.

"Oh, she is," Zyne replied. "The loveliest lady in all the world. After she rescued me, she took me back to her home in Frolly. It was the most magical wetland place hidden among the mountains. Covered in tall grasses, lily pads, and lotus flowers. People dressed in colorful kimonos, their dwellings built on floating rafts along the rivers. Floating bridges connected everything in their circular village. Wooden canoes and glittering Koi fish. A magnificent waterfall poured into the main river, casting rainbows without end." He closed his eyes and took a deep breath. When he spoke next, his excitement had dampened into sadness. "And there we lived together. Until..." His face contorted in regret.

"Until?" Percilla asked, both curious to know what happened and worried by the implication of that last word.

"Until the prior Council of Dignitaries came to us." Zyne's song suddenly changed, its rhythm slowing into drawn-out, crawling notes in a minor key. "I left my home one morning to find myself facing the backsides of five people wearing dark purple waistcoats with tails and striped pants of various colors. A group of Frollians had gathered in front of them. They thought me part of the group in front of me and threatened all of us, accusing us of stealing Gangleton's Eye of Rou."

"Did the Frollians have it?"

"No, the Frollians have their own Eye of Rou. But that didn't stop the people of Gangleton from suspecting them of thievery. That night, dark magicians set teepees, bridges, and canoes ablaze. Everywhere, people screamed and jumped into the water to escape the flames. The elders' magic stopped it from spreading any farther, but the damage had already been done. Frolly was ruined."

"Just like Gangleton," Percilla remarked sadly.

"No," Zyne said. "*By* Gangleton."

Percilla looked at him. That was not at all what Frida had told her. "The Frollians attacked Gangleton," she objected.

"No, Gangleton tore Frolly apart. In the dead of night, they came and burned our peaceful home to the ground with their magic. In their fury, the Frollians burned the bonds of community and harmony that had held them together for so long. Half of those who remained wanted to attack Gangleton in retaliation. But the other half wanted only to settle on new lands in peace. Barna and I joined those peaceful villagers, and together, we departed from Frolly in what few canoes were left to us. That was the last time I ever saw the other Frollians. Barna and I have been traveling together ever since."

Zyne's tale stirred a deep regret in Percilla's heart, but his own heart carried a heavier weight. He fell to the ground and broke down into tears. "Until today," he added through a muffled cry, "when they captured her. My love!"

"It's okay," Percilla said, trying to comfort him as best she could. "We'll find her. Where we're headed, I believe we might find people who can help... I hope."

"You promise?" Zyne asked, tilting his head up toward Percilla with huge, pleading, glistening eyes.

Percilla opened her mouth to reply, but then the whispering voice returned, and she stopped.

'Percilla... tra-nas maka...'

Without so much as a sound of approach in warning, Percilla was swooped up from about the waist and lifted high into the air. It took her a few moments to realize she was now being transported at the top of a unicycle. Then she looked up to see a young man in a detailed vest of red and gold beneath a fedora, who held her tightly against him as his legs pumped away at the pedals. She was keenly aware of his muscular arm wrapped around her waist, and his sparkling white teeth glistened in the sun from behind his perpetual grin. He pedaled furiously, propelling the unicycle wherever he fancied as effortlessly as though he were gliding on air. Not even scooping up Pricilla had brought him remotely close to losing balance.

"Zyne!" Percilla cried as she was swept away from her new companion into the Barrens.

"Percilla!" Zyne leapt up from the ground to chase after her. He zipped as fast as he could, but even his abnormal swiftness could not match that of the kidnapper's unicycle.

"Put me down," she yelled, but the man only pedaled faster.

Zyne shouted her name again as the distance between them grew with remarkable speed.

"Put me down! He needs me. I promised him." Tears welled in her eyes as she thought of all the promises she had made and was now reminded of all those she had yet to keep.

The final call of her name from Zyne's lips was a soft, hollow echo before his figure vanished behind her and her kidnapper into the Barrens.

"Zyne. I promise," she whispered. At this speed, the wind buffeted her face, carrying away her tears the minute they fell. Percilla held on tighter to the warmth of her kidnapper, more afraid now to fall than she was of him. The odd care with which his strong embrace safely held her brought an unexpected comfort to her entire being. When she realized he carried her rapidly toward the source of the music she'd followed, she wondered if this man might in fact not be an enemy.

He said nothing, and just when she was about to ask, he pointed ahead for a split second. She followed his gesture, only to stare in awe at what rose before them. Shapes she'd thought were mountains in the distance quickly revealed themselves as a massive gathering of tents. Faster and faster they rode, until Percilla had to close her eyes, gripping tighter to the strong arm around her waist.

Finally, they slowed, and Percilla's eyes fluttered open. Her jaw dropped at the sight of so many colorful, ornamented tents of various sizes, held up not by poles or stakes but by blue falcons fluttering there in the sky within this particularly empty expanse of the Barrens. An array of people had come together in this most unexpected gathering. A festively plump woman in a fanciful dress exited a purple and blue tent, two porcelain teacups resting in her hat. Stepping directly over her and then the unicycler were two more women on stilts, their striped costumes extending all the way to the ground and their faces

painted with extraordinary makeup. To Percilla's left, a bare-chested man in a gold vest blew fire in the shape of a phoenix. A group of petite women dove and tumbled right in front of the unicycle before rolling into a large green tent. A curious man with a pointed mustache and a top hat intensely observed Percilla's kidnapper from his tent, and behind him, seven women had formed a living sculpture of a human skull. Almost every person Percilla saw had one strange quality or another, and there were far too many to count by herself.

Her skilled kidnapper weaved around them all atop his unicycle, spinning in circles and jumping off ramps with an easy flair, making a show of his feats for all to see. Many people seemed to recognize the man and cheered him on, his acrobatic performance growing more and more difficult the closer they drew to the densely packed center of the community.

When they came to a long, straight stretch of space between the tents, a crowd cleared themselves swiftly from the unicycler's path. But one woman with dark hair and enchanting eyes stood in the way. Percilla's kidnapper pedaled faster toward the woman, his speed increasing rapidly. Still, the woman refused to move. Percilla clutched her kidnapper tighter and shut her eyes, bracing for impact. When nothing happened, she opened her eyes to see the woman had lifted into the air, presumably at the last second, and now hovered above where the unicycle would have hit her. When she saw Percilla's mouth drop open, the woman burst into laughter.

Percilla applauded, no longer frightened but instead impressed and entertained by the ongoing show in this strange and fanciful place. At least her kidnapper had been thoughtful enough to bring her where she'd wanted to go. The man in question laughed when he saw she was no longer afraid, pedaling next toward a little girl in a pale blue dress holding an orange balloon. Percilla gasped when she saw a man's face glowing upon the balloon when it turned in the air to face her. The man appeared sophisticated and knowledgeable, his curly brown hair hanging neatly under his perfectly tipped top hat of plum-and-green plaid. His bright blue eyes sparked, and when he caught sight of Percilla, he offered her a whimsical grin.

"Welcome to Dawookrunk," the balloon head said. "I hope Matik didn't frighten you. He enjoys showing off. That's why he's one of our best performers. Thank you, Matik. I will take care of our new friend from here."

"Very well, Symon," the unicycle rider replied. With all the confidence befitting his skill, he slipped Percilla from his hold around her and gently lowered her to the ground.

The orange balloon burst with a loud pop, and from it leapt Symon's entire body. The man shimmered with a charmed aura, dressed in a finely made plaid waistcoat with matching striped vest and trousers. Taking note of Percilla's troubled state, he wiped the remnants of tears from her face. "You must be parched," he said. "Care for some tea?"

"Please," Percilla replied. "This whole day has me beyond parched. I don't even know—"

"You don't have to," Symon said, taking her hand in his. "We'll talk about it over some tea. Just breathe for now and know you're safe here in Dawookrunk."

Symon led Percilla through the many colorful tents scattered about the circus village of Dawookrunk. The man with the pointed mustache who'd watched Matik and Percilla earlier passed her and Symon now, glaring at her with beady eyes and no attempt to hide his suspicion. Percilla could not help but stare back at him and wonder what she had done to provoke such a reaction.

"Don't mind Daldor," Symon said. "He's been a little bitter since one of the women in his troupe was caught in a force field."

"That's unfortunate," Percilla said, wishing not to cross paths with him again.

"Someday, he will let evil go. He really has quite the big heart... when he forgets what's been done to him," Symon assured her. She found it difficult to believe.

After a short time at a brisk pace, Symon brought her to a richly colored, three-tiered tent from which a constant stream of multi-colored smoke floated into the sky. They entered the tent, where they faced a large, ornately carved wooden cabinet, its hinged doors splayed open to either side. Small jars with all manner of unknown liquids filled its shelves. Below that was a three-tiered chest carved in the same design, its one hundred small drawers each marked with their own symbol. At the end of the tent sat a large wooden bar from behind which a panther with captivating eyes prowled toward them.

Symon gestured for her to take a seat in front of the bar, and while Percilla thought the sleek beast approaching them odd, she felt little fear. By this point, she was certain Symon would not put her in harm's way. He'd had plenty of opportunities to do so by now, if that was what he wanted. The man spoke directly to the curious panther, who'd stepped closer for a better sniff at Percilla's head. This she did think entirely too close for comfort.

"Times like these, we must look beyond the mask. Deep inside the eyes. Isn't that right, Vogle?" Symon asked with a grin.

The large feline sniffed Percilla loudly, tilting its head around hers as it did so. Trying not to show her discomfort, Percilla leaned closer toward Symon and hoped the look she gave him quite obviously said, *Get this cat off me, please.*

Symon cleared his throat. "Vogle, I would like to introduce you to Percilla. Just arrived from the Barrens. Quite parched."

Instantly, the panther's body shifted, its hind legs taking on human shape while its paws became hands. Its pelt grew into long black hair and a black, well-fitted linen ensemble. Finally, the creature's intimidating head became that of a striking woman. "Fine creature you are, Percilla," Vogle said, getting a good, long look at her. "What type of concoction do you fancy?"

"Concoction?" Percilla asked with a tilt of her head, still taking in the transformation she'd just witnessed. The sight of magic outside Gangleton continuously fascinated her.

"Ah," Vogle replied. "First visit to the apothecary. Let's have a consult, shall we? How are you feeling today?"

"Flown out of my limits," Percilla replied. "I just lost the only family I have left. I've made more promises, which I don't even know are possible to keep, and people's lives are at risk." Now, she found it harder than ever to hold back her tears.

"Unfortunate events. Hmm. Some strong adaptions will fix that with a little bit of pearl for that pale complexion. While I do that, you just hold these." Vogle placed a white selenite crystal and rose quartz in front of Percilla.

Percilla shrugged and picked up the stones. "Whatever works."

"Mama Vogle will take care of you, little one. You'll be feeling good in no time," the woman said with a wink. Then she whisked around to collect the necessary ingredients, pulling dried herbs from drawers, pouring liquids into vials, shaking and stirring containers filled with magical solutions. She ground up herbs and mixed them together.

Percilla fell silent in amazement, tightly gripping the stones. Beginning to feel a lightness in her being, she inhaled deeply. The heavy weight of the tears in her eyes lifted, and her mind ceased its racing. Fully in the present moment, her attention turned to pondering the most curious of things most relevant to right now. "How did you know my name was Percilla?" she asked Symon.

"You told me," Symon replied, not looking at her once as he pointed to Vogle. The woman poured a pink liquid that sparkled every time it moved from one copper cup to the other.

"No, I didn't," Percilla argued, sure she'd never even met this man before in her life.

Vogle whisked the gobleted elixer in front of Percilla to set it on the bar, and the minute she withdrew her hand from the cup, she was a panther once more. "There you are, lovely. Drink up." Her human voice rising from the panther's open mouth made Percilla's jaw drop.

"Oh, a name, a face, a person," Symon said as he turned to Percilla with an amused smile. "I simply just know them." The man glanced back toward the tent's entrance. "One moment." Symon stood and called, "Will you join us for a little journey inside The Gold?"

Percilla turned as well to see Matik's fedora slipping through the tent's entrance before the rest of him. "Absolutely!" the man replied, then ducked his head with a sheepish smile, as if he hadn't anticipated his own outburst. "I was just—"

Vogle popped up in panther form beneath him, making the muscular unicycler jump forward. "Whoa! Hey, Vogle," he said. "I need something to give me zest all night." He tipped his fedora at her.

"Ooo... all night. How do you feel about deer antler?" Vogle asked, sounding more human than panther.

"Sure. You're the master alchemist."

"Yes, that's right. I *am* the master." Vogle leapt behind the bar and shifted back into human form to begin the concoction for Matik. She retrieved a stick of deer antler from behind the bar and ground it into a fine powder, which she thoroughly mixed into a cup of blue-violet tea. When it was done, she slid the drink across the counter toward the muscular acrobat and shifted into her panther form once more. Then she hopped onto the bar to sniff around Percilla.

Percilla turned slowly toward Symon again, getting used to Vogle's intrusive mannerisms. "What were you saying about looking deep inside the eyes?" she asked, incredibly aware of the panther's sharp claws resting on her shoulders as Vogle sniffed her head.

"The Look Beyond," Symon said, his eyes growing wide in suspense. "Fabulous technique. Matik, Vogle, will you help me in a demonstration?"

"Of course," Vogle replied.

"I need you in your human form," he said. "And will you please quit disturbing our guest with all the sniffing?" Vogle's human shape reappeared, and she grinned at Percilla. "Matik," Symon continued, "in front of Vogle, please." The two approached each other in the middle of the tent and bent forward so their faces nearly touched. Symon ushered Percilla with him to observe them closely. "Percilla, step right up. Don't be shy. Get your head almost touching theirs."

"What exactly am I looking for?" Percilla asked, not sure in the least what the Look Beyond was even supposed to be.

"You'll see," Symon assured her. "Matik and Vogle, close your eyes." They did as he instructed, shifting just a little closer, chins tucked to their chests so their noses didn't get in the way. "Now... open."

The demonstrators gazed at one another, focused on nothing but the other's eyes, which Percilla thought were far too close for them to see anything. But then a quick, faint light burst from Vogle's eyes toward Matik's.

"Do you see the light connecting their eyes?" Symon asked, pointing between the two of them.

"Flown!" Percilla exclaimed. "Is—"

"This always happens," Symon interrupted, "but we usually intuit it as a feeling. Vogle, I want you to lie to Matik."

"Matik, the concoction I served you will make you fall asleep in an hour," Vogle said. The light between their eyes faded the moment she spoke her lie.

"Now, watch Matik's eyes," Symon continued. Matik's pupils grew under the fading light. "Matik, reestablish the connection."

"Vogle, your concoction will give me zest and make me ready for the performance tonight," Matik said. The man's pupils returned to their normal size, and the light flashed again between his eyes and Vogle's.

"Flown," Percilla whispered. "The light's back."

"Precisely. Matik reestablished the level of truth," Symon explained.

"Level of truth?"

"The eyes create a pathway from one person's truth to another. It's the outer layers which interfere with the pathway, usually disturbed by evils."

"Evils," Percilla said softly, remembering her conversation with Frida earlier that day; it felt so very long ago. "My great aunt spoke about them."

"That will be all for today's lesson," Symon said. He almost said more, Percilla thought, but then his eyes fixated on something only he could see through a gap in the apothecary tent. "Excuse me for a moment." He hastily left the tent without another word, leaving Percilla, Matik, and Vogle to their concoctions.

"What do you think of Dawookrunk?" Matik asked as he stepped away from Vogle and turned to Percilla at the bar, sitting next to her with his drink in hand.

"I'm not sure yet," Percilla answered, finding even more of her own questions. "I mean, it seems nicer than the place I came from."

"Wait till you see the show tonight. People come from all around to see us." Matik spread his arms in an all-encompassing gesture.

Before Percilla could say another word, Symon returned, his lips pressed tightly together and his voice filled with subtle urgency. "But first you must experience The Gold."

"What's The Gold?" Percilla asked.

"You will see. Now, sip. Sip."

Percilla had barely taken one drink of her tonic before Symon clapped his hands loudly together.

"All right. Let's be off, shall we?" Symon motioned for Percilla and Matik to leave with him as he stepped outside. When they took too long, trying to finish off their drinks, he poked his head back into the tent and shouted, "Come now, you two. We mustn't skimp on the sunlight while we have it."

CHAPTER 12

Reminiscing

PERCILLA COULDN'T HELP her fascination when she gazed up at the large blue falcons in the sky, still holding aloft the colorfully ornamented tents of Dawookrunk's lively, nomadic village. She didn't look away until she heard the most joyous music. The passionate sounds tickled her mind with memories of the Cherry Orchard. For a moment, she closed her eyes, listening to the accordion hold an all-too-familiar sound. With it, a few tears slipped from the corners of her eyes, even when she tried hard to hold them at bay. She was happy to think of her friends but deeply saddened by their absence; she hadn't the time to realize how much she missed those sounds until hearing them now.

A light touch on her shoulder reminded her where she was, and she opened her eyes to see Matik smiling at her. He wiped away a tear from her cheek, then took her hand and led her with much excitement toward a clearing in the tents. As they walked into the open space there where the whole of the community gathered, Symon moved ahead of them, greeting people and smiling but in no way stunting his fervent pace. Percilla naturally stopped to take it all in—the sights, sounds, and smells. Matik stood at her side all the while.

The performers and eccentric characters of this circus community milled around the firepit ringed with stones at the clearing's center. A man sat atop a flying carpet playing the fiddle beside the woman with the accordion. Others danced in celebration around the fire, stomping their feet upon the earth, clapping their hands, and adding to the music with their voices, clearly improvising at every turn. Pockets of conversations passed around the gathered groups, each new face and voice as eccentric as the last. Two young girls carried baskets of vegetables to the outdoor kitchen, where a woman and a man chopped up food and stirred bubbling pots of stew.

Percilla was eager to see what would happen next, for she finally felt a sense of ease here with the familiar sounds amid jubilant people; she wanted to soak it all in as long as she could, though Symon made it clear with a light whistle directed toward her and Matik that they had other places to go. Matik motioned Percilla forward so he could follow. Understanding yet a bit reluctant to leave this fine setting, she slowly made her way through the gathering, hoping to return later.

Symon waited for them beside a small black tent. When they stopped in front of him, he looked at Percilla and muttered, "This is Oan's tent. Dawookrunk's elder." He raised an eyebrow, as though asking if Percilla understood the level of respect this visit required. She nodded, and with a quick smile, Symon drew back the black curtain and ushered Percilla and Matik inside.

Within, Oan, the elder of Dawookrunk, sat cross-legged in the center of a glittering circle of finely cut crystals. He was an old man, appearing wrinkled with age despite what Percilla now knew was the slow passage of time beyond Gangleton. His gentle eyes and warm smile bore the signs of true wisdom, and merely being in his presence felt like basking in a wellspring of spiritual knowledge. He wore simple, black and white linen clothing with a golden charm hanging from a chain around his neck. The belt around his waist boasted numerous pouches filled with all manner of spiritual materials, the purposes of which only an elder would truly know. Across from Oan inside the circle was a full-length mirror within a golden, clawfoot frame.

Symon signaled for Matik to enter the quartz circle, motioning him forward with an outstretched hand and a bow. Matik approached and sat with his own legs crossed in front of Oan. The elder lit a fire between his fingers and touched it to the base of a small vessel, within which rested a white, sparkling resin. He stared at Matik intently through half-shut eyes.

As the vessel heated, smoke rose from the resin. Oan took a feather from his belt and fanned it toward Matik, engulfing him fully in the smoke. Matik in turn took a long, deep inhale. Percilla gasped, seeing for the first time an elder performing the ritual she and her friends had conducted so many times. Ecstatic, she watched and learned so she could bring this next phase home to the others when she returned.

Oan stood in front of Matik, producing a rhythmic breath that soon became a hushed whistle filling the tent with a harmony of its own. He took a bundle of feathers and herbs from his belt and fanned them all around Matik, ending the motion above the unicycler's head. Matik maintained a respectful silence and did not say a word. Oan then stepped aside and invited Matik to approach the mirror, motioning him forward the same way Symon had. The unicycler stepped toward the gold-framed mirror, then straight into it, passing through the reflective, shimmering surface as though it were made of water. Then he disappeared.

Percilla marveled at the sight until Symon then signaled for her to enter the crystal circle. Bursting with excitement, she stepped into the ring and sat cross-legged in front of the elder. There was so much she wished she could ask of Oan, but she had no idea whether that was allowed. She held back her desire to tell him of her friends and the ritual and the many questions surfacing about what he was doing now. In her best attempt to remain composed, she took a deep inhale of the sweet pine smoke, bringing her back to the peacefulness that was her life before this whole journey began.

Oan continued the ceremony, his breath swirling around her, lifting her mind out of her body. As she closed her eyes, the elder added a soft, rhythmic whistle while fanning feathers and herbs up, down, and around her. She felt light again, all the weight of her journey and all that had occurred washing away from her, leaving her cleansed of the past and the future. She felt the smoke filtering into her nose; the subtle caress of the feathers fanning around her; the swirling of whistling; the drumbeats faintly heard from outside the tent dancing in her head; the fresh air on her skin. Her whole body seemed to now keenly sense and take in the whole of her environment. Though when Oan's feather reached her hat and the elder paused for a long moment, Percilla found a self-conscious anxiety about what she had been holding secret. Oan carefully eyed the hat with a perceptive stare. She dared not move for fear of jostling her ravens into a frenzy and alerting Oan to their presence. After what seemed a long moment of whistling and fanning around her hat, Percilla was elated and relieved when the elder stood aside and signaled for her to enter the mirror.

Percilla immediately stood, bowed to Oan, and jumped straight through the mirror. She emerged in an ancient setting of overgrown plants climbing the walls and covering the remnants of elaborate stone structures. Vines draped over the open spaces like curtains. Sweeping these away to see more, she looked out in awe. There, in the distance, a rainbow arced over a large waterfall emptying into a clear blue river. This river flowed past tall outcroppings of draping willow and bodhi trees. Exotic and colorful flowers grew from every surface like a garden of rainbows in the city of gold. Extravagant homes built right into the trees twinkled with flickering lights. Magnificently colored flying creatures of all shapes and sizes filled the air and spirited across the sky. Percilla's jaw dropped at the wonderland before her very eyes. The words Victoria had spoken of the Tale of Rou rang true. There was no mistaking it. This place in which she now found herself could be no other.

"The waterfalls. The rainbows. I've found it," she muttered. "Rou!"

"Sorry, love," Symon said, passing through the mirror. "This is not Rou."

She turned to stare at him, watching him walk past her until she couldn't help but gaze up at the incredible place around her. "But it's exactly as Victoria described," Percilla replied.

"Some things in life aren't always as truthful as they seem," Symon said, his lips pressed solemnly together.

"Plus, we have no way to get back to Rou," Matik interjected with a frown.

"You mean you've been there?" Percilla asked, hoping these new friends could assist her on her quest.

"No, but Oan created this from his memories of Rou," Symon explained, motioning his arm toward the wonders of the paradise and pointing upward toward an island in the sky. Atop the floating island, Oan sat cross-legged with his eyes tightly shut, whispering ancient words to himself in a sacred ritual. A golden light emanated from the center of his forehead as he performed the ritual, illuminating the space around him.

"Come now," Symon said lightly. "I've something to show you."

Symon led Percilla down a dirt path along one of the many clear streams running freely through the simulated Rou. This most euphoric setting intrigued her more with each step. Looking up and around to take it all in and forgetting to watch her feet, she tripped over a root. Matik grabbed her around the waist and set her back on her feet before she'd even begun to fall. "Thank you," she said.

"I got you," he replied with a wide grin. "Enjoy the sights." A group of butterflies circled around her head, caressing her with their wings, which tickled her nose and made her giggle. Then she found herself fully laughing, and the sound of Matik joining her made it even better.

"In Rou," Symon explained, "all things live in harmony. People exist together as one, despite their differences. It is a true paradise, Percilla... What a lovely name."

"My grandmother named me," Percilla said.

"Of course. Always a taste for beauty." Symon's voice filled to the brim with nostalgia of times long since passed.

The dirt path brought them to a grassy clearing where two grand cherry trees rose from the soil. A hammock had been tied between them, and lying in that hammock was none other than Frida, blissfully napping the day away with her hat tilted down to half cover her face.

"I know that hat," Percilla exclaimed. "Frida!" She ran to the hammock, holding back tears. "Frida," she whispered.

Frida grunted with a dismissive wave of her hand. "No business now. I'm balancing my energy bodies. Later... maybe."

"I thought that force field—"

"Percilla!" Frida shouted, recognizing her grandniece's voice and rousing herself from her slumber. She whisked the hat from over her face and sat up to stare at her grandniece. "Hello, love. No, I'm fine. Just resting. Thank you, Symon," she added with a gracious nod toward him.

"My pleasure." He offered a short, whimsical bow.

"You know each other?" Percilla asked.

"From long ago in Gangleton," Frida answered.

"Luckily, Frida stepped into our force field," Symon explained. "We set them up to claim the lost in the Barrens and keep them safe from the Dignitaries."

"I was going to go back and get you myself," Frida continued, "but he assured me you'd be in good hands. True?"

"Beyond true," Percilla replied with a laugh.

"You are both welcome to stay as long as you like," Symon prompted.

Percilla wanted dearly to accept his offer and stay in the simulated Rou with Frida, but in her heart, she knew she had a duty to her family and her friends to complete her journey. "We have to continue to Rou," she said with a rekindled purpose, seeing now what was truly at stake if they did not find Rou before it was too late.

"You need rest," Symon advised with a kind smile beneath a frown of concern.

"I have people waiting for me in Gangleton."

"Are you sure he's still there?" Symon asked, and Percilla blinked, staring at the man and wanting to say she did not know of whom he spoke. That would not have been true.

"Let's stay the night," Frida suggested. "Rest is good."

Percilla might have been able to resist the advice coming from Symon but not from Frida. She relented with a reluctant, "Fine."

"You'll get to see tonight's show," Matik said with excitement. "Wait 'till you see my new trick."

"Marvelous!" Frida clasped her hands together. "It's been centuries since I've seen a good show."

"Why don't you join?" Symon suggested. "I'm sure you have something in your bag, Frida. And Percilla, you can be Matik's assistant."

"I have just the thing," Frida said, digging through her bag.

"I'd have no idea what I'm doing," Percilla said, unsure of her ability to assist anyone with an acrobatic maneuver.

"I got you," Matik promised again with a wink.

"There will be time to discuss this at length later," Symon said. "For now, let me show you the greatest sight in all of The Gold."

Symon led Frida, Percilla, and Matik to a cliff overlooking the imitation Rou. Here, she realized why this placed was called The Gold. The full majesty of this seeming paradise took her breath away. Rainbows gleamed in the mists of an expansive waterfall valley, shimmering over the aqua rivers. Birds, butterflies, and dragonflies flew around freely, their own energy blending with that of the land itself. A luscious green jungle filled the valley, vines draping from columns and remnants of ancient buildings coated in moss and eroded by the currents of even older rivers. Magnificent flowers sprouted from the land and dotted the surface of the waters, making a glorious garden of the whole of Rou's memory.

And yet, Symon could not help but sigh. "I don't think we could ever truly recreate Rou's magnificence."

Percilla found herself filled with a sudden and intense purpose; she would do whatever it took to ensure Rou was never forgotten. "Come with us," she insisted.

"To Rou?" Symon asked, turning his head toward her with wide eyes.

"Victoria left me the Eye of Rou and urged me to bring it back," Percilla explained.

Symon sighed yet again. "I know."

"How?" Percilla asked. She couldn't fathom the reasons or the ways Symon could possibly know so much.

"Stay," Symon said with a solemn stare. "We can protect the Eye of Rou here. The Dignitaries haven't suspected us since they stripped us naked and marched us out of Gangleton."

His words made Percilla's heart ache. "Why did they do such a thing?"

Symon turned to look over the image of Rou—the freedom of the past they'd all lost. "To set an example for everyone else. To show them what happens when one speaks against them."

"Flown!" Percilla shouted, her disdain for the Dignitaries growing more and more with each passing word of their treachery.

"Stay," Symon repeated, and his eyes flashed with momentary hope.

Percilla turned away from him, unable to look him in the eye when she replied, "I have to—"

"Symon, you know we can't," Frida interjected. Percilla couldn't have been more grateful for her great aunt's attempt to save her from saying aloud what was already so painful.

Symon bowed. "As you wish."

Relieved he had relented in his proposal yet not ready to meet his gaze, Percilla let the sights of The Gold reclaim her purpose and dispel Symon's interjection. She stepped away from the group and looked out to admire the memories of Rou made very real. Across the valley's river, she caught sight of a woman dressed in one long, flowing garment of silk tied about the waste with a belt of the very same. The woman stared at either her reflection or something beneath the surface within the clear, running water.

"Who's that woman by the river?" Percilla asked.

"A Frollian," Symon replied. "She came in just before Frida did."

It only took a few seconds for Percilla to put the pieces together—a Frollian woman, alone, who'd been supposedly captured by a force field and actually brought safely to Dawookrunk and then The Gold. If she was right, staying in Dawookrunk a little longer might not be such a bad idea after all. "I'm pretty sure I know who that is, and there's a zany little man longing to see her. What's the best way to get down to the river? I need to speak with her."

"Matik, do you mind assisting Percilla?" Symon asked. "I have some business to discuss with Frida."

"Gladly, Symon." Matik nodded for Percilla to follow, and they started off down an overgrown trail into the valley.

While Matik escorted Percilla through the lush and vibrant jungles toward the valley's river, Symon led Frida across the ridge. He stopped at its edge, and the minute she stood beside him, the earth on which they stood broke away to rise into the air and carry them with it. The breathtaking glow of sunset's reds and oranges shimmered on the waterfalls dropping down from cliffsides and into clear-flowing rivers. The sight was pure ecstasy for Frida, who admired the water as one might a beautiful work of art. But her elation soured the longer she looked upon what was nothing more than a highly convincing reproduction.

"Our ancestors traded this for a new life," she said, ashamed of how far their world had fallen and how little they had done to prevent it.

"Trade?" Symon said. "No. It was a choice to go out into the world. The evils can be a tricky business."

"Oh, I know," Frida said. "I've been living in the middle of it all. Alone."

"Loneliness only exists in one's perspective of it. Rou has always been in your heart." Symon paused, then took her hand in his and gazed into her eyes. "And you've always been in mine."

"And now we are here together again," Frida said, slowly caressing his cheek with her other hand. "I've missed you."

"This is the moment we've been preparing for." A determined flame flickered in his eyes. "We can actually make a stand now."

"Percilla is a good omen for that."

"You know she has no training."

"She doesn't even know the spell book." Frida sighed.

"How does she expect to protect herself?"

"I suppose that's why she found me."

Symon tilted his head and gave her a sad smile. "I can't join you. But I will do everything I can to help you safely to Rou."

Together, they looked out over the memory of Rou before them—their past, a past that, by fate's blessing, they might soon regain. They had only to hold tightly to the courage and the strength to persevere through the challenges ahead.

"Someday, we will have our home in Rou," Frida said.

"Our cloud," Symon replied, pulling her closer.

The pair floated away on the island in the sky, heading for the sunset in each other's arms.

Hexed Invaders

Later that night, after everyone had left The Gold and prepared for their performances, an audience of people from all across the Barrens gathered inside the huge, main tent. There, a circus marching band played with boisterous flair around a brightly lit center ring. Frida emerged from backstage in a puff of smoke, swerving and looping while hanging upside down on a flying carpet. She did a headstand, then sat on the carpet, poured a piping-hot cup of tea from a rather considerable height, then sipped it and flew away all while upside down. The crowd cheered their appreciation for her miraculous maneuvers.

After the applause died down and the crowd was ready for the next act, Matik rode into the ring atop his unicycle with Percilla balanced on his shoulders. He rapidly pedaled toward a ramp, easily supporting their combined weight, and rode right up the wooden prop to launch them through the air and land skillfully on a tightrope. He pedaled across the rope with perfect rhythm, not even wobbling while balancing his weight and Percilla's. At the end of the tightrope, they rode down a long ramp toward the ground, where they spun around three times to slow their momentum. Percilla tossed a handful of cherries up into the air and recited one of the few spells she knew. "Flisp ta-pow." In an instant, the fruits were transformed into brightly colored sparks of light that filled the ring with a warm glow. With a few tiny, popping explosions, the lights whizzed through the air and fizzled out. Again, the crowd hooted and applauded the performance, loving the pair's wonderful combination of acrobatic skill and magical talent.

Then, much to the audience's surprise, the lights in the ring flickered on and off, then went out completely, bathing the tent in pitch-black darkness. A sole light appeared, illuminating first the tip of the staff from which it originated and then Symon, who now stood alone in the center of the stage, gripping the staff in front of him.

"Where do we come from?" he asked the crowd. His voice echoed all the way to the very edges of the tent. "What are we living for? Let me entice your minds with a truth not so far removed from our existence." More light shot from the prismatic crystal fixed to the top of his staff, projecting above him an image of Rou. "Rou, where to live is to be one with all that is. You may wonder, 'Does it really exist?' Question then is, 'How well do you know yourself?' Look beyond for the connection within everyone else—"

A terrified scream broke out from the back of the crowd. From within the darkness, a figure dressed in a dark-purple outfit stormed through the tent, pushing his way toward the

stage as those gathered leapt away from him and shouted in confusion. At first, many assumed he was part of the act, but then he cursed and glared at those around him, scaring them away with his erratic behavior and the strength with which he shoved others out of his way. He wore a derby hat, and his long trench coat brushed the floor. The man dashed toward a girl in the crowd who, Percilla only had a few seconds to realize, looked remarkably like herself and grabbed her, lifting her up over his shoulders. Before anyone realized who this man was or what was happening, the kidnapper rushed out of the tent, pulling the poor girl out into the shadows of the desert.

"To sense those who are consumed by Evils," Symon concluded, not appearing surprised by what occurred, just perturbed it had happened so soon. "I believe they are here." Then the light on his staff fizzled out completely.

This seemed to be a rather effective signal for the audience. Everyone gathered moved into hasty action at once, clearing the tent with a few startled shouts and a frightened cry. Backstage, Percilla looked out into the crowd with both confusion and an almost crippling fear. She had seen the terror in the girl's eyes when the kidnapper had taken her from the tent, as if she'd been staring into a mirror the whole time. Matik shielded her with his body and poked out his head from the back of the main tent to make sure it was safe.

"They came for me," Percilla whispered. "The Digs."

"We don't know that," Matik whispered back, trying to ease her fears and keep the evils at bay.

"Then why are you keeping guard? Who were they after?"

Symon appeared from the shadows, seeming to fade into the back of the stage with an eerie speed. "Matik, take Percilla to her tent."

Matik nodded and moved to guide her, but before they left, Percilla demanded, "Who did they take? Who did they steal in my place?"

Symon stared at her for a moment, making her think he wouldn't tell her. Then his eyes softened, and he dipped his head in consent. "Someone who looked remarkably like you."

Percilla frowned with grief and allowed Matik to escort her to a tent within the middle ring of Dawookrunk dwellings—somewhere between the outer rings of the traveling circus village and the large clearing at its center. Once inside, Matik offered a little bow and told her, "For now, you should stay here. I'll be keeping watch just right outside if you need me."

Her fear still pumping through her, Percilla could not rest easy, even within the safety of this new shelter and her allies. She sat motionless in front of a standing mirror in the corner of the tent, searching for some sort of guidance she could not find within herself. And, like an answer to a prayer, she heard a voice in her head, enchanting her mind with that alluring whisper.

'Percilla... Percilla...'

As she listened to the voice, she found herself staring at her reflection and the golden light she saw shining from beneath her hat.

'Frik-nas tan,' the voice said, tempting her with words she did not understand.

Unable to stop herself, as if she were nothing more than a puppet, Percilla removed her hat and exposed her ravens to the cold night breeze and the fears inhabiting it. The black birds uncurled from beneath her long black hair, stretching their wings in readiness to fly. They cawed madly after their release from beneath her hat, now flapping their eager wings.

The entrance flap of the tent was whisked aside, and Matik stepped through again. "Percilla, is everything okay?" he shouted. "I heard—" Percilla met his gaze in the mirror's reflection, and she knew he'd seen the ravens. How could he not? "Where did those birds come from?" he asked. "Are they... are they your *hair*?"

'Tra-nas maka net masyan,' the voice whispered again in her mind, and if Matik had said anything else, she didn't hear it. Her ravens took flight, slowly at first so she just hovered above the ground inside her tent. But she knew where they'd be taking her. Percilla glanced down at her own airborne feet, and in the mirror's reflection, she saw Daldor come trampling through the tent entrance, followed by Symon and Frida, all three of them looking furious and ready for action.

"Lasa-mae Eek-tren!" Symon shouted. The ravens ceased their flight and curled to rest under Percilla's hair. She dropped the few feet back to the ground, stumbling to her knees, and felt as if her mind had returned to her.

"Traitor!" Daldor screamed. "I knew it the moment I laid eyes on her. *Traitor*." His beady black eyes grew wide, filling with rage and fear that engulfed the whites around his irises.

"Leave her alone," Matik protested, placing himself between Daldor and Percilla like a shield.

"*Traitor*," Daldor continued. "You stay away from my ladies, you... you—"

"She hasn't done anything to you," Matik interrupted, his finger pointed at Daldor looking rather like a sword.

"She will bring us right into the thick of evils—"

"Enough!" Frida yelled. With a twist of her fingers and her whispered spell, the man's lips and moustache curled themselves into a tight, muffled knot.

"Daldor, instigating fear is not tolerated," Symon said. Then he turned to Frida with a frown of disappointment. "Frida, using magic on the community is not tolerated either, I'm afraid. Unbind him."

Frida reluctantly did as she was told, reversing the twist of her fingers before Daldor could open his mouth again. Then the angry man backed out of the tent, glaring at Percilla and Frida until his beady eyes were the last thing to be seen disappearing around the corner of the tent's opening.

"I can explain," Percilla said, finally finding it in herself to stand.

"We must cut them off," Symon said, his words almost as sharp as that hypothetical blade.

"No!" Percilla shouted, blinded by her lifelong attachment to her avian companions. "I need them to get back to Gangleton after we find Rou."

"Forget it."

"I made a promise."

"That was your choice."

Frida approached Percilla and placed her hand on the girl's shoulder. "It's time to free them, Percilla," she said, her voice carrying all the empathy and compassion Symon's had not. "It's not safe for them to stay. Or us."

"I…" Percilla fluttered with indecision. She saw the concerned faces of those who cared for her, and yet their concern still wasn't enough. "I can't," she whispered.

"Then we must leave you here." Symon closed his eyes and nodded, as if reminding himself he made this hard decision for a reason. "The livelihood of our community cannot be put at risk."

Frida sighed.

"I'm sorry," Percilla said, forcing herself to look Symon in the eye.

"As am I." Symon stepped toward her and rested a gentle hand on her arm. "But before we part, let me prepare you a gift for the morning."

CHAPTER 14

The Honorable

WHEN EVERYONE AWOKE the next morning, Symon gathered Frida and Percilla at the center of the circus and bid them wait just a moment while he prepared his gift. With a flick of his wrist, the whole of Dawookrunk was lifted from the ground—all except one storage tent, into which Symon swiftly disappeared. The traveling circus in the middle of the Barrens briskly dispersed into an enormous gathering of trunks, onto a mass of flying carpets, and into a fleet of air balloons. The happy bustling of the night before was now a mad scramble as objects and clothing zipped by in the air, rushing around Percilla and Frida. They had to duck and dodge trunks, baskets of food, and trinkets all flying toward where they belonged. Some tents closed in on themselves, folding into perfect, travel-sized packages; others remained upright and intact to serve as protection from the blazing sun and were carried by the blue falcons. Performers walking on stilts raced to gather their belongings, taking long steps over Frida and Percilla's heads on the way to their floating tents.

In mere moments, the entire community was packed up and ready to move to new lands, where the show would go on. All in attendance either paraded under or alongside the draping tents or happily sat themselves in their own air balloon baskets or flying carpets. Together, the traveling circus village headed off, as they always did and always would. The sound of brass music faded away into the distance, where Dawookrunk soon disappeared into the morning horizon.

It was then Symon emerged from the last remaining tent, which lifted and packed itself up just as a crew of Dawookrunk handymen carried out a deflated air balloon draped over their shoulders and its large basket above their heads. The men plopped the unfilled balloon into Percilla's hands and set the basket on the ground at her feet. Then they jumped on their flying carpet and took to the sky to join the rest of the floating circus.

"I promised you I would get you there," Symon said. "Here is a start. This basket was made from a durable, enchanted wicker." He winked. "And the air balloon will take more than just flame and gas to fuel its ascent. Frida will know how to operate it."

"Thank you, Symon," Frida said. Her brows drew together in a type of pain Percilla didn't know her great aunt had ever felt.

Symon stepped toward Frida and wrapped her in his arms. "I'll always be with you." To Percilla's surprise, the man pulled her great aunt in for a long, lingering kiss, then stepped back and bowed. "Until next time, loves," he called as he floated into the air. "Don't let those birds keep you from Rou." In that very moment, his arms transformed into wings and his feet into talons. Symon, as a raven, flew off with the rest of the circus.

Frida and Percilla stood alone in the Barrens with their basket and deflated air balloon, silent and motionless. There was little Percilla felt she could say after her blunder the previous evening. Finally, she looked up to see Frida staring after Dawookrunk, which could no longer be seen, with suddenly old eyes that had seen too much loneliness over the course of their many long years.

"You just couldn't part with those stupid birds, could you?" Frida asked, though she did not turn to look at her grandniece.

"I—"

"As if anything on this journey wasn't about you."

"I'm sorry." Percilla stared at the ground, her arms sinking limply by her sides.

"Of course you are... That's why you wouldn't free the birds."

"I need to save my friend." Percilla did not wish to argue with her great aunt, but the truth was that this journey did not stem purely from duty and destiny. She'd left behind people for whom she cared deeply and whom she would never abandon. Never again. Not like with Victoria.

Frida grunted. "Attachments." She rummaged through her bag, sticking her head inside as if she were looking through an extremely large closet.

"What are we going to do with this thing?" Percilla asked, staring at the deflated air balloon in her arms.

"Fill it with air and fly," Frida responded curtly.

As Frida continued to search for something that would get their air balloon ready to ascend, Percilla looked out across the sprawling expanse of the Barrens. From over the hump of a far-off sand dune, a wavering streak darted, sending up a long plume of dust in its wake. It moved incredibly fast—so fast, by the time she realized it was headed straight toward them, the thing was nearly there already.

"Percilla!"

She recognized Zyne's voice immediately. He zipped right passed Percilla and Frida, who at first hadn't noticed his approach at all, then still darted around and around so quickly, the women soon stood in the center of his manufactured dust storm. When he finally came to a full stop in front of them, he pulled the tight-fitting goggles from his eyes before they smacked back against the top of his head.

"I found you!" he exclaimed, grinning ear to ear.

"I have good news," Percilla replied, just as happy as he looked.

Zyne's eyes widened with anticipation. "You fixed it?"

"Yes!"

"Where? Where is she? Is she okay?"

"Slow down," she said with a chuckle, knowing full well that was probably the one thing Zyne could not do. "They just left, but she's in Dawookrunk. I met her and told her I knew you, too. She's fine. And she's with the circus."

Zyne's eyes shimmered with tears. "You really found her!" he cried out, then jerked his head around to scan the emptiness of the Barrens in every direction. "What circus?"

"They headed straight that way," she said, pointing to where Dawookrunk had disappeared. "Ask for Symon and tell him Percilla sent you. Listen for the music."

Without another word, Zyne took off, sand spraying everywhere behind him.

"Tell them your love is in The Gold!" Percilla shouted happily, waving her arm in farewell.

"Thank you!" His voice echoed only briefly behind the incomprehensible speed of his departure.

Apparently not all that interested in the goings on outside her bag, Frida removed a small bottle from it and stuck her finger in the air. After testing the wind, she dumped yellow and orange dust from the bottle into her hand and motioned for Percilla to hold open the air balloon. Frida opened her palm and blew the dust into the great contraption.

"Trip-tan-as Frim-pos-eeum."

The dust inside the balloon ignited to fill the space with air, slowly inflating it for flight. As Percilla went about attaching the balloon to its basket for travel, Frida looked to the sunrise to check the skies for any signs of trouble. The air was clear, calm, and good for flying today. "Percilla," she said. When Percilla looked up, she found her great aunt holding a spyglass to her eye. "Did your friend forget something?"

Percilla turned around to see another cloud of dust churning furiously in the distance in the same direction Zyne had sped away. "I don't think so..." she said, squinting to see anything in the cloud of sand.

Frida leaned forward with her spyglass, and a grin spread across her lips. "Ah. Never mind."

In seconds, the streaking figure was close enough now for Percilla to make out Matik atop his unicycle, headed for them at top speeds. He had a satchel slung over his shoulder beside a bow and quiver, and an ornate scabbard hung from one side of his belt. A coiled lasso swung from a leather loop at the other side of his waist. Frida chuckled.

"Matik," Percilla exclaimed, glad to see him again but confused by his sudden return. "Is everything all right?"

"I'm going to help you find Rou." Matik offered quite the formal bow, peddling back and forth on his unicycle to keep it upright. "What do you need?"

"Let's get this thing up," Frida ordered, already stepping over the edge of the air balloon's basket.

After Matik attached his unicycle to the basket, he joined them inside the contraption, and they waited for the air balloon to finish inflating. Once filled, it lifted them into the air, and Percilla looked over the edge to watch the ground slowly slip out of sight. Then they drifted farther up into the clouds and disappeared inside the fluffy nimbus around them. Sunlight overwhelmed them when they popped through the layer of clouds. Squinting against the sudden brightness, Percilla recognized, after a few seconds, a second balloon piercing through the field of clouds behind them. This one was white, its basket black, and it came at them with a wicked speed. Her heart pounded in her chest at the sight of the Dignitary Nylz alone in that black basket closing in on them fast. The woman leered at them and let out a blood-curdling cry of triumph.

"It appears we've attracted a Dignitary balloonist," Frida said with remarkable calm.

Nylz pulled down on a lever fixed to the basket, and her balloon picked up even more speed, dispersing clouds of black fumes. Grinning, the Dignitary loaded a crossbow and aimed its bolt at the trio's own balloon. "Percilla," she shouted, "I've come to claim my prize!"

"Get down!" Matik yelled. All three ducked below the top of the basket, but it hadn't been necessary. The crossbow bolt pierced through the wicker, latching itself onto the basket. Their airborne vessel jerked backward, as if being pulled. Matik rose from his crouch, pulled his sword from its sheath, and sliced down upon the rope. His blade did nothing but glance off the Dignitary's rope as if it were also made of metal.

Looking out toward Nylz, who now held them in tow, Matik asked, "Frida, do you have a shield in that bag?"

Frida dug through her bag with a few quick jerks, then swiftly removed a round, iron shield far larger than her bag's opening. "Here."

Matik snatched it from her with a nod and untied his unicycle from where he'd secured it to the basket. He jumped onto the basket's wicker rim, then mounted his unicycle atop the rope leading to the Dignitary's balloon.

"What are you doing?" Percilla asked, rising only for a moment from where she'd crouched to the basket's wicker floor.

"There's only one way to end this," he said, then pedaled across the rope. Shield extended before him, he made his way toward Nylz, who had abandoned the lever propelling the unnatural speed of her air balloon to take up the crossbow again.

"I wonder if you can fly, circus boy," Nylz shouted, then fired a volley of three shots at him as quickly as she could load her weapon. The first missed its mark, whizzing past Matik's face, but the next two landed squarely in his shield.

"You obviously don't know who I am," Matik shouted back. By the time the third arrow landed, he was already halfway to the Dignitary's balloon. "I am Matik, star performer of Dawookrunk."

In swift, astute movements, Matik reached her basket and leapt toward it, abandoning his unicycle to the sky. Nylz swung at him, but he'd launched himself high enough to avoid the blow, then landed nimbly in the basket behind her. He drew his sword, and Nylz whirled around.

"A duel it is!" Nylz released a rage of ceaseless strikes at a hexed speed, thus pinning Matik in the corner of the basket. He sprang up onto the edge of the black basket and swung around its corner bars, lifting his legs to strike the Dignitary square in the chest. Nylz flew across the basket, and the air balloon shuddered when she crashed against its far wall. Then Matik jumped back down, only to narrowly avoid the woman's spinning kick as she lashed out at him like a striking snake from where she'd landed.

Frida squinted and studied the Dignitary's rope. After a brief moment of hesitation, she grabbed hold of it and closed her eyes.

Percilla peeked her head over the rim of the trio's basket to watch the fight, her heart thumping as the sound of blades slicing through air and clanging against each other rang out in the sky. "Get us closer!" she shouted to Frida. "We have to help!"

"I need to understand the hex on this rope first," Frida replied rather calmly. "This balloon and its rider are of a dark magic I've not often come across."

Percilla's stomach clenched at the sight of Matik now hanging with one hand from the Dignitaries' basket, his sword clenched tightly in the other. "Frida, we need to get closer."

"I've almost got it. The spell upon this rope is of a tongue no longer spoken."

Aboard the Dignitary vessel, Nylz raised her blade high above her head, preparing to finish Matik with one last, powerful slash. "This is not a circus ring, *boy*."

Percilla gasped when she saw Matik let go of the basket's edge. But he'd only slipped with acrobatic grace down the side of the basket to now cling to its underbelly before Nylz could bring down her sword. "Everywhere is a circus ring," he shouted. "And your act is a flop." He thrusted his sword upward into the basket and sliced through the wicker bottom.

Nylz nearly fell all the way through, but to Percilla's dismay, she caught herself on the edge and dangled there by one hand. Matik heaved himself up the other side of the basket to climb the stabilizing ropes to the air balloon's very top. Nylz sheathed her sword in one quick motion and followed Matik up the same path.

"Aha!" Frida shouted, and the impenetrable rope in her hands slackened immediately. She rummaged through her bag once more, then brandished a sharpened dagger. Seizing the disenchanted rope, she brought the blade slicing down against it and released their air balloon from the Dignitary's. "Now time for a rescue. Hang on." Frida drew a symbol in the air, then pushed her hand through it, casting a force that propelled their basket toward the dueling pair.

The Dignitary hacked and slashed with unbelievable speed,
her eyes wide and blazing with the heat of battle. It seemed she
might press Matik off the edge of the balloon until he flipped
over her head, just barely skimming her blade. Bellowing out a
wicked growl, she whirled around to face him again.

While the pair balanced on the tremulous height of the
balloon, slashing, lunging, and parrying in a deadly dance that

might as well have been on a tightrope, Frida had managed to pull her and Percilla quite close to the Dignitary's aircraft, lifting their basket at a level with the fighting pair. Matik glanced back at them to see Frida guiding the basket toward him, then stepped swiftly backward until he stood close enough to jump to safety. He managed just in time to parry Nylz's next crushing attack, and though he kept his balance on the balloon's sloping edge, his sword flew from his hand to spin end over end through the sky. Matik unhooked the lasso from his belt, whirled it around to open its noose, then slung it over the Dignitary's head. When he pulled it tight, Nylz grunted in surprise, her arms pinned to her sides.

Frida dug into her bag yet again and removed a delicately constructed crossbow of her own with a single golden bolt already loaded. "Would you like to do the honors and put an arrow to that cursed balloon?"

Filled with both an urgency to help Matik and a surprising desire to rid herself of the Dignitary pursuing her, Percilla grabbed the crossbow and aimed for Nylz's white balloon.

"Your evil is your own demise," she heard Matik shout, and the certainty in his voice only steadied her concentration. From the corner of her eye, she saw him leap from the other balloon toward her, and she pulled the trigger. The crossbow's golden bolt soared into the white balloon, ripping two massive holes through its enchanted canvas with a gasp of hot air. Both the restrained Nylz and the Dignitaries' air balloon plummeted from the sky right in front of her.

"Doesn't look like she was expecting to lose her power so quickly," Frida said, peering over the edge of the basket. "Little does she know I've studied all the ancient languages."

Percilla slowly lowered the crossbow and turned to see Matik standing in the basket once more, grinning at her before bending into a low, flourishing bow. "You *are* a star performer," she told him, feeling a little breathless.

"And you have quite the shot."

Their basket lurched in the sky, and the trio stumbled to keep their footing. Then their air balloon turned in a wide circle, picking up speed. Percilla leaned over the basket to see a dark funnel rising from below, which had caught their air balloon in its grasp and now spun them around like a top. The trio struggled to hang on, clutching at the edges of their basket as they were pulled down by the shadow vortex.

"What's going on?" Percilla shouted.

Frida peered over the basket as well, raised her eyebrow, and offered a nonchalant shrug. Then she daintily lifted her pinky finger and the ring upon it set with a black gemstone. "Wisp-ken-ta!" she yelled over the raging winds. The vortex howled as its spinning force reversed, and the first wisps of black clouds snaked over the edge of their basket to trail into the gem on Frida's ring. "Hang on!" Frida yelled, gripping her wrist now with her other hand as the sky rocked with the force of such a turbulent, devious hex being sucked entirely into the ring itself. In the next instant, the basket stilled, the sun shone down upon them once more from within a blue sky, and silence overwhelmed them.

The trio waited a moment, still gripping the basket should any other unknown attack be thrown their way. Finally, Percilla released her tight clutch on the wicker frame and heaved out a sigh. "Why do the Digs always know where to find me?" she asked.

Frida twisted the ring on her pinky to center it again. "They work with evil," she explained. "One spell can cast all darkness upon a single person."

Percilla groaned, holding her head between her hands. "What did I fly myself into?"

"It's our family's destiny. Just be thankful we can do it together."

Matik cleared his throat, inspecting the balloon for any damage before asking, "Where to, ladies?"

"Percilla?" Frida asked, dusting herself off.

Percilla pulled the map from her satchel and placed her pendulum over it, revealing the lay of the land. "Find Rou," she said. The pendulum guided her hand to the north, and with that, she announced their journey's course. "Straight ahead." Matik opened a compartment under the burner to reveal a silver propeller, and with the pull of a lever, the propeller engaged to steer them in the direction Percilla now pointed.

CHAPTER 15

Stealing Tricks

DRENDLE MOVED HASTILY through the mountains bordering Gangleton. He rode his motorbike and pulled the trailer concealing the girl he'd kidnapped from Dawook-runk. The mountain path was ill-trodden, filled with sharp rocks and deep chasms connecting ravines of untold depths. Broad patches of thorny cacti grew everywhere, their prickly arms reaching out to snag intruders. Loose stones tumbled down the cliffsides as the wheel of the trailer skimmed the edge of the pass. It was terrifying terrain to travel, but for this Dignitary, the greatest trial was not the terrain itself but his orientation and sudden detachment from headquarters. Drendle poked at a radio transmitter built into his contraption, nearly breaking it off with his huge fingers as he struggled to get it working. Perplexed beyond usual, he looked around for any sign to guide him.

He found the rising pinnacle of rock shaped like a meerkat and grinned. They'd arrived.

It had been hours since Drendle had snuck off from Dawookrunk, and the morning sun was already rising high into the sky. But now, they finally arrived outside the Caves of Seoj, where the rest of the Dignitaries planned their next move and awaited Drendle's arrival within the confines of their cavernous chambers. Drendle dismounted from his motorbike and approached the cavern's entrance, dragging his bound captive with him, keeping one eye on her always. The entryway into the Caves was covered with a massive boulder immovable even with Drendle's considerable strength. A lone cactus grew next to it, inconspicuously placed beneath the shadow of the cliff above.

"I have returned," Drendle whispered as he leaned toward the cactus.

"Where have you been?" Franc's voice blasted back from inside the cactus, muffled with static from the transmission.

"On mission 'Get the Girl'," Drendle replied, confused.

"Well what took you so long?"

"I-I'm sorry, ma'am. I got lost in the mountains on my way here."

"Imbecile. Do you have Percilla?"

"Yes, ma'am," Drendle answered.

"Well then, bring her in!" Neither Franc's frustration nor her eagerness were dampened even by her voice erupting from the cactus.

"Right away, ma'am." Drendle turned toward the cave door and said, "Flisim-gwee." The boulder blocking his path rolled aside with the crushing grind of stone against stone. A thick shadow filled the Caves' entrance, but as Drendle stepped foot inside, a light rose within the tunnel to illuminate his path. He entered the Caves of Seoj, forcefully dragging his confused and frightened abductee behind him, the way ahead steadily revealing more of itself with each step they took. He moved through the twisting caverns, following the light back to the central chamber where the rest of the Dignitaries—except Nylz—had already gathered for a meeting.

Drendle stepped into the large chamber and saw Franc, Ons, and Lyken looking over a large table map of all the communities in the Barrens and their corresponding miniature figurines. It was masterfully crafted of metal and magic, displaying all the notable topography and figurines representing each community as they moved about in the world. Next to the map, Vahn sat exhausted and tied to a chair, completely silent. The boy craned his neck toward Drendle and his prisoner.

Franc turned to face Drendle when she heard him enter the chamber. As her gaze passed over the girl abducted into the Caves, her eyes lit up with a dark giddiness. "Good day, Miss Bomqui. We were worried about you."

"Who are you people?" the girl asked, her eyes wide.

"You poor child," Lyken moaned, stretching his legs grotesquely across the chamber's obsidian floor. "Have the Barrens been too rough on you? They tend to be quite unforgiving to traitors."

"What are you talking about?" The girl jerked away from Drendle in a futile attempt to wrest herself from his ironlike grip.

"Don't play games with us," Lyken hissed.

"This is my first time out of Krinkton. I don't know what you want."

Franc's glare narrowed. "Krinkton?" she asked quietly. "Why have you been in Krinkton?"

"That's my home," the girl answered with a small whine in her voice. "My name is Daisy. Daisy Etsen of Krinkton."

"We've watched you your whole life," Lyken exclaimed. "Your name is Percilla Bomqui. Do not lie to us, sweetie."

Vahn chuckled, rocking back and forth in his chair. "That's not Percilla," he gasped through his glee.

"What do you know?" Lyken slinked to Vahn's side and loomed over him. The Dignitary's thin, greasy hair slapped against Vahn's face.

"I grew up with Percilla," Vahn said, his laughter fading away as he pulled his face away from Lyken's disgusting hair. "I know her voice."

"Nonsense," Ons remarked. He scrambled toward Drendle, adjusted his monocle, and tore the map from Drendle's satchel. He unrolled the map and revealed the X representing Percilla— still far away from the Caves of Seoj, moving slowly through the Barrens. He tossed the map to the cold floor of the cavern and pinned it beneath his cane. "Drendle, why did you bring us this girl?"

"She..." Drendle thought for a moment, caressing his beard and looking down at Daisy, whom he still held firmly in his grip. "She's Percilla?"

Vahn laughed again, quieter this time.

"And what makes you think this is Percilla?" Ons inquired, sounding remarkably patient.

Drendle knew Ons wanted answers—good ones—so he tried to choose his words most carefully. "She matches the picture," he said. "And the X was at Dawookrunk, where I found this girl."

"This is not Percilla!" Franc shouted, slamming her palms down onto the table.

Drendle glanced at the girl, highly confused, and blubbered, "But she looks like the picture."

"I don't care!"

Ons sighed and briefly adjusted the monocle over his left eye. He tapped his cane against the X on the map lying at his feet. "This little X on the map. *This* is Percilla."

Drendle stared down at it, pressing his lips tightly together and furrowing his brow in anxiety. "Sorry." His shoulders slumped.

Ons rolled his eyes and brushed past Drendle to leave the chamber, shaking his head.

"Have you no mind at all?" Franc shouted. "Leave and do not return until you have Percilla!" Drendle bowed in obeisance with a rekindling determination.

Lyken left Vahn's side to approach Franc and softly assured her, "Nylz will bring her soon."

Drendle saluted and turned to exit the chamber, almost stepping right into the other Dignitary when Ons returned with a new map in his hands. "Nylz is... on her way back," he announced. "It appears she does not have Percilla." He pointed to his map. Just then, a bright light flashed around the Percilla lookalike before she blinked out of existence. Vahn erupted in another bout of laughter.

Hesitantly lifting his head and waiting for her outburst, Drendle noted the visible twitch of fury around Franc's eyes. The cavern filled with silence for a brief and awkward moment before she finally screamed, "Can *nobody* get this pitiful girl?" Her hands came crashing down again on the table, flinging all the figurines onto the chamber floor. "Ons, I want you to get in her mind now! Use all the energy storage. I don't care where that leaves us. Just bring her here! She obviously has allies now, and they all must know we mean to take her down. *And* all of Rou. This is *our* world."

"At once," Ons affirmed, then immediately left for the Cuckoo Clock Tower. Drendle scuttled from the cavern after him, leaving the rest of the Dignitaries to face Franc's wrath.

CHAPTER 16

Mind Ruse

PERCILLA AND FRIDA slept with their backs against the air balloon's wicker basket as the sun's rays shone down on them amid a clear blue sky. Matik piloted the balloon, being the most experienced with it. Traveling with Dawookrunk had also given him a much greater understanding of the lay of the land. The afternoon sun brought its usual intense heat, but now that they no longer had to walk to Rou, he noticed the group's disposition much improved. Not one bead of sweat nor a twinge of discomfort marred their faces. And most importantly of all, in the sky, they traveled safely above any of the dangers lurking on the ground below.

Matik found solace in the soft howling of the wind and the peacefulness of his companions. He felt a certain satisfaction in protecting Percilla, knowing she was safe from the wrath of Nylz and the other Dignitaries. And he'd hoped to continue in that way until they reached their destination. Matik appreciated the purity and devotion Percilla represented. Now, as she rested, he took the moment to fully admire this beautiful young lady—the delicacy of her lashes and the soft color in her cheeks. Then, as if his gaze disturbed her, a small, muffled groan escaped her. When Percilla furrowed her brow, his admiration gave way to concern. Percilla shifted against the basket, as if trying to turn away from whatever bothered her. When she whimpered louder, Matik could not ignore the cautious alertness flaring up in him.

Then her eyes shot open. "I want off this balloon," she announced, launching herself violently to her feet and setting the basket to swaying dangerously.

"What?" Matik asked, both wondering what had caused this sudden change and trying to find the right response.

"I don't want you to follow me anymore. I want down. Now!" Percilla clenched her fists and glared at him.

Matik glanced at Frida to see the sorceress had awoken at her grandniece's shouts. Then he looked again at Percilla and swept aside his hand to gesture at the sky. "Why? We're perfectly safe up here."

"I want you to land this thing," Percilla insisted.

"Percilla," Frida asked, "are you not feeling well?"

"Take me down and leave me," Percilla shouted. "Both of you!"

"Why the sudden change?" Frida cocked her head and studied Percilla, but she did not stand from where she leaned against the basket.

Percilla's mouth opened, closed, then opened again with a whisper. "Tri-nis... rin... ta..."

The sky darkened in an instant, black clouds coalescing to create one massive thunderhead towering directly above them. It swirled rapidly, twisting itself into a dark vortex. The screeches of mad, unseen creatures within it echoed around them, and at the storm's center, a black hole opened, growing like a vile mouth stretching wide and pulling the air balloon toward it. As a smoky staircase descended from the black hole and stretched toward the basket, Percilla stepped up onto the wicker edge. Without stopping to think why she would do such a thing, Matik lurched forward and grabbed her by the waist to pull her back. The girl ripped his hands away as quickly and easily as swiping away an insect.

The black hole churned just beyond their air balloon, and Percilla stepped up onto the edge of the basket again, holding the corner bars for balance.

"What are you doing!" Frida shouted.

Matik knew Percilla was not in her right mind, though he had no way to know what she was thinking right now or how he could protect her. Then she jumped from the wicker ledge toward the black staircase beside their balloon, and in the same instant, he launched himself over the edge of the basket after her. He hooked the toes of his boots against the wicker edge before their combined weight could drag him out with her, and he managed to just pull them both back to safety. Percilla snarled at him, kicking and squirming before she broke free of his grip. Then she shoved him away with an unnatural strength and pounced on him like a feral animal.

Her eyes glowed with malevolent energy. "Don't ever touch me, you scab!" she shrieked.

Matik froze, terrified by both her warning and the violent light in her eyes. He did not want to hurt her, either, so he let her go. When Percilla seemed to recognize he was no longer a threat to this bizarre thing she wanted, she turned away from him again in another attempt to climb up the staircase toward the portal.

"Percilla," Frida said, "look here."

Percilla turned toward the sorceress, and when Matik looked up at Frida, he found the woman held a green potion vial between herself and Percilla. Before Percilla could react, a thick puff of emerald smoke fumed from the vial's mouth, trailing over the girl's face and into her mouth, which had opened in surprise.

"Loctis-hic maan," Frida said, and the glow in Percilla's eyes dimmed before she fainted, falling backwards over the edge of the air balloon. The sorceress grabbed her arm just in time, though Percilla was left dangling in the air as the emerald smoke dissipated and Matik regained his footing in the basket.

When he looked up, he saw looming from the dark portal a terrifying number of large, demonic, winged creatures, their eyes also glowing with that same malintent. With an earsplitting screech, the creatures took flight, leading a seemingly endless swarm of the same pouring from the portal to swoop around and around the air balloon.

Matik quickly rushed to help Frida pull Percilla back into the safety of the basket, only to find one of the demons had shot up from below with a shriek and grabbed Percilla's foot in its razor-sharp talons. It yanked and tugged at her, furiously beating its wings.

"Hang on to her!" Matik yelled. He pulled his bow over his head, nocked an arrow, and shot it straight into the demon's eye. The creature screamed but still held fast to Percilla's foot. The awful sound shot a bolt of pain through Matik's head, and he stumbled back for a moment to cover his ears. He saw Frida's mouth moving in an unheard whisper, and the demon's racket stopped short. Then the sorceress blew a long breath toward the vile thing, which shook its head and attempted to shriek once more. No sound released from its struggling throat, and as Frida opened her mouth wider and blew more violently, the demon twitched, shuddered, then burst into a cloud of swirling black smoke.

With the creature vanished, Percilla fell below the basket's edge, nearly pulling Frida out with her. Matik grabbed Frida about the waist this time to haul her back, and together, they managed to drag the still-unconscious Percilla back into the basket. There they stood above her, back to back, blocking the creatures' attacks in their haste to reach the girl. With each arrow pulled from his quiver, nocked, and released, Matik effectively held off the demons, but there were too many to fight one by one.

Frida turned to her bag and withdrew a crystal wand, the pure white gem affixed to its intricate shaft blazing with mystical energy. "Fran-tum gruae!"

A glowing nebula of white light pulsed from Frida's crystal wand, spreading outward to form a protective barrier around the basket. The demons screeched and howled as they tried to avoid the blinding glow, and those caught within Frida's cleansing magic instantly disseminated into black smoke. The flock fled to the top of the air balloon, evading the light at all costs. They tore at canvas panels with their claws, the shredded holes whistling with fleeing gas and air.

"*Frac-tus brono-mak!*" Frida shouted.

Her wand's light expanded even farther to surround the entire balloon and basket, thus engulfing the demons around them. Screams of pain and low, vicious growls rang out in unison before each creature was reduced to smoke, the terrible echoes filling the silence left behind. What remained of the monstrous flock scattered and wheeled back into the closing portal, which then shrank down to nothing and disappeared. The swirling air stilled, the dark clouds parted to reveal the sun's brilliance, and the trio was once more alone in the skies.

The balloon, however, was still losing gas and altitude with concerning speed. Frida sat in the basket and lifted Percilla's head into her lap. Then she turned to Matik and said something he realized he couldn't hear above the wild ringing in his ears. "What?" he yelled back, though he did not catch the sound of even his own voice.

Frida waved him toward her, and when he crouched into a squat beside her, she leaned toward him and whispered what must have been another spell. The ringing stopped. "Land this thing," she said.

CHAPTER 17

To See or not To See

PERCILLA FELT A warmth upon her forehead, then a flare of white light made her eyes flutter open. When she did, she watched the pulsing glow retreating into an open palm held steadily over her eyes and forehead. She blinked quickly, the hand moved away from her, and she stared up into Frida's concerned gaze above a relieved smile.

"What are you doing?" Percilla asked, feeling remarkably tired and not entirely sure why she'd been asleep.

"Helping you find peace," Frida answered. "How do you feel?"

"Terrible." Percilla realized her great aunt held her head in her lap, and she huffed out a breath when she pushed herself up to sit beside Frida. "What happened?"

"Another horrible trick." Frida let out a heavy sigh. "The next time you hear something, you tell me, yes?"

"Hear something?" Percilla tilted her head, then she gained a full awareness of the things she'd been hearing almost this entire journey. "That *voice*."

"Yes, that voice," Frida repeated. "You put us all in danger. Keep that in mind."

Percilla nodded sheepishly at her great aunt, not believing what she'd nearly gotten them all into; she remembered the dark staircase, the portal, the creatures, and yet it all felt so much like a nightmare. She thought she'd heard that enchanting voice in a recent dream as well, but now she couldn't tell if that was true or if the voice had called to her right before the dark portal had appeared. "Promise," she whispered and tried to push the terrifying event completely from her mind again.

She turned to look up at Matik, who extended a hand toward her with a silent smile. Percilla took his hand and let him help her up. Without a word, he pointed over the side of the basket at what she could only assume was their next unwilling destination on the ground.

The air balloon descended toward the ruins of a village in the middle of the Barrens. A murky veil of clouds completely hid the center of the ashen remains from view, though its outer edges of crushed stone and burnt debris made an intimidating sight. Everything had been drained of color and life, not even a single tree left standing around the outskirts of the village. Not a sound could be heard from within the destruction save for the howl of the wind.

"We'll be walking from here on, ladies," Matik announced as he gently landed the air balloon outside the ruins on flat, rocky ground. The torn balloon itself could not have held them airborne much longer anyway; as soon as the basket thumped against the ground, the balloon's canvas deflated almost entirely to fall against the basket's side.

Percilla retrieved the map from her satchel, unrolled it, and used her pendulum to track Rou's location. Luckily, they remained on track, but Rou was still an exhaustibly far distance. She sighed, not wanting to walk one more step, but quickly snapped back into action when she saw Matik and Frida both looking at her for direction.

"Well, which way?" Frida inquired.

"We have to go through there," Percilla said, pointing toward the destroyed village and its gated entrance lying on the ground in a pile of rubble.

"Oh, good." Frida rubbed her hands together. "Maybe we'll find some ancient artifacts."

"Are you sure you have room in that bag?" Matik added. He stooped to relieve a measure of rope from the deflated air balloon. At one end, he tied a swift, deft knot to form a lasso, then he coiled the rope and latched it through the loop in his belt.

The sorceress smirked. "I was just going to have you carry whatever I find."

The three left their deflated air balloon and walked through what remained of the stone arches surrounding the ruins. From the sky, the place had seemed completely devoid of life. Now that they were closer, though, they found vines growing up the edges of the demolished, white marble architecture. In the aftermath of whatever destruction had come for this village, it seemed new life had found room to grow, turning the drab gray of the rubble into a thriving forest of overgrowth. Greenery, flowers, and tall grass covered the loose stones set into the ground. Roofless cobblestone buildings had been reduced to little more than half-existing frames. Fallen stone walls and shattered marble pillars littered the ground, blocking off alleyways and whole streets. A few remaining columns appeared sturdy, still supporting perilously detached archways. At the edges of the ruined village turned desert oasis, an age of blowing sands had nearly built a wall around such ancient remains, as if the Barrens themselves had wished to preserve both the history of this place and whatever abandoned artifacts lay hidden beneath it.

"What could destroy such a place?" Percilla wondered aloud.

"The Dignitaries, no doubt," Matik said.

"More likely just one of their schemes," Frida added.

Within the silence, the faint sound of dangling wind chimes echoed from inside the ruins. With it came the hollow resonance of wind blowing across an open vessel and the deep toll of a gong in nature's metered rhythms. A tambourine jingled, following the tune of the wind.

"Is that music?" Frida asked.

"I think it's coming from that way," Matik replied, pointing ahead and cocking his head toward the sound.

"Let's investigate." Frida grinned, seeming remarkably excited by the prospect.

Frida and Matik started toward the music, heading deeper into the ruins. Percilla moved after them, but a flash of movement beside her made her stop. When she turned to glance that way, she found herself staring at Vahn. No doubt it was him, standing at the edge of an alleyway, half covered in the shadow of a ruined wall ripe with vegetation. Filled with joy at the sight of him, she opened her mouth to call to him, but Vahn disappeared down the alley before she could say a word. Without thinking, she chased after him, slipping away from Frida and Matik while they followed the music.

Frida and Matik quickly worked their way over the uneven ground, walking through cleared alleys and into a courtyard. The fallen stone walls around it formed a perfect ring with a dry stone fountain at its center. Dead leaves blown from the creeping ivy tumbled across the courtyard's cobbled stone.

Around the fountain danced an old man in a long black cloak, his wide-brimmed hat concealing most of his face. Though a long cane rested on the ground beside the fountain, the man's light, fragile movements imitated a fallen leaf as he swayed and fluttered in circles. He played a broken tambourine missing two of its cymbals, periodically shaking it ever so lightly whenever the winds changed. The wind chimes hanging from columns of stone tinkled in time, and the wind whistled over the open lips of empty clay jugs scattered about the courtyard. The man flicked his hand toward a gong at the edge of the ring, which released its low, reverberating echo on cue. Then he sang in a deep, raspy voice:

Do you hear?
I say do you hear?
The message of the breeze.
Do you hear it stirring through the leaves?
Speaks a secret kind of tongue.
Only the silent will receive.

Do you hear the message of the breeze?
It wonders why there's no peace.
Why the people don't speak?
Freedom can be their choice.
Their silence is their cage.
Have they forgotten they have a voice?
Do you hear the breeze?

"Do you hear the breeze?" he asked, his voice falling into a normal timbre, his eyes closed. "Do you hear the breeze?"

"Who, me?" Frida asked, pointing to herself.

"My dear, that is clear. Do you hear the music?"

"Of course."

"Does it sooth you? Do you feel it move through you?"

"Sure," Frida replied, though now she found the man's line of questioning particularly odd.

"A soothing sound heals the soul. Wakes the spirit to take control. Why didn't it stop the fight which drew out long past five nights? Didn't anybody hear? No. Why? Fear... fear killed the harmony."

"I'm not sure," she said. "We've only just arrived."

"I've been waiting." The old man smiled and sat cross-legged in front of the fountain.

"What do you mean?" Frida glanced quickly at Matik, who gazed about the courtyard with wide eyes. Then she slowly approached the seer.

"A message for the girl."

"Who?"

"The one with the Eye of Rou," the old man replied, as though his meaning were obvious from the start. Then the oracle opened his eyes for the first time, revealing their permanently clouded irises and hazy pupils.

"I am not sure what you're talking about," Frida said slowly, stopping dead in her tracks when she saw those eyes. She did in fact consider turning right back around the way they'd come, realizing the man knew too much about their journey. "But we mus—"

"You fear me, Frida?" the oracle interrupted. "Trust in me, dear."

Frida stood her ground and narrowed her eyes at him, still not convinced he meant well at all. "What have you for the girl?"

"Secrets," he answered. "Matik, fetch the girl you desire."

Frida whirled round, realizing she had neither heard from nor seen Percilla for some time. "Percilla!" she shouted, fearing the worst.

"Many guardians watch over her," the old man crooned.

Matik leaned toward Frida and whispered, "I'll find her. You keep an eye on this seer." He nodded at the oracle, then rushed back through the ruins of the village.

Symon had found them again the minute the balloon touched solid ground. He'd expected their flight to have lasted a little longer, but when his astral spirit had seen the torn shreds of the balloon and the trio moving off into the ruins of this ancient village, he understood the danger had not left them for long.

Now, he followed Percilla through the rubble, shifting from his physical raven body to a spectral being to help her here in any way he could. She followed the shadow of a young man— the very same to whom he'd only briefly revealed himself in the Caves of Seoj—who darted through the decimated streets, turning corners with unnatural speed before Percilla even got a chance to speak. Symon recognized illusions when he saw them, but the girl seemed either too tired or too unfamiliar to suspect a thing.

As Percilla ran, a black fog seeped from the ground at her feet and sprawled across the path, pursuing her as if it were alive. Its flickering tendrils slithered without sound through the air, crawling from the shadows of the ruins, growing with every step she took. Percilla followed the illusion of the boy to a dead end, where he disappeared through the wall as if he had never been there at all.

She stood there—physically alone but not entirely—and examined the wall in front of her with a confused stare. As if she expected to find some lever or secret door, she ran her hands through the vines and along the wall's rough surface. Behind her, the black fog rose from splintered cracks in the ground, coalescing into a black snake rearing above the unwitting girl's head. It opened its maw and let out a low hiss like the rattling of wind against stone. Daggers of obsidian fangs glistened between its jaws, the things eyes two deep portals into an infinite abyss, watching Percilla with voracious, wicked intent. She was prey standing in the jaws of evil, only moments from being swallowed.

Symon drew himself into a more corporeal form—though only just—and raised his palm toward the snake. The symbol appearing in his hand could only be seen by himself and this dark hunter; the snake turned to see Symon's sigil, falling victim to its captivating power.

"Til-mee ay-son," Symon said, speaking in tune with the breeze so Percilla could not hear. He would not let any harm come to her—not now, when there was hope.

The blue light radiating from Symon's palm grew until it pierced the snake through to its shadowy core and obliterated it. The monstrous creature writhed in agony, losing its physical form and twisting back into a black fog before dispersing into so many strands of thin smoke.

Percilla turned back from the wall in time to see nothing at all. She unknowingly stared straight through Symon, who would not make his presence known to her right now. As she turned away, he produced a sheet of parchment and whispered, "Kat-ama." The wind he'd summoned blew forth and swept the paper from his fingers, and when he motioned toward Percilla, the paper followed. It fluttered against her leg and caught there, even when she attempted to shake it off. Forced to kneel, she peeled the paper away and lifted it to read its contents. Symon also knew what existed there—Percilla's face depicted in black ink above the text that read:

Danger: Percilla Bomqui carries the lick of evil. Report any sightings at once, for you are in danger. Exorbitant Rewards.
– Dignitaries

Symon drifted up to the roof of a nearby building and took on his raven form. He perched there for a moment, gazing out over the destroyed village and everything within it. Frida sat with Vincent the oracle at the fountain, speaking of events and visions yet to pass. Matik ran through the broken streets and alleys in pursuit of Percilla, finally drawing close. Seeing that Percilla would now be safe, Symon made his final act of departure and let out a startling caw. The girl turned toward the building only to see him flap his wings and take flight before he disappeared into the gray clouds above.

When Percilla looked away from the raven in the sky, she found Matik racing toward her down the alley, panting heavily and slick with sweat.

"Thank goodness you're safe," he gasped.

"Of course I'm safe," Percilla replied. "What's got you all flown?"

"An oracle has news for you."

"A who?" Percilla asked, distracted again by the warning scrawled on the paper and half deaf to what Matik had said. "Look." She flipped over the paper and held it out for him to read.

When he did, his eyes grew wide. "You'd better talk with him."

After a few minutes, Matik finally led her to the courtyard and the fountain. There they found Frida and the oracle deep in conversation, neither of whom seemed to notice that Percilla and Matik had returned.

"What happened here?" Frida asked.

"If anyone should know this type of destruction, it would be you, Frida."

"Why do you say that?"

"Your village fell prey to very much the same. *This* village, however, rejected whatever aid evil offered."

"Not everyone suffered Gangleton's fate."

"This is true," the old man agreed. "Gangleton was easily swayed. A misfortune only the fearful create."

"Our community was deceived and split from the inside. No one knew whom to believe."

"Your destiny with Gangleton has not ended," he warned her.

Thinking they'd come upon the fountain unnoticed, Percilla was entirely surprised when the old man turned his filmy gaze upon her and said, "Come, Percilla. There is something you must see."

Percilla glanced at Frida. Her great aunt nodded, though it did not lessen Percilla's hesitation. Slowly, she approached the old man and knelt in front of him before he placed his hand over her eyes and instructed her to breathe deeply.

Following his direction, she let the winds howling through the village fill her lungs. Almost immediately, a blurred vision overcame her sight—a dark, cold dungeon. Chains hung from the stone walls lit only by the ominous blue aura of light with an unknown source. Water dripped slowly from the ceiling somewhere and echoed through the semi-darkness. Cages filled the cavern, but only one in the corner drew Percilla's attention. A woman sat completely still on the floor of the cage, hidden in shadow. Percilla heard the oracle's voice in her mind as clearly as she heard her own thoughts.

'Go to her,' the old man instructed.

Percilla did as she was told and approached the motionless woman. As her eyes adjusted to the darkness, she realized nothing could have prepared her for this image before her now. The woman was ragged and disheveled, quickly losing her elegance in the cruelty of the dungeon, but the serenity and focus on Victoria's face was as unwavering as it had always been. Percilla sensed with a keen knowing that every bit of her grandmother's inner strength remained, even in such a dark and lonely place as this.

Victoria sat cross-legged, her eyes closed as she focused inward and shut out her surroundings. The door behind Percilla creaked open and slammed against the wall with a clang. Franc entered the dungeon, looking both bored and irritated. She stood in front of Victoria, lifting her hands in the air before reciting, "Onh-niktis." A beam of red energy leapt from her fingers toward Victoria's head, but it elicited no response. Victoria remained silent and motionless. Franc tore her outstretched hand away from Victoria and roared with anger before giving up and exiting the cell.

"Victoria!" Percilla shouted.

The vision quickly dissipated, as if being sucked into the dark beyond, and more images flashed in Percilla's mind almost too quickly to process—her parents running through the Cherry Orchard in Gangleton, swinging her as a child around in their arms; a fire burning high above the village as a pillar of black smoke clouded a night sky; Victoria running from a burning building with Percilla wrapped in her arms; two gravestones in the Gangleton cemetery both marked with the Bomqui family emblem. Then Percilla's sight slowly returned to the ruins of the courtyard as the oracle removed his hand from her head.

Her jaw dropped as she let out a huge gasp and leapt away from him. "Is it true?" she asked, her eyes filled with tears. "Victoria is alive?"

"Alive!" Frida shouted with a grin.

"She will remain alive until they can break into her mind," the oracle replied in a grim rasp.

"How do you know?" Frida asked.

"How can we trust you?" Matik added hotly, positioning himself between Percilla and the old man.

"I have no need to lie." The oracle smiled as the wind blew a soft tone on the chimes.

"Are you working for the Dignitaries?" Frida inquired, folding her arms across her chest.

The oracle's grating laughter seemed to prompt Matik into lifting his bow from over his shoulder and nock an arrow to it. "I work for no one. I only help those who need my assistance."

Percilla wiped the tears from her eyes with renewed determination to rescue her grandmother. She stared at the oracle and demanded, "Where is she?" Pushing Matik out of the way, she approached the old man again. "How can we save her?"

The oracle smirked. "She will remain in the Dignitaries' dungeon inside the Caves of Seoj. I suggest you make haste to Rou if it's your grandmother's memory you wish to save."

"What if they break her?"

"If you go to save her now, it will be too late. If you go to Rou first, you'll change her fate." The wind blew, playing the chimes and clay jugs. The old man danced and played his tambourine, circling around the back of the fountain as his eyes glazed over once more with the white haze of a deep trance. He flicked his wrist toward the gong before a resounding clang filled the courtyard.

"What do you mean?" Percilla shouted, chasing after him. "Why is my face on a warning letter? Tell me more!"

Frida grabbed Percilla's shoulder. "He's gone," she said. "Flown off with the wind."

Percilla's hands balled into fists, and she did everything she could to hold back her tears. Victoria was *alive*. The knowledge filled her with both a profound sadness and a hopeful joy; her grandmother was in the Dignitaries' dungeons, yet she could still be helped. In that moment, she couldn't tell if she wanted to feed that sadness or that joy, but at least she had the choice.

Matik returned the drawn arrow to his quiver and once more slung his bow over his shoulder. He took a glance around the ring of toppled stone, then peered farther toward the outskirts of the village. "We obviously haven't any time to lose."

CHAPTER 18

Pursuit Awry

THE ASHEN CLOUDS looming overhead colored everything with a pale dimness as Frida, Percilla, and Matik
approached the edge of the demolished village. Even still, a
new hope held firm in their hearts. Victoria was alive, and that
news alone was enough to keep Percilla going for as long as
she needed. She knew Frida would go to any lengths to rescue
her sister and to help Percilla find Rou first. And while Matik
had never met her grandmother, Percilla was starting to feel
he would follow her anywhere if it meant he had the chance to
protect her.

Just as they stepped beyond the banks of sand around the
ruins, the sky darkened above them. Percilla had just enough
time to notice Matik had slowed before he rammed against her
and sent her flying from where she'd stood. She sprawled across
the ground, confused and panicking, with the breath knocked
from her lungs and her jacket torn. Then she looked up, only to
see a conspiracy of ravens had descended from the sky to drop
a net upon Matik that was most assuredly meant for her. The

ravens swooped toward him and hooked the netting with their beaks and talons to carry him away.

Percilla rolled onto her back, and at the sight of the ravens attempting to lift the net with Matik inside, she pushed herself to standing and meant to do something about it. She realized the Eye of Rou around her neck had slipped from its hiding place only when a beam of golden light—the very essence of Rou itself—shone through the crystal gemstone and into the attacking ravens' eyes. Percilla glanced down at the Eye in surprise and, without any hesitation, lifted it toward the birds. The light flared to envelope her, Matik, and the creatures trying to cart him away, then flashed in a brilliant surge of energy before returning to its place within the gemstone. When the light subsided, the ravens released the net entirely, launched swiftly back into the sky, and disappeared into the clouds.

"My, Percilla. You sure have quite the way with ravens," Frida said with a wink as she reached the others.

"I didn't do anything," Percilla said, staring down at the Eye in her hands. Then she remembered Matik still caught in the net and headed toward him. "Are you all right?"

"A little stuck," he replied with a smile.

With a wave of her hand, Frida lifted the net and tossed it to the sand beside him.

Percilla sat beside Matik, her heart still pounding from the harrowing encounter. She wondered briefly if she was actually trembling a little or merely imagining it. Looking down at the Eye of Rou in her palm, she turned it from side to side, watching the light within the sky-blue gem shimmer. "This thing *does* something," she mused.

"It's the Eye of Rou," Frida said. "Didn't I free Shru so you could study that spell book?"

"I am..." Percilla started, then stopped that lie in its tracks before it grew too much. Perhaps some part of her had wanted to study its pages, but the weight of her responsibility had overwhelmed her, and she no longer held the inclination to even so much as peruse the all-important tome. Not that she'd had any time recently with so many potentially life-threatening incidents.

Frida sighed. "Yes, yes. Okay. Please read up on the Eye of Rou before we go anywhere... and..." She froze, squinting in Percilla's direction. "What is that thing on the back of your neck?"

"What thing?" Percilla touched the back of her neck in concern—perhaps she'd find an insect there—but felt nothing out of the ordinary.

"I saw something glowing at your hairline."

"I don't know," Percilla said; this might have been the first time she'd ever worried about being in her own skin.

Frida stepped toward her and pulled down the collar of Percilla's jacket. She ran her fingers along the base of Percilla's skull, let out a small hum, then announced, "I think I know how the Dignitaries get inside your head."

"What's wrong?" Percilla couldn't help but imagine a bug *inside* her neck now.

"Someone's inserted a tiny chip just beneath your skin."

Percilla's eyes widened. "Get it out!" she pleaded, not knowing exactly what a chip was but of course wanting it removed all the same.

"I've never done this sort of operation before," Frida murmured. "But you should be fine."

"I trust you," Percilla hastily replied. If the Dignitaries had done this, she wanted even less to do with it. "Just get it out."

Frida rummaged through her bag and produced a small, round black stone humming with energy. "This is a magnetic stone," she explained. "It ought to pull that nasty little bit right out."

"Just do it."

Frida slowly pressed the stone close to the back of Percilla's bare neck.

Percilla squeaked at the sharp pinch, then rubbed the back of her neck and peered at the stone in Frida's hand. "How long has that been in me?"

"Hard to say." Frida offered her a better glimpse of the small, square piece of metal. Percilla was surprised to find it did not look as gory as she'd expected after being removed; there was no blood at all. "Study the book," Frida added, "and let me figure out this device."

The sorceress went to work inspecting the Dignitaries' chip with a variety of tools from her bag. She started with a magnifying glass and quickly moved on to a crystal. Matik dusted himself off and stood to scan the horizon with a watchful eye.

Percilla retrieved her spell book from her satchel and opened it to the last page she'd read. She slid her finger along the text as she softly read aloud, "When the eye is open, the path to Rou is clear." She looked away to examine the Eye of Rou in her open palm, then recited the words listed beneath the passage. *"Al-bista trun-ona dimos-ka."*

The very air itself around her charged with an unfamiliar frequency, and the Eye of Rou glowed with a golden light, its energy pulsing at her touch. When she looked up from the page once more, she was no longer in the Barrens. An almost blinding glow permeated the space around her, illuminating this otherworldly dimension of colorful and sacred geometry. Where she sat existed an enchanted portal, magic rushing back and forth and all around her. She could just faintly make out the desert sand at her feet, which seemed the only thing to ground her as the energy currents surged around her, spinning so many geometric shapes of the air itself in a kaleidoscope of hues and patterns.

Directly in front of her, where her focus seemed most pulled, she saw the bright gates of pure gold and beyond them the energy of Rou itself freely flowing. She felt the rivers running through verdant valleys, the lush overgrowth and rich soil from which it grew, the vibrant, glistening sky, and all the creatures flying through it. This same essence she held herself now within the Eye of Rou, and it source—all of it—lay beyond those gates.

Percilla closed her fingers tightly around the Eye of Rou once more, and just as suddenly as it had appeared, the brilliant dimension around her faded away into the bleak ashen sands and cracked earth of the Barrens.

"Flown," Percilla exclaimed. "I saw the Gates of Rou!"

Frida grinned at her. "A vision? Lead the way, Raven Eye. Matik and I will be the only ones following you now." She extended her hand to Percilla and opened her palm to reveal the Dignitaries' chip, laid flat and no longer glowing. "This is a tracking device most likely inserted at birth. A dark enchantment had previously rendered it undetectable... but not to my trained eyes." She nodded once, looking quite pleased with herself.

"Flown!" Percilla exclaimed once more, then stood and stepped away from the chip in her great aunt's palm. "Let's get away from *that*."

Frida tossed the chip over her shoulder, where it slipped through a dry crack in the hard earth and vanished from sight.

"How shall we travel now?" Matik asked.

"How else?" Percilla sighed and gazed northward. "We have no choice but to walk. And without delay. Time is of the essence."

They gathered their things and set forth once more toward Rou.

CHAPTER 19

Reckless Junctions

T IME PASSED SLOWLY through the Barrens and the endless expanse of flat, cracked earth, distinguishable only slightly by the scattered sand dunes, long-dead trees, and spires of tattered buttes littering the impossible landscape. Their progress could be tracked only by Percilla's map, pendulum, and their growing shadows cast by the stagnant arc of the sun. They were hot, they were hungry, they were thirsty, but most of all, they were tired. It had been a long day, and it showed no sign of ending any time soon.

"I don't think I'll ever get used to all this walking," Percilla groaned, sweat rolling down her forehead, cheeks, and neck. Then she thumped against Matik's outstretched arm and stumbled backwards. He'd stopped her this way on purpose to keep her from moving any farther. Annoyed at first, she glared at Matik, about to demand an explanation, then noticed the rather stern crease of his brow. When she looked up, she found a lone figure walking toward them. The heat and brightness of the sun had grown so intense at this point, no one in their group of three could see a thing but the figure's long, pitch-black shadow. Matik glanced at Frida, one arm shielding Percilla and the other whisking his bow over his head to be at the ready. Percilla caught them nodding at each other.

The sorceress moved with slow, alert steps toward the stranger, who did not change his course toward them. When they approached each other enough for the hazy veil of brilliant sunlight to lift, Frida let out a tiny gasp and doubled her speed toward the figure.

"What are you doing?" Percilla shouted, still held back by Matik's defensive arm and unable to see whatever it was her great aunt had discovered.

"It's Drendle," Frida replied over her shoulder. "And he's alone."

Percilla could not believe what she was hearing. "Are you flown, Frida? He's a *Dignitary*."

"That's not who he *really* is."

Frida ignored Percilla's cries and hurried after the Dignitary. When she reached him and stopped directly in front of him, Drendle merely walked around her and continued without so much as a glance or a pause to acknowledge her presence.

"Drendle," she shouted with a smile.

The Dignitary turned around to face her. "What? Yes. Excuse me." Then he spun around again and just kept moving across the desert.

Not one to ever accept being ignored, Frida grabbed his shoulder and pulled him back toward her, forcing him to look her in the eye. "Drendle, remember me?"

"Can I help you, madam?" he asked. It sounded polite enough, but he brushed Frida's hand from his shoulder.

"Frida..." She enunciated slowly, pointing toward herself just to be perfectly clear.

But Drendle only fixed her with a blank stare before blinking slowly. "I don't you know, madam."

"Surely you remember." Frida dipped her head to catch his attention. "It's me. Freedum..." Though she studied the man's lack of response in her normal, critical fashion, she could not help the tremble in her voice or the fluttering ache in her heart as she looked into the eyes of a man who no longer knew who she was.

"Madam, I am a Dignitary," Drendle stated proudly, pointing at himself in the same manner. Then he enunciated very slowly, "Dignitary."

"They've muddled *your* mind?" For a moment, disbelief shattered her composure, and then she dug anxiously through her bag once more before producing a pink spray bottle.

"Madam, I am a Dignitary of Gangleton," Drendle repeated.

Frida brought the bottle right up to Drendle's face and unleashed a chalky pink mist that immediately sank into his pores. She waved the bottle from front to back and top to bottom, spraying vigorously to be sure she thoroughly coated his body.

But Drendle did nothing more than wave away the spray with an agitated swipe of his strong hand. He coughed and spat out a cloud of mist. "Stop that!" he shouted. "Stop spraying, this instant."

"Kas-wana," Frida said, bewildered to find nothing happened.

Drendle finished waving away what remained of the pink mist and said with quite obviously forced etiquette, "Madam, if you don't mind, I have things to do."

The lone Dignitary turned to leave, but Frida once again grabbed him by the shoulders and spun him back around. She locked eyes with him and tried again. "Mio lo-ton."

"Madam, please move away," Drendle warned.

"They got you completely," she whispered in defeat, finally realizing there was nothing she could do to get through to this man.

"Good day," Drendle shouted, brushing Frida's hands off his shoulders once more and whirling round to be on his way.

He left Frida standing there, alone and devastated, watching his shadow stretch long and heavy beside him. Matik and Percilla hid behind a boulder to give the man a wide berth as he shuffled onward, then rushed toward Frida. The sorceress watched her old friend abandon her in the desert, not even a shred of memory left of her within the confines of his mind.

"What did you say to him?" Percilla muttered, her eyes wide with amazement and a smaller flicker of fear as she stared back and forth between Frida and Drendle.

But Frida's devastation would not let her answer. In some ways, Drendle's fate seemed even crueler than death. Now he walked the earth, a shallow husk of his former self, overtaken by darkness still corrupting the very essence of his being. But then, as if she'd spoken her mourning aloud, Drendle paused, one foot suspended halfway through his next step.

Slowly, he looked back over his shoulder at her, his gaze moving hesitantly from the hot sand to her face. "Did... did you say your name is Frida? Are *you* Frida?"

"Yes!" Frida shouted, daring to hope something of her spells had landed with him.

Drendle dipped his chin toward the front pocket of his jacket, his eyes narrowing now into angry slits. "Activate Quadrant Fifty-Four."

The ground rumbled beneath their feet, and Frida's hope shattered into despair. Percilla ran toward her, Matik close on the girl's heels, and the cracked earth split in two and crumbled away before them. Between the trio and Drendle now gaped a black pit, and the crevasse widened until Percilla, Matik, and Frida now stood on a tiny island of rock, bits of the earth slipping into the yawning abyss surrounding them. Dark fog seeped up from the darkness below, materializing into skeletal arms and hands that crawled and wriggled across the dirt toward them. Matik drew an arrow and nocked it in preparation. Frida, however, sank to her knees on the unsteady ground collapsing all around them.

"They've taken his mind," she muttered.

"Frida..." Percilla called out, clutching both the Eye of Rou and her spell book as tightly as she could, trying to return Frida to her senses and preparing to fight, if it came to that.

The hexed, clawed tendrils launched viciously toward them, one of them instantly grabbing ahold of Percilla's legs. Matik loosed his first and second arrow into these incorporeal beings, momentarily shattering their advance. Freed from their vile clutches, Percilla raised the Eye of Rou and readied herself for more. But Matik could only do so much with his piercing weapons; whenever one of the black, coiling tendrils fell, two more returned in its place, quickly giving birth to a horde of enemies that could not be killed by normal means. Percilla flipped through the pages of her spell book, desperately searching for anything that could save them. But her frantic urgency made it impossible to comprehend both the words staring back at her and their purpose.

As the ground gave another thunderous quake, Frida finally rose, forcefully wiping the tears from her cheek with the back of a hand. Then she plunged her hand into her bag, training her angry glare upon the shadows crawling over the crumbling landscape.

Just as she removed her crystal wand and extended it toward their slithering enemies, a loud, shrieking whistle pierced the dry air of the Barrens. They all turned toward the sound to see an enormous chain of black steel barreling toward them like a stampeding rhino. Clouds of thick, acrid gray steam billowed from the massive steam engine racing across the Barrens on seemingly nothing but air and speed. The engine charged

straight for the troubled group, smashing through the horde of dark appendages as its whistle sounded again. Another thick blast of steam burst through the air, pummeling away the darkness and disrupting the fog's reformation. Percilla barely had time to understand what she was seeing before rough hands reached out and swept her, Matik, and Frida into the train itself. Drendle leapt out of the way, barely avoiding a head-on collision with the powerful engine. He tumbled into the sand and scrambled back to his feet, but when he turned again toward his prey, they were already gone. The barreling machine sped off into the Barrens, leaving nothing but sprays of dust, puffed columns of steam, and a chorus of triumphant howls echoing across the wasteland.

Inside the train, the trio lay sprawled across a worn, dirty, hardwood floor. Percilla gazed up at the train's steel interior, her vision clouded by the partially transparent haze of steam filling this particular car as well. Long copper pipes zig-zagged along the walls, softly rattling amid the turning cogs and subsequent thumping of the train's wheels outside. Empty, overturned barrels served as seats around wagon-wheel tables, and deep red curtains draped over long rows of windows looking out into the wasteland. Dim lights hung from the ceiling, gracing the train with a soft glow and dark shadows. Crates of food and jugs of what she hoped was water settled haphazardly at the back of the car.

Dominating the car with their yipping and howling, the group's three saviors celebrated their daring rescue. Each of them wore a different ensemble of long-sleeved, ruffled blouses layered under individually fashioned, leather shoulder holsters, discolored and nicked by long use. The only woman among them stood in the center, ornate goggles fixed over her wildly pinned-up burgundy hair within which a variety of trinkets intertwined with her curly locks. Her face was tanned and weathered by the Barrens' harsh climate, her wild green eyes lending her a surprising ferocity despite her short height. Each man beside her stood a good two feet taller, both wearing stained leather boots and thick, wide-brimmed hats. An assortment of apparatuses and trinkets the likes of which Percilla could hardly decipher hung from loops on both their trousers and holsters. The man with the yellow-lensed goggles resting over the green bandanna tied casually around his neck was inordinately lanky, his clothes nearly dangling from his frame. Percilla thought he looked around the same age as the woman. The other man was younger and of much greater physical stature, his own ensemble clinging to his muscular arms and his goggles with blue lenses strapped on top of his hat.

All three strangers gave their new arrivals a hand and helped them to their feet. The floor of the car rocked back and forth as the train plowed through the Barrens. Steam billowed from the locomotive's chimney and the steam-powered whistle, which shrieked again and trailed thin clouds of pungent vapor past the windows. Percilla found it difficult to steady herself on the swaying floor beneath her at first, though seeing Frida stumble once as well made her feel a little better about it. It took them both a moment of awkward adjustment, but Matik squared himself against the wobbling wooden floor and took to the motion immediately.

"Now, Frida," the woman said, "what were you thinking creeping in on that one? Don't you know he's a Dig?"

"I do," Frida replied. "Hard to see people you love fall."

"That's why I been keeping my eye on you since you left Fridanda."

Frida cocked her head. "Am I marked?"

"Only by Symon," the lanky man interjected.

"Symon told you where we were?"

"Thankful he did," the younger man replied with a smirk. "Entertained us for days."

"Brought a lot of acts to the stage," his skinny counterpart added.

"Sure was a hoot."

"He did give me a genuine device that tracks you," the woman blurted with a laugh.

"He *what?*" Frida shouted.

"Couldn't tell ya." The redheaded woman shrugged. Her eyes fell on Percilla, then, who still wished she could stand in the rocking car without the urge to reach out and grab ahold of something. "You must be Percilla. Very lovely."

"Thank you." Percilla struggled to reply politely as she finally gave in and steadied herself against one of the overturned barrels.

"And the strapping Matik," the woman continued, eyeing him with a grin. "Prized performer of the Dawookrunk circus."

"Pleasure," Matik replied with a succinct bow.

"You can call me Deena," the woman said. "This here pile of sticks is Calvin. The youngin' goes by Jance." She spread her arms, propped a booted foot forward on its heel, and gave a half bow. "Welcome aboard the Wonkt Train. Now, second order a business." She straightened and snapped her fingers. Calvin produced a rolled parchment from his satchel, unraveled it, and revealed yet another copy of the Dignitaries' missive marking Percilla as a threat to the Barrens, complete with her sketched likeness in black ink.

"The Digs be looking for yas and askin' everyone in the Barrens to help," Deena explained.

"Where did you get that?" Percilla asked, her urgent surprise momentarily overcoming her growing nausea.

"Find 'em everywhere," Deena replied.

"Lucky nobody really care for dem Digs," Calvin said. "So they ain't eva' gonna find ya."

"Unless you go talkin' to 'em again," Jance added. "That was just plain goofin'."

"Yes, I know." Frida let out a rather defeated sigh. "I thought… Doesn't matter." The sorceress shook her head quickly, then nodded once at Deena. Even still, Percilla caught the glint of what looked like deep regret in her great aunt's eyes before it was forced back beneath her composed exterior.

"Sure doesn't," Deena replied with a knowing, sympathetic stare. "It's in the past."

"And we still gonna love ya just the same," Jance hollered. "How's 'bout a drink?"

Deena howled in delight. "Now dat's what I need. Grab dem cups, Calvin. Time for a celebration."

Jance howled back, yipping and shuffling his feet in a little jig. "Here's to outsmartin' dem Digs!"

Calvin retrieved six glasses nearly overflowing with a sparkling blue drink and distributed them all around. Everyone raised their glasses for a toast.

"Here's to the times!" Deena exclaimed.

"Here's to Rou!" Frida added.

"To Rou!" everyone shouted and downed their glasses. Percilla eyed her drink afterward; it tasted of lemon and elderberry mixed with honey and a dash of ginger—sweet, sour, and a little tingly. That was the way Victoria had always described it. "The perfect remedy to boost your immune system and warm your tummy." Percilla let the memory of her grandmother's voice sooth her mind as she closed her eyes, remembering all the times Victoria had made this very drink for her when she was ill.

Deena let out a deep sigh of satisfaction and said, "Rou. Is that where y'all be headin'?"

"Makes sense why the Digs want ta take ya in," Calvin added.

"Ya know which direction ya be goin'?" Deena asked.

"Yes," Percilla replied, her eyes reopening in determination.

"Ain't that a bless," Jance said.

"Sorry, can't take ya there," Deena said. "We got to be setting up for the annual Reckless Barrens gathering."

"S'posed to be the grandest yet," Calvin added with a grin.

"What's that?" Percilla asked, taking small, savored sips of her beverage.

"The one place a Dignitary would never dream to show their face," Deena boasted.

"Won't ya join us?" Jance asked, apparently oblivious to the severity of Percilla's task.

"After we get to Rou," Frida added, shooting Percilla a supportive nod.

"Y'all the first folks I hearda actually going there," Calvin remarked in disbelief.

"You gotta join the party tonight, then," Jance said.

"Jance, they just got in," Deena interjected. "Let 'em see the place first. No sense in just keepin' 'em in the lounge car all night."

"Well lets show 'em 'round, then," Calvin exclaimed. "'Cause the party already goin'."

"Ha. You boys know the party be goin' on til it ends. No need to be rush." Deena winked at her companions and waved them along.

Calvin and Jance followed Deena from the car and beckoned their visitors to join them. Deena led them on a tour through the train, entertaining her guests with tales of wonder and bravado. They passed through the music car first, where instruments of all kinds haphazardly hung on either wall. Brass, string, drums, accordions—the Wonkt had them all. Some were newly acquired from trading outposts and craftsmen, but most were worn with old age—not that the Wonkt minded. Any instrument was a good instrument for the frisky nomads.

In an open circle at the center of the music car, a group of blissful and finely ornamented players carried a spirited tune. They danced, hooted, and hollered with delight, stomping their feet against the floorboards so loudly and heavily, Percilla thought they might fall right through. On the left side of the car, a bar served drinks from fashioned rows of colored glass bottles with corks to seal in the flavor. In the corner of the car, two foreign ladies sat at a table, talking quietly among themselves. One wore a dark, hooded robe and the other a bright pink cape.

"That's when the spitfire slipped out the dragon's lips," Deena recounted, "swirling through dem golden blossoms, dancin' across the trees, aimed directly for me. So, did I run?"

"Yoo-hoo, Frida!" The two women at the table shouted in unison from across the room, waving and wiggling their fingers. Frida froze, eyes wide, then she turned slowly toward the table and seemed to assess the situation. Moving much slower than her usual self, she briefly looked at Percilla with a thin smile, shrugged, and reluctantly turned to approach the women's table.

When Percilla saw that Matik had also left her side to grab an instrument from the wall and wander off to join the festivities, her attention returned to Deena and the tour now being given to only one. Very soon, they entered the sleeping car at the back end of the train, where a variety of beds made long rows all the way from one end of the car to the other. Typical of the lively Wonkt folk, all the beds were empty. This car was the only one without electric lighting, instead illuminated only by strands of pale moonlight slipping through the gaps in large curtains covering small windows above each bed and nightstand. In contrast to the rest of the train, there was a silent comfort in this car, the distant noises of celebration only a soft vibration now in Percilla's ears.

"Finally, I come to a door in the ground," Deena said, still not finished with her story, "and down pulls me a little old lady. Guess I found myself amongst the Krinkton folk."

"Krinkton?" Percilla asked, recalling the name from her map.

"Kind folks," Deena remarked fondly. She stopped when she came to the biggest and softest bed in the sleeping car—like a billowy cloud of loosely packed feathers. Fluffy white blankets draped neatly over the mattress within the mahogany frame. "Take this bed for the night or choose whichever comfort suits ya. I can tell you're not used to this traveling business."

"Thank you," Percilla replied, truly grateful to finally be able to sleep in a nice, cozy bed again.

"Bless dreams." With a slight bow, Deena departed silently from the sleeping car, leaving the girl to her slumber.

Percilla plopped onto the bed, letting its comforting warmth and softness overtake her. Sliding between the smooth sheets, she wrapped herself in a fluffy blanket. It seemed such a long time since she'd slept in a bed as large as this. Perhaps it was even bigger than the bed she'd had in Gangleton, but she could no longer remember. She could be sure of nothing in her memories of home. So much of it had been a lie. But the people were real, that much she knew. And the people she had met on her journey were real as well. They were kind and generous, giving her so much in return for so little. She would repay them if she

could, for that was all she could do. With those thoughts drifting through her mind, Percilla closed her eyes and fell asleep.

"How are your lessons?" Frida asked, composing herself in the
booth beside Beatrice.

The woman's sister Janet, who wore the dark, hooded robe,
replied, "We've nearly completed."

"One final community," Beatrice added.

"Once we boarded the Wonkt Train, it became a lot easier
to find them."

"And when we told them you were our mentor, everyone was
thrilled."

"That's lovely," Frida said hastily. "Well, was a delight to see
you ladies. You'll have to excuse me, though. I've got important
things to tend to." She stood from the table and nodded. "May
your spirits remain high and your journey be blessed. See you
when you've completed your training."

"Wait!" Beatrice shouted. "We have gifts for you."

Frida stopped and turned back toward the woman in the
pink cape. "Have you now? What sort?"

"Ancient. Very ancient," Janet said.

"Join us," Beatrice continued. "It would be an honor."

Frida studied each of her former pupils for a moment, then
smiled. "Ancient. My favorite sort. The honor's mine."

CHAPTER 20

The Quiet Voice Inside

MATIK PERFORMED A passionate flamenco dance in the music car, his movements inspired by the live music and the power it held over his body. A crowd of musicians with various instruments surrounded him, all gathered to watch the renowned skills of Dawookrunk's star performer. Not a soul in the Wonkt Train had not heard of him or dared pass up a chance to see him perform outside the Dawookrunk circus.

Frida sat with Janet and Beatrice, chatting the night away at their table in the corner. While they appreciated singing and dancing, their interests on this particular night fell to things of a magical and political nature. They discussed the recent goings on in the communities Janet and Beatrice had visited for their training, the spells they'd mastered since the last time they'd spoken with Frida, and most importantly, the devious actions of the five Dignitaries.

"The Digs have taken in people from all across the Barrens to settle there," Janet said.

"Yes, I've heard," Frida replied, sipping at her drink. "All the poor souls who stumble into their control."

"But have you heard why?" Beatrice asked, leaning closer over the table.

"I assume for more power." Frida had never imagined the Dignitaries would desire anything more than just that.

"You're only hovering over the real reason, love. How do you think the elders knew Gangleton was the place to settle?"

"Well, that part of the story is simple. Gangleton is an oasis in a wasteland. Grandmother made it seem as if Rou itself guided them there."

"You're getting warmer." Beatrice giggled at the chance to reveal something her mentor didn't know. Then the woman seemed unable to stop her laughter.

"What's so funny?" Frida asked. "Surely you're not tittering at me."

Janet nudged her sister in the ribs, which only barely hushed the snickering. Then she leaned toward Frida and glanced quickly about them before whispering, "Do you know what sits under Gangleton?"

"Oh, under?" Frida leaned in closer. "Are you suggesting the tunnel systems actually exist and I could have had access to them the whole time I lived there?" Beatrice's fit of giggles burst out even louder. "Is that some sort of secret code for yes?" Frida snapped. "Or are you truly laughing at me?"

"Yup-naw," Janet said, motioning toward her sister's hat. The accessory pulled itself down over Beatrice's face, muffling her laughter. Beatrice's hands flew to her face, where she tugged and tugged at the hat but could not remove it. "You'll have to forgive her. She's experimenting with a new substance."

"That explains it. Alchemy is so unpredictable compared to sorcery. I swear, everyone of that sort who has come to Fridanda has either been in a state of complete madness or has brought with them the most magically strange and unpredictable potions and offerings I've ever seen. Now, tell me what more is under Gangleton but the tunnels?"

"Together we fly!" Matik shouted from across the room. "Arm and arm we kiss the sky. Dream and die. We live the eternal life." The circle of Wonkt folk surrounding him erupted into cheers and took long, full swigs of their drinks. They followed this with another cheer and a long, low howl of all their voices rising together.

Janet snapped her fingers to release the spell holding her sister's hat over her face. Smiles bloomed upon both sisters as they bestowed their gifts. Beatrice slid a small, heavily full pouch across the table, and Janet presented a golden headpiece interlaid with ruby, emerald, and sapphires.

"Oh, my," Frida said with her own wide-eyed grin. "That *is* ancient."

Matik interjected once more with the lines of a common singalong, which all of Wonkt knew. "A fool to the rest is a fool at its best. For a fool is no fool who knows it's all a jest."

"I hope Percilla is able to get some sleep," Frida mused, glancing back through the car as she removed her hat to don the gifted golden headpiece. Then, settling back into her conversation with the sisters, she dipped her hand into the pouch and revealed a heaping handful of blue gemstones.

Nestled in the corner of the sleeping car, Percilla dreamt uneasily, tossing from the visions plaguing her tired mind. In her dream, Victoria sat once more in the darkness of the Dignitaries' dungeon, cross-legged and with her eyes closed. She wore tattered rags highly unfit for someone of her status, her hair raggedy and unwashed, and she'd grown so thin from hunger and pale from thirst. Though she appeared physically exhausted and malnourished, whatever the Dignitaries needed from her apparently wasn't worth harming her further to get. Percilla approached her grandmother slowly, not knowing if this was true waking sight or the cruel temptations of her slumber. Either way, she did not want the vision to end.

Victoria's eyes opened at Percilla's approach, darkened with unrest and anxiety but still retaining a glimmer of hope and the vestiges of willpower. She smiled fondly at her granddaughter, stretching her shaking arm out to caress the girl's face. Percilla knelt and felt the warmth of her grandmother's touch on her cheek.

'Percilla.' She heard her grandmother's voice without the older woman's lips ever moving. 'You must not waste any more time. The Dignitaries will try anything to stop you.' Despite her appearance, Victoria's voice was strong, passionate, exactly as Percilla remembered it. 'Listen to the quiet voice inside. It is your truth. And read the spell book. There is still more to know about the Eye of Rou.'

Then Percilla felt a light, warm pressure in the center of her forehead, though her grandmother had not touched her this time. Her vision faded quickly, and she reached out to touch her grandmother. "Victoria!" she shouted just as she jerked awake and her eyes sprang open. She closed them again immediately, hoping to return to the vision—to remember, to see, to ask— but the vision of her grandmother was gone. Had it only been a dream? No, it seemed far too real. Her eyes welled with tears. She could barely stand to see her beloved grandmother in such a state. Percilla had so many questions, and they needed answers; she had no time for crying while everyone she loved and cared for was in trouble.

She looked around to find nothing in the sleeping car but Frida and Matik in their own beds on either side of hers and all the other passengers filling the beds around them. She rubbed her eyes, wiped away the last bits of her dreaming, and wondered what time it was. Hours had passed since their cele-bration, and now the whole of the Wonkt Train was silent in the deepest part of the night. The only person not here was Deena, who had her own personal quarters. Percilla considered trying to go back to sleep, but as she shifted, she felt something pressing against her lap. There she found her spell book emitting a light from within. She looked around again, clutching the Eye of Rou and not knowing what to do.

"Read the book. You must know how to use the Eye of Rou."

She heard it clear as day—Victoria's voice, telling her what she needed to hear. "Victoria?" she whispered, trying not to wake the other passengers in her excitement. "Where are you?"

"In your heart, my love. Please... find Rou..."

Before she could ask any more questions, a blue, swirling orb whizzed from somewhere behind her and darted directly toward

the window over Percilla's bed. When it vanished through the glass and disappeared into the night, she had the oddest sensation of being left alone in the car full of sleeping people.

Percilla picked up her spell book, opened to the glowing pages, and scanned the illuminated words, their sapphire glow filling her vision. There was so much to learn and so little time to learn it. The duty overwhelmed her, but it did not break her spirit. So when she began, she read the pages with a determined mind; her purpose was essential to saving so many lives, not only of the people she loved but all those who had been deceived by the Digs.

CHAPTER 21

The Illuminated Path

DEENA STOMPED INTO the sleeping car, thumping against the hardwood floors and making them creak beneath her. Then she flung open the closest curtain to bring the morning sunlight spilling into the car. "Rise and shine," she announced to the sleeping passengers. "Hope ya got some good rest." Some of the eager early birds popped out of bed, while a few disgruntled sleepers covered their heads with pillows.

Percilla hastily closed her spell book and hid it within her satchel. She trusted Deena and the Wonkt people well enough, but after so many run-ins with the Dignitaries and their allies forged by evils, she'd realized she could never be too careful.

Frida yawned and stretched in the bed beside her.

"We're about to turn." Deena said, sitting at the edge of Frida's bed. "Which way you headin'?"

Frida yawned again, then rubbed her eyes. "Percilla?"

Percilla pulled the map from her satchel and took note of their current position in the Barrens. "You're turning?" she asked. "We'll have to get off the train, then. We're going straight to the middle of this land." She pointed to the center of the Barrens, the deepest and oldest part of the dry wasteland, where Rou's Golden Gates now stood and awaited the Eye of Rou's return.

She, Frida, and Matik wasted no time in gathering their belongings before assembling in the Wonkt Train's lounge car where they'd initially boarded. Jance, Calvin, and Deena saw them off, passing out warm food wafting cooked spices and wrapped in handkerchiefs. The hospitality of the Wonkt could certainly not be understated.

"Figured y'all be needin' some fuel for the road," Deena said kindly, patting Frida on the back.

"Take care out there," Jance said, shaking Matik's hand.

"Remember ta come find us when yer done," Calvin added.

Percilla happily accepted the gift of food, gracefully shaking each of their hands and thanking them for all their help. "How will we find you?" she asked, hoping to see them again in times less dark.

"That's easy." Deena laughed. "Just have a want ta find the Wonkt Train."

And just as she said that, the train came to a full stop, steam billowing from its chimney with a long, loud whistle. Frida, Percilla, and Matik stepped down off the train and back onto the cracked earth of the ashen Barrens. The morning sun was hot as always but tempered by what remained of the cool night air. After sleeping on a real bed for the first time in days, Percilla felt wholly refreshed and ready to continue her journey.

"Thank you for your hospitality," Frida said with a fanciful bow.

"Our pleasure, sister," Deena replied. The train's whistle sounded again, signaling its departure. "Take care!"

The adjustable staircase from which they descended folded up and snapped back under the train. Finally able to see the whole of the Wonkt Train, Percilla realized it did not actually touch the ground at all. Then, with a loud howl, the pistons pumped and churned the locomotive, briskly moving its wheels hovering above the earth before it sped off on its way again. She watched the train's inhabitants turning back inside as they yipped and howled, starting yet another long day of cheerful, carefree celebration.

Percilla opened her palm and the Eye of Rou nestled there to the hot desert sky above. The blue gemstone shimmered ever so slightly and produced a thin blue aura. Whereas before, the Eye of Rou seemed little more than an ancient trinket, it was now clear the gem possessed a powerful magic far beyond anything she'd ever imagined. And if she were to complete her quest, she would need to learn how to utilize its essence.

The air was warm and pleasant against Percilla's skin. Even the ground itself seemed to soften beneath her footsteps, as if Rou's concentrated essence within her hand had changed it. If she could discover how to fully commune with this gemstone, she had a feeling nothing would then keep her from rescuing Victoria from the Dignitaries' prison—and most likely

Vahn, too, if she had to guess what the five had done with him. Perhaps she might even save the whole of Gangleton. Certainly, the guardians of Rou would offer their help.

"Are you all right, Percilla?" Matik asked, turning around to look at her. Both he and Frida had walked ahead as she'd lagged behind and stopped now to let her catch up.

"It isn't safe to expose the Eye of Rou so frivolously," Frida warned. "The Dignitaries could be watching from anywhere in the Barrens."

Percilla's brow furrowed with unease at the passing thought of meeting another Dignitary before they reached Rou. They'd barely managed to escape from Drendle with the help of the Wonkt Train and its passengers. "If we're going to survive this journey, we need to know more," she announced.

"Know more about what, love?" Frida asked.

"The Eye of Rou," Percilla answered. "When I used it that first time, it was like... like it transported me to a completely different world. I don't know how to explain it, but the spell book said it was a portal. That it illuminates the path to Rou." She frowned. "The book also said more was supposed to happen. I think I left the portal too soon."

"Well done, Percilla," Frida said. "You're becoming a fine leader. If anyone here knows how the Eye should be used, it's you. Do what you must. We will watch over you." Matik nodded as well, his bow already in hand again as he faced the horizon before them and kept watch.

Percilla could not help but smile. She was glad she had someone as powerful and supportive as Frida with her, as well as the honorable Matik. Without them, this journey would surely be a lost cause. She would have most certainly been lost somewhere in these reckless lands, or up on the Sky Way, or worse—trapped in a prison of the Dignitaries' making, waiting to be found by them and taken right back to the place she'd been trying to leave behind. And with that thought, she had to believe that this journey and everyone in it were part of her destiny to find Rou.

Recalling the glowing words she'd found in her spell book the night before, Percilla prepared herself to learn more about the portal and the path to Rou. With a deep breath, she extended the Eye of Rou before her. "Al-bista trun-ona dimos-ka."

The Barrens disappeared again, replaced once more by a dimension of colorful, sacred geometry. The ethereal shapes shifted as they stretched in front of her and narrowed her focus in one direction within a kaleidoscopic tunnel. At the end, the grand, Golden Gates of Rou glowed. Within the shifting patterns, Percilla noticed three objects scattered in a row on the path before her. The first was a statue of a winged stallion, pristine and pure white. The second was an ornately painted, broken wooden boat. The third and final object was a lone, barren tree at the foot of Rou's glistening gates. It seemed to be as just as old, taking in the rainbow of color surrounding it yet retaining a constant sheen of glittering gold. All the leaves had fallen from its branches, leaving them empty and perfectly smooth.

Something moved across the sky, and Percilla looked up to see a golden dragon soaring gracefully through the shifting patterns and colors of the portal. Awestruck by its regal presence, she could not look away as the creature glided over her head, leaving a trail of golden sparkles in its wake and falling all around her. These particles coalesced into a slightly more material form, wrapping around Percilla until she stood within a column of glittering gold. Then the dragon itself circled her, speaking something barely audible and completely foreign. Symbols formed along the walls of her glittering cocoon, glowing ever brighter and spiraling up and down, around and around the girl in the portal. The dragon wheeled and flew back into the night sky. Percilla watched it until it seemed to disappear into a star, and she felt the strongest sense of belonging in her life when that same star flashed toward her and wrapped her in its brilliance.

For a moment, she stood there with her eyes closed, basking in the sense that something new and powerful had been unlocked within her. A gentle buzzing filled her ears, and when she opened her eyes, she saw a bumblebee whizzing about her head, spinning in tight circles, as if it shared her revelation. Then it flitted toward her hat, disappeared, and the buzzing ceased.

Feeling in her heart that her purpose in this dimension had been fulfilled for now, Percilla closed her eyes one more time and closed her hand around the Eye of Rou. When she saw this had returned her to the Barrens and her companions, she pointed toward where she'd seen the Golden Gates through the portal. "That way."

"Looks like you got a little stowaway in your hat," Frida remarked with a smirk.

A muffled buzz sounded from over Percilla's head, and Percilla shrugged. "I guess it came to help us find Rou."

A calm breeze blew across the Barrens as the morning sun reached its peak, brightening the wasteland.

CHAPTER 22

Inhale of Evil

ONLY THE DIM green glow of an unnamed aura lit the dark caverns within the Caves of Seoj, giving just enough light to see movement and shadow. Vahn sat with his back against the iron bars of his caged prison, where they'd left him in the darkest corner of the dungeon. He was tired and defenseless, but his will held strong.

Quick footsteps echoed through the cavern, then a looming figure appeared before him. He heard the jangling of keys and the clicking of the lock before the cage door swung open. Then a low voice ordered, "Follow me."

Vahn's eyes took a moment to adjust even to the dimmest lights in the chamber, and he realized now that Lyken stood in front of him, beckoning him out of the cage. Although Vahn refused to cooperate with the Dignitaries, he had no way of physically resisting them. Reluctantly, he forced himself to his feet and followed Lyken down a long cavern snaking deeper into the mountains.

The farther they went, the darker the Caves became, and all sound vanished save for the distant echoes of water dripping from the stone ceilings. Then at last, a light flickered against the wall just ahead. Turning the corner, they came to the opening of a much larger chamber, where Vahn found himself staring at a finely kept alchemy lab stocked with vessels, vials, substances, and tools for every kind of magical concoction imaginable. At the center of the lab, Ons poured a metallic liquid into a round-bottom flask atop a clay stove. The other Dignitaries watched his work with twisted grins. Their attentions turned to Vahn when they noticed him enter, and he clenched his fists at his sides, trying not to let them see his fear of what they had planned for him next.

"Have a seat," Lyken instructed, jerking Vahn forward by the arm until the young man stumbled into the metal chair at the center of the lab.

When he tried to get back up, an unseen force threw him back into the seat and kept him there. He glanced over his shoulder to see Franc eyeing him, who seemed to have appeared behind him from thin air.

"We mean to protect Gangleton from malevolent influences," Lyken explained. "And unfortunately, your friend is a threat."

Franc thrust her open palm toward Vahn as she prowled around the chamber. He felt a dark force press his body tightly against the cold steel chair. Ropes of shadow rose from the earth below him and bound his arms and legs in place.

Liquid from Ons' flask on the stove steadily rose through a tube to a separator funnel. Ons placed a second tiny vial below the funnel and twisted open the stopcock. A thick, bright-orange liquid slowly dripped into the vial until it was half full. Vahn saw what the Dignitaries had prepared for him and desperately tried to free himself from the chair, but Franc's magic was far too strong for him to break away.

"It is quite in your best interest to help us," Lyken assured him.

Vahn spat in Lyken's face, mustering what meager resistance he could in the face of the villains before him.

"Last offer," Lyken growled.

Vahn forced a laugh, desperate to hold onto what little autonomy he had. "I wouldn't help you if my life depended on it."

"Let's test that theory," Franc said, motioning toward Ons for the man to proceed.

Ons swirled the bottle in his hand, and the liquid within it sparked and spurted from the top of its new container. With a slow, ominous gait, he approached Vahn from the side and lifted the bottle to the young man's nose just as his other hand slammed down over Vahn's mouth. Vahn let out a few muffled protests as the fumes emitted from the effervescent liquid drifted up into his nose—through which he'd now been forced to breathe—and cursed his senses. He could not stop from inhaling it, no matter how hard he tried to avoid it.

In seconds, he felt something awful and powerful overtaking him—a force he struggled desperately to resist. Every muscle in

his body clenched and twitched violently, and when he glanced down at his arms pinned by nothing to the chair, he found a hideous black network of his own veins spreading down his arms toward his fingers. A sudden, sharp pain struck him from within his very core, and he stared with wide eyes at the Dignitaries, all of whom watched him with those sadistic grins.

What began as gasps of discomfort quickly rose into screams of pain echoing throughout the Caves of Seoj until, at last, they finally came to an end.

CHAPTER 23

Guardians of the Pure-Hearted

THEY WALKED UNTIL evening, where vibrant twinkles of stars blinked in the darkening sky overhead. The moon in its new cycle would not be seen on this night, giving the stars more space to beam their radiance. Percilla yawned, exhausted, and almost felt it necessary to call their day's travel to an end and set up a makeshift camp before it grew too dark for sight alone to guide them. She looked up to scan the horizon, and then she saw it, no longer hidden behind a lone spire.

The statue of the winged stallion stood staunch and sturdy right there before them in the Barrens, surrounded by a ring of large rocks. Percilla hastened her step toward it, and the others followed close behind. It was exactly as it had been in her vision, enormous and pristine. What little of its marble exterior showed through the vines climbing up it appeared unblemished, as if the years and the elements had done nothing to wear it down. Scattered all around the foot of the statue were things half-buried—swords, bows, axes, shields, and helmets from all ages lay rusting and broken.

"Quite the place," Frida remarked. "Must be filled with interesting artifacts. Good for trade, you know. Can never have too many. Everybody has their own taste." Pulling a fuchsia umbrella from her bag and popping it open, she muttered, "Lammaste." The umbrella lit up like a lantern, illuminating the area around them. "Better, yes?"

A heavy buzz rose again from Percilla's hat, and the bumblebee took off toward the front of the statue. Percilla followed, drawn to the statue by her quest and her vision. All her exhaustion had vanished now that she saw this thing existed right in front of her. Whatever importance the statue held, there was no doubt in her mind that it was vital for her journey to Rou. She stepped over armor and weapons alike, paying little heed to the remnants in her path. The last light of the sun disappeared beneath the horizon, and the ensuing darkness settled upon the Barrens like a black cloak.

At the foot of the statue, the bumblebee landed on the hilt of a sword thrust deep into the sand. What was visible of the sharp blade glinted in the umbrella's light, shining as brightly as if it were freshly forged. Unlike the rest of the weapons and armor littering the ground, this particular sword appeared untouched by the passage of time. There were no marks or brittle chips in its edge from battle, nor did a single speck of rust mar its excellence. The hilt was crafted from gold and engraved with an impeccably detailed dragon. The large ruby at the top shone as brightly as if it were freshly polished. And at the center of the sword's crossguard, the symbol of Rou had been branded into the metal with as much detail as it had been burned into the cover of Percilla's spell book.

The hilt tantalized Percilla with its warm lacquer finish. Though she had never been trained in the art of swordsmanship, she reached out to grasp the sword and pulled it from the ground. Its sharp edges slid from the dry earth as if she drew it out of water, and when she held it aloft, the shimmering blade almost glowed in the darkness of the desert. The weapon was remarkably heavy—not only physically but in its destined responsibility—and Percilla struggled to hold it upright and steady even with both her arms.

Something within Percilla demanded she attempt to wield the blade properly despite its bulk. Holding the sword's grip with both hands, Percilla took a feeble forward step and swung her wobbling arms downward. The blade's weight toppled her balance, nearly sending her face first into the statue, but her feet shuffled beneath her, and she stood. Turning her back to the statue, she practiced these swings again and again, making little progress in her skills. Her arms were not accustomed to such a heavy weapon—or any weapon—and her own lack of training amounted to little more than wildly waving the blade around.

Frida and Matik quickly approached her with frowns and eyes wide with concern. "What are you fighting?" Frida asked, glancing about them and lifting her umbrella for more light.

"I'm not fighting anything." Percilla let the tip of the sword sink toward the ground in her already tired hands. "But I guess I might have to."

Matik blinked when he saw her weapon, then his eyes widened even more. "What a beautiful sword. The inscription..." His eyes wandered to the sword's hilt and crossguard. "Is that..."

"The symbol of Rou," Percilla said, completing Matik's sentence for him.

"Do you... do you mind if I see it?" he asked, looking from the blade to Percilla and back again with obvious excitement.

Percilla glanced down at the weighty blade and back up at Matik, who reminded her of a child anticipating a present. She gladly handed him the sword, and he raised it effortlessly in his own hand, twisting it back and forth to admire the craftsmanship. When he had seen every part of the blade, he stepped back and slashed at the air with graceful ease, the steel flashing in the light with each precise maneuver. Matik's mastery of form and footwork seemed emboldened by the sword from Rou, as if it had been made only for his hand to wield it. Both Percilla and Frida watched the show in awed silence. When he finished his spectacle, he bowed to his audience of two, laid the blade flat between his palms, and offered it back to Percilla.

Having seen his skill with a blade again and remembering the one he'd lost to the skies in his battle with Nylz, Percilla nodded at him. "I think it's meant for you."

A grin burst across Matik's face, and he bowed to Percilla once more. Beside where she'd pulled the sword from the earth, he stooped to retrieve a fine black scabbard that fit his new weapon perfectly, and he took a moment to fasten this to his belt.

With an abrupt, droning buzz, the bumblebee took to the air again and bounced between the trio in noisy circles.

"Tibs agrees," Percilla said, not having realized she'd thought of the insect as one more addition to their party until she'd said this aloud.

Frida raised an eyebrow, and her attempt at a smile looked a little more like a playful wince. "Tibs the bee?"

Percilla shrugged, then nodded at her great aunt with a little chuckle. "It seemed like a name *you* would have chosen." She smiled at Frida, the one person she knew to maintain a playful nature amid the chaos of the world, which Percilla found to be one of the most admirable things about the woman.

"Exactly what I would have named it." Frida grinned and dipped her head toward the bumblebee. "Good to meet you, Tibs."

Matik smiled at the bee, following its swirling circles in front of him. "Nice to meet you, Tibs."

The bee stopped in front of Matik's face, hovering there for just a moment with a short buzz before returning to Percilla's hat.

A piercing shriek whistled toward them from the sky, faint at first but growing louder and closer by the second. A shadow moved across the twinkling stars, and when Percilla looked up, she shouted, "What is *that?*"

A wriggling mass of black nearly darkened the entire sky, masking the blinking starlight behind a veil of shadow even darker than the night. Its sickening form was barely visible, and as it approached the trio, the stars winked out at its passing.

Frida urgently closed her umbrella and dug through her bag to retrieve a large, pyramidal quartz. She set this on the cracked earth at her feet before plunging into her bag six more times to produce six more of the same crystals. Despite their speed, her movements were fluid and precise, fueled by necessity, until she'd placed all seven quartzes in a circle around the trio. The crystals glowed with a soft white light, warding away the darkness and illuminating the half-buried and rusted armaments at their feet. Next, she produced a pointed ruby and pinched it between her fingers. A fire seemed to rage within the gemstone, burning with an enchantment and visible even within the consuming darkness of the Barrens. "Those would be Siren beetles and a seemingly large force of evil," she said, her voice surprisingly calm and collected despite the approaching black cloud. She lifted the ruby above her head and toward the cloud, chanting, "Na-Yama-Sha."

The energy within each of the seven crystals erupted into a stream of wavering light drawn instantly toward the ruby between her fingers. The streams of energy merged at the gemstone, and another flash of white light crossed over their heads to coalesce into a barrier. It filtered down around the trio until they stood within a domed shield protecting them from the darkness beyond its border.

Through this shimmering light, Percilla watched the dark mass wheel closer. Electric currents flashed like lightening inside it, illuminating wisps of shadow whipping through the cloud like a feral beast. Shifting demonic shapes swelled within the blackened depths, as if countless creatures fought to escape from beneath the hazy surface. Then Percilla noticed a second, constantly fluctuating swarm directly under the first, moving with the larger cloud and yet almost distinctly separate. This second cloud, however, was not composed of roiling shadows but thousands of beetles, just as Frida had described. Flashes of light shone upon their glistening black carapaces and glinted off their wings moving with haphazard, insectoid disorder.

Another blaring shriek of the Siren beetles rose again, and Percilla tried to gulp down her fear.

The black cloud swept toward the massive statue of the winged stallion and spread itself over the earth, encircling the force field Frida had summoned. Even the light of their shield was dampened by the cloud's thick darkness, and the shadowy surface settled for a moment. Everything fell incredibly still and silent, and Percilla felt a cold chill creeping through her bones. If it weren't for the white glow of the crystals and the red blaze of Frida's ruby, her world would have been complete darkness.

Percilla jolted when a hand of shadow lunged from the black cloud to claw at the barrier, trying to press through toward its victims inside. Countless other hands joined the first from all sides, banging and scratching against the shield. But they could not pierce the strength of Frida's spell, which would only keep the trio trapped here as long as Frida maintained the barrier. Writhing, shadowy beasts emerged from the darkened mass— shapeless horrors with waving tentacles, piercing talons, and snapping fangs. They floated around the force field like horrible specters, shrieking and roaring and screaming in rage.

Despite the safety of Frida's shield, Percilla's heart pounded in her chest, her head throbbed at the terrifying noises around her, and she clutched the Eye of Rou with all her might, desperately hoping for some miracle to rescue them from this nightmare. But there was no one coming to help them this time—not this deep within the Barrens. If they could not ward off this evil, Frida's strength would eventually dwindle, and this monstrous enemy would then consume them within its shadowy depths where countless horrors dwelled. As Frida concentrated on maintaining the spell, her outstretched hand and the ruby within it thrust toward the black cloud, Matik stepped closer to Percilla. His gaze swept over the terrifying mass all around them, but Percilla saw his hand had moved to the hilt of his new sword.

The beetles' grating scream came again, this time painfully loud. Percilla slammed her hands against her ears, and with a low grunt of pain, she hunched over in fear, clenching her eyes shut against the horrors outside. Whether from terror or the deadening cold seeping into her being, she started to shiver. A deep, whispering laugh echoed outside the force field, and all manner of creeping shadows and slithering silhouettes grew within the black cloud. The ranks of chaotic monstrosities raged and bucked, their shadows licking at Frida's shield, searching desperately for a way inside. The blows of their fists and claws were now enough to shake the foundations of Frida's barrier.

The crystals shuddered where they stood in their protective circle.

"They can't harm you," Frida said, her voice soothing with reassurance. She reached out with her free hand and clasped Percilla's to draw her closer. "Don't feed them with your fear."

As if to contend with Frida's words, the evil around them rose darker and louder. The cloud swirled with storming speed, the shrieks and screams doubling to a deafening roar that made even Frida blink rapidly and squeeze Percilla's hand. But then the sorceress pulled Percilla closer still and shouted over the furious beasts, "You have to stop feeding them your energy! Close your eyes and think of Rou!"

Frida's voice was like a calm breeze amid a raging storm. Percilla shut her eyes and soothed her mind, concentrating on visions of golden light, twinkling blue crystals, waterfalls with rainbow mists rising into a perfectly sunny sky. They were not memories of The Gold she'd entered in Dawookrunk; these were visions of something pure, something so great and wonderful that she could hardly hold this utopia in her mind. Then, as if summoned by her call for help, the golden dragon appeared in her mind. Its long, majestic body flew across the rainbow skies she envisioned, over valleys of pure, luscious forest where clear rivers flowed. Once again, the regal guardian disappeared into a bright, shining star of gold hanging in the sky like a divine ornament. It glimmered with purpose, lighting Percilla's way through the darkness, leading her ever forward past the evils in her path. And in that moment, all the fear in her vanished; as long as Rou watched over her, no evil could ever harm her.

When Percilla opened her eyes, the swarming cloud surrounding them had transformed into little more than mere strands of shadow. Now, these fluttered pitifully against Frida's summoned barrier. With no fear to feed it, what was left of the cloud whisked away into the veil of midnight. Directly beneath the cloud, the swarm of beetles followed it intently, their final, waning shriek nothing more than an echoing memory across the Barrens.

Frida breathed a sigh of relief and lowered the ruby. The connected lights from the surrounding crystals split apart as she returned the ruby to her bag, and the force field disappeared with it.

"Nasty creatures," Matik said with a cringe.

"The Siren beetles only make that noise to warn of evil," Frida replied as she stooped to collect her crystals from the circle. "They *are* helpful."

"Seems like they found the source," Matik retorted.

"Exactly. Let's get out of here."

They both turned to Percilla, who focused now on her slowing heartbeat and returning to the present from her vision of Rou. Then she found her eyes drawn to the sky by a new glimmer among the stars. There, she saw a golden star greater than the others—the exact one she had seen in her mind just moments ago. It felt right that this star would be the guardian dragon watching over her—maybe even Rou itself. Either way, she knew within her core that this star would be her guiding light toward Rou for the rest of their journey.

"This way," she announced, pointing toward the star.

When Frida looked up to see the bright light overhead, she winked, and the golden star flickered. "Hello again, Mother," she whispered.

CHAPTER 24

Trickster's Fate

I N THE MIDST of the dark Barrens, Frida stood atop an enormous sand dune and lifted her fuchsia umbrella. The tiny light at its tip blinked continuously until Matik and Percilla joined the sorceress at the sandy height. Then a bright glow expanded across her umbrella and illuminated the area around them. From where they all stood, they could now see the rolling hills and towering waves of sand much different than the flat, dry, cracked earth they'd previously traveled.

Percilla looked up to find the golden star again. The farther they traveled toward it, the brighter it seemed to glow, hopefully signifying the end of their journey. Ready to continue moving and staying beside Frida's light, they slid down the sand dunes and ever onward. They'd agreed to keep going as long as they could, both as a precaution against more lurking evils and in an eagerness to complete their quest as soon as possible.

As they walked, Percilla finally found herself ready to ask the question that had bubbled in her mind from the moment she'd met her great aunt. "Frida, what happened to your ravens when you cut them off?"

Frida eyed Percilla's hat. "Would you like me to release yours?" she asked with a mischievous smile.

"No," Percilla quickly replied. "I'm just wondering if the ravens will go back to the Dignitaries." She couldn't help but feel attached to her ravens and concerned for their safety. They were a part of every single memory, every facet of her old life, and though they might have been more trouble than they were worth, they were friends in a strange way. More than that, she'd only just discovered how to control them before leaving Gangleton, which she'd thought would be the easiest way to return to save her friends once her duties in Rou were fulfilled.

"Not my ravens," Frida boasted. "Victoria and I cast a spell to set them free."

"Panya!" Matik shouted, pointing into the distance where a menagerie of colors had gathered on the horizon.

There among the stars was a community of colorful, illuminated air balloons glowing brightly enough to light the night sky, like a rainbow swaying gently in the air.

"The air balloons?" Percilla said. "I saw them when I was on the Sky Way."

"Great place to people-watch," Frida remarked. "I suppose Shru took you up there. No wonder I didn't notice you two entering Fridanda. Yes, the air balloons are the Panya community. They are of Rou as well."

"It's too bad we can't hitch a ride with them," Percilla said with a small frown.

"Should we ask?" Matik winked.

"If they weren't going the opposite way we need to go, I'd definitely say yes." Percilla shrugged.

Frida smiled as they pressed onward, traveling under Panya's rainbow lights on their path to Rou.

Above their heads, the giant, brightly colored air balloons were lit with the soft, warm glow of their burners, blanketing the sky with wonder. People moved to and from the ships below the balloons across tightly bound rope and sturdy wooden bridges, the entire floating village connected by such walkways.

From one of the largest balloons at the center of Panya, a rope descended, sliding soundlessly into the clouds below.

"Keep your hands to yourself, you dirty thief!" a woman shouted from inside the balloon.

Shru jumped from the ship and grabbed onto his magic rope with a triumphant laugh. "That's Shru ta you, madam." Then he tipped his hat and slid down the rope. Shouts of frustration echoed into the sky as Panya also slid from Shru's view, replaced by the darkened sand of the Barrens below him. He passed through the clouds and landed with a soft jump before his magic rope coiled itself back into his coat. "Thanks for the ride," he said, grinning. "And the glasses."

He popped a pair of fancy spectacles with copper rims and sparkling lenses out of his coat pocket and examined them with a mischievous smirk—another treasure to add to his collection. Spinning around, he placed the glasses over his eyes to find his vision completely blurred, obscuring the wasteland before him. In the distance, he saw three figures moving across the sand under Panya, but he couldn't tell what they were.

"What kinda glasses *are* these?" he muttered, then removed the glasses and gazed again at the figures. Two of them he recognized. Even from a distance and in the darkness of the night, the trained eyes of a thief keenly identified Percilla's blue hat, and Frida's umbrella light made them stick out like a sore thumb. The man with them he did not know, but he would soon enough.

"Eh..." Shru tossed the spectacles onto the sands and rushed to catch up to his newly acquired interest. He made no effort to conceal himself, his loud, running gait alerting the group to his approach far before he reached them. "Wait up, my fair ladies!" he hollered. Percilla and Frida both groaned when he slowed behind them. "Glad ta see ya made it out alive, Frida," he said with a toothy smile.

"I'm sure you are." Frida rolled her eyes and turned away from him.

"What do you want?" Percilla snapped.

Shru backed off a little, wisely detecting the hostility in both women's voices. "Naw, ladies, no need ta demean a man. I just wanted ta check in with ya. Make sure ya all right."

"They're fine," the man interjected, motioning toward the gold-hilted blade in the scabbard at his belt.

Shru narrowed his eyes at the man. "Looks like you got yourself a tough guy," he scoffed. "Don't mind me, sir. I was just passin' by."

"Fine," Frida said. She paused and held out her arm to stop her companions as well.

"Come on, Frida," Shru said in his weakest-sounding voice. "That's not too kind. I never wronged you, did I?"

Frida gave the man a look of pure disbelief, as if she couldn't comprehend that anyone could possibly be so shameless.

Shru shrugged. "Yeah, yeah... whatever..."

"We would like to continue, Shru," Percilla said. "If you wouldn't mind." Her tone lacked the etiquette of her words.

"No, I don't mind." Shru raised his hands and feigned turning back, but he tried to catch Percilla in his gaze and entrap her as he had the first time they'd met. The girl immediately looked away, and the man in their party pulled his sword just a few inches from its scabbard.

"Mind if I join?" Shru asked, still daring to hope they'd accept him again.

"No!" Percilla shouted. "You don't care about anyone but yourself."

The man with the sword steadied his hand and stepped between Shru and Percilla. "It's the path you chose," he said.

"Eh." Shru shrugged again and lowered his arms. "I got more important things ta do anyways."

"Good," Frida stated with a curt nod.

"At least I know where ya are." Shru smiled to himself and pulled a small umbrella from his coat. At the flick of his wrist, the thing expanded, and when he'd tipped his hat to the trio, the contraption lifted him into the sky.

As he ascended, Shru noticed Frida digging in her bag before placing a few items on the ground. Curious as to what the sorceress was up to now, he pushed a lens attachment connected to his hat over his eye for a better look. Three small musician figurines with a sousaphone, clarinet, and trombone grew to human size. The band marched with the trio, and Frida danced along, kicking sand into the air with each skipping step.

Just before he slipped away into the clouds, he noted the rest of the party joined in the celebration. "Yeah, yeah. Celebrate me leaving. But ya shoulda let me join, 'cause now I got reportin' ta do."

Shru stepped foot onto the Sky Way, brushing stray bits of sand from his clothes. In the middle of his next step, he found himself unable to move, frozen before being spun around like a top. Standing directly in front of him was the Dignitary Franc.

"You don't seem to take your job too seriously," she said, her voice filled with malice.

"I found the girl, didn't I?" Shru definitely panicked, but he thought he hid it rather well.

"Do you have the Eye of Rou?" Franc asked. "Perhaps you forgot whose time you are on?" She extended a hand toward him, manifesting a glowing orb. A hazy light swirled beneath its surface, and an image of the Cuckoo Clock Tower illuminated in the center. "Fail me again, and I will take you to a place where you won't be able to forget the time or your position," she hissed. "You'll even get a new name." Then she released him from her magical grasp, dropping him back onto the Sky Way as a conspiracy of ravens descended onto Franc's shoulders and lifted her into the air.

"I'm a Dignitary!" Shru screamed, regaining his footing as Franc's ravens flew her away. "I'm a Dignitary! You made me one yourself. I got *rights*."

Franc's voice boomed inside his head, sending him flailing back against the transparent walkway in terror. '*There are no rights.*'

CHAPTER 25

Rise and Shine

ONS EAGERLY PULLED a lever in the Cuckoo Clock Tower's control booth. Enraptured by his schemes, he let out a wheezing, venomous laugh. Gazing upon the massive black orb pulsing with energy at the center of the Tower, he clenched his fists tighter as the pulses intensified. After receiving Shru's information, Ons wasted no time in reuniting with the Tower's control booth, for his true expertise could now be put to good use. His previous attempts to thwart Percilla and her companions on their journey had failed, but only by chance. Now, as the group moved deeper into the Barrens where no life lingered, they would have only themselves to rely upon when he made his next move. Finally, he would have the chance to electrify and rouse his most prized apparatus.

As his contraptions grew to life, spinning energy faster and faster around the Tower, Ons' fists rose into the air with another wheezing cackle. A button flashed on the panel in front of him. He slammed his hand upon it, and a projected image of Frida, Percilla, and Matik appeared on the black orb's glowing surface. They were exactly where Shru said they had been headed—Quadrant 99, at the edge of a basin where the sands ended and became a long, flat plain of dry rock. The morning sun shone brightly on the traveling group, vanquishing the night from their sight as they danced with Frida's enchanted marching band. Ons ground his teeth into a crooked smile at the sight of the oblivious trio. He zoomed in on Frida, centering on her forehead.

"I've got you now," he whispered. Then, replacing the monocle over his left eye with a black lens, he let his fingers do their long-awaited dance upon the buttons of his most esteemed creation.

A haze of hexed energy swirled around the black orb as the projected image displayed on its smooth surface remained locked onto Frida's forehead. An ominous hum vibrated throughout the Tower as the haze spun faster and faster at unperceivable speeds—around and around until at last, the orb itself disappeared into a glowing vortex. Its intensity only heightened, painting the Tower's whole interior with bright rays of energy twisting around the instrument. Lights flashed across Ons' reflective goggles, dousing him in colors. He counted the seconds under his breath, then yanked the cord he'd been anxiously waiting to pull. Instantly, the vortex was sucked into the black orb, now fully illuminated from the inside out as the harnessed energy spun, growing stronger by the second, increasing with each press of his finger. The supernatural hum throbbed in sync with rising levels of energy permeating the orb, filling the Tower with vitality.

"You won't be dancing much longer," Ons said, letting out a final breathless chuckle as he pulled a large lever in the Tower's control booth.

Though nothing apparent happened, Ons' twisted smile and childlike glee assured there was trouble brewing below the surface. Inflamed with malicious intent, he kept his hand tightly gripped around a lever and flicked a trigger at its base with his thumb, beginning the next phase. The concentrated energy inside the black orb shot both up into the air and down into the earth in a tall, black ray. It flew through the domed, glass roof of the Tower, piercing the Force Field as a second bolt darted into the floor through a symbol engraved into the stone. The thick black ray streamed from the orb, no sign of Ons' madness diminishing. He stared at his work with eyes ablaze, watching the projection of the traveling group still wandering into the basin.

"It is our time. Rise, my demon of death. Rise. Rise!" Ons' shouts cut off into another bout of wicked, panting laughter. The man could not have been more anxious to see the impending destruction wrought upon the enemies of the Dignitaries.

Percilla, Frida, and Matik danced into the basin at the edge of the desert. The ground was easy to traverse compared to the thick sands they'd traveled across the night before. It was still soft from the remnants of silt, left behind from days when this basin had once been filled with water. But there was not a drop of liquid to be seen here; it had dried up under the heat long ago. Stretching cracks ran along the ground, exposing the contents buried beneath. Trinkets and treasures once lost to the basin's waters were now laid bare in the blazing sun—gold coins, jewelry, broken apparatuses, and even eroded gemstones graced the earth, half buried inside the hardened ground. Percilla noticed a sunken boat lying splintered and cracked at the center of the basin—the same boat she had seen in her vision.

"We're getting closer," she told the others, her voice lifting with excitement. "After we cross this, we should find Rou."

"Then we'd best keep moving," Matik said. His sword hand rested on the pommel of his newly gifted sword; it seemed even Percilla's optimism was not enough to lower his wary defenses.

"Tin-za win-ke," Frida said, nodding toward her enchanted marching-band figurines. The musicians shrank back down to their original, hand-held sizes at Frida's feet. She knelt and carefully picked up each one, dusted the sand off their legs, and put them back into her bag one at a time. "Until next time, my little music-blasters," she said. When she'd returned the last one, she stopped.

Percilla slowed down to study her great aunt, seeing the beads of sweat already dripping from Frida's brow beneath the hot sun. The sorceress tilted her head toward the sky and shielded her eyes with a hand over her brow. Then she winced and looked back down at the ground, blinking quickly. "Everything all right?" Percilla asked. She'd never seen Frida look so physically uncomfortable.

"I... I think it's too hot..." Frida said. She met Percilla's gaze and waved the girl forward. "I'll be right with you."

Percilla caught up with Matik just as a loud, alarming thunk made her stop and spin around. Frida had dropped to her knees and was gazing down at the pale, dry skull of a buffalo half-buried in the ground and baking in the desert heat. "Too hot for you too?" the sorceress asked, smiling weakly down on the skull as she ran her hand along its horns. "My, you were a magnificent creature. You'd fit quite well in my collection." Percilla frowned at her great aunt, thinking something felt quite odd about Frida's responses. "I'll just..." Frida swayed, her eyes rolled to the back of her head, and she fainted there on the dry earth without a sound.

"Frida!" Percilla shouted, running toward her great aunt before she had time to think. As soon as she reached Frida, the ground beneath them rumbled with a violent, unnatural lurch. Percilla and Matik struggled to maintain their balance, and Percilla dropped to her knees, clutching at Frida's jacket and dress to keep her close. "Frida," she cried out again, praying her great aunt would hear her. "Wake up. Wake up!"

The rumbling only intensified, releasing loose trinkets from the basin's cracking rock. Then the land itself split in two, separating along an enormous fault line spanning the full length of the basin. To make matters worse, each half began to sink inch by inch, as if summoned by what lay at the depths below. Slipping through the cracks and out of the now massive crevice, swarming black clouds rose from the abyss, forcing the ground apart with its potent energy. With another mighty tremble, the two halves of the basin lurched apart, separating Matik on one side from Percilla and Frida on the other, the gap growing immensely wide between them.

"Percilla!" Matik shouted, reaching futilely toward her.

Percilla glanced up at him in terror and saw only determination on his face when he took a few steps back and paused. Then he sprinted toward the gap in the earth, picking up incredible speed with each long stride. The ground rumbled at his feet, tumbling into the abyss, and when he reached the edge, he leapt across the divide to vault over the breach and the destructive energies below.

He seemed to almost fly through the air, but as he passed the center of the crevice, a mountainous black snake reared up from the abyss to intercept him. Matik smacked against its face and flickering tongue, scrambling now to grip onto armored scales for dear life. Percilla let out a startled shriek at both the abruptness of Matik's leap cut short and the terrifying sight of the wicked beast. Its striking red eyes and black pupils darted to focus on Matik. A forked tongue flickered outward to taste the intruder, and the snake hissed furiously at the man clinging to its scales. It thrashed about, violently twisting and coiling with enough force to loosen even the mighty grip of Dawookrunk's star performer.

"Matik!" Percilla yelled, watching in horror as Matik was catapulted through the air toward the other side of the divided basin.

Skidding across the quaking incline of the fragmenting bedrock, Matik scrabbled to find a hold among the crumbling landscape. But each piece of jutting stone and root he grabbed only held him for a moment before it broke. Percilla screamed as the earth trembled once more and the stone Matik was hanging onto broke away from the earth. Again, he slid down toward the edge. Watching fearfully as the slope increased and her closest ally neared its edge, Percilla closed her eyes to wish for a miracle and ask the guardians of Rou for help. Placing her hand over the Eye of Rou hanging over her heart, she whispered, "Guardians of Rou, please help. Help Matik. Save him." When she opened her eyes, Matik had just managed to catch himself at the edge of the crevice by a thick, tightly dug root jutting from the crumbling edge of the cliff. His body dangled over the shadows below as he struggled to grab hold of anything else with his free hand.

"Matik!" Percilla cried. "Just hold on!"

Then the snake turned its attention toward her and Frida, slithering through the shadows after new prey.

The fragment of land on which Percilla huddled beside the unconscious Frida sank lower and lower still, and when the snake slithered onto it, the earth shuddered beneath its weight. The beast's massive body shifted side to side as it moved over the shaking ground, its low hisses echoing off the walls of the jutting cliffs surrounding them, as if it were taunting its prey with laughter. Percilla stared at the thing drawing ever nearer, shivering in fear as the serpent's maw gaped terrifyingly wide to reveal fangs far larger and sharper than any blade. The slimy ichor of the snake's venom dripped from its mouth, and it coiled back for one final, deadly strike. Percilla closed her eyes once again and placed her hand over the Eye of Rou, silently wishing for the guardians of Rou to help and knowing full well there was nothing else she could do at this point. Only her faith in Rou kept her strong; the guardians had been with her throughout this journey, and they surely wouldn't abandon her now.

Percilla felt a grim cold emitting from the snake's maw as it snapped open and darted toward her. She clenched the Eye of Rou and screamed, but then the thunder of toppling stone drowned out even her own voice. Peeking one eye open at a time, she saw the snake had reeled away from her, hissing in fury as it thrashed about, crashing its massive body into cliff-sides and shattering them under the sheer magnitude of its weight. Then Percilla noticed a long rope swinging in the air, one end connected to the arrow buried in the serpent's eye. And when she searched for the other end of the rope, she saw Matik swinging across the quaking gap toward the snake. He leapt onto the serpent's back and with nimble feet dashed up the scaly hide toward its head. The snake reared high into the air, darting its head back and forth in an attempt to reach the unwanted passenger. Matik had already drawn his sword, and with a curdling battle cry, he vaulted into the air, heaved the blade over his head, and swung it mightily down. The sun flashed against the honed steel, and the force of Matik's blow brought him to his knees atop the serpent's back, where his blade sliced cleanly through armored scales, flesh, and bone without fail.

The serpent's severed head dropped to the ground with a sickeningly wet thud, landing just behind Percilla and Frida in a cloud of dust. Green blood oozed from the end into a smoking puddle in the dirt. Matik leapt from the limp beast, flipped

through the air, and landed atop the snake's head, where he sheathed his sword again and bowed. What remained of the serpent's lifeless body slipped over the edge of the earth and into the abyss, disappearing into the shadowy ruins of the basin. The quaking ground stilled, the land ceased to sink into the pit of shadows, and the roar of chaos from below them subsided. All these were minor reliefs for Percilla compared to the fact that she could now focus on tending to her great aunt.

Percilla held onto Frida's unconscious body and broke into tears. The battle might have been won, but the Dignitaries' trap had still ensnared the most powerful of their group. "Frida," she sobbed. "Frida, please. I need you." When she received no answer, she turned to Matik and said, "She won't wake up. I don't know... I don't have her powers." Only once before had she felt this helpless, and that was when the Dignitaries came for Victoria. She'd thought now things would be different. What was the whole point of this journey if she still couldn't even save the people close to her? That thought brought the sadness and anger welling up inside.

Matik placed his hand on Percilla's shoulder and met her gaze. "You have the Eye of Rou." His voice held nothing but confidence. Percilla realized he was not making some simple guess to cheer her up; he truly believed she could save Frida.

"I don't know if it can do anything," she replied, calmer now as she lifted the Eye of Rou from around her neck and examined it for any clue as to how she might help her great aunt.

Tibs flew out of Percilla's hat and dipped in circles in front of her, buzzing and swerving. Then the bumblebee landed just between Frida's brows and stayed there, buzzing a few more times in short spurts. Percilla looked to the Eye of Rou once more and understood what Tibs meant for her to do. When she moved, the little bee flew back into her hat, and Percilla gently placed the Eye in the same place upon her great aunt's forehead. When the sacred gemstone touched Frida's skin, a blast of golden light shot from it, dazzling Percilla and Matik with its brilliant purity. In an instant, the blaze disappeared, and Frida's eyes flew open, followed by a long gasp. She gave herself a shake, then pushed herself up to sit beside Percilla and gazed around until she settled upon her grandniece.

"Hello, love," Frida said with a crooked smile.

Percilla gasped in both shock and joy. "You're all right." She had expected her voice to be weak after such an ordeal, but she sounded as jubilant as ever.

"Would you expect me any other way?" Frida's brows drew briefly together, then she hoisted herself up to her feet and dusted off her garments.

"No. But—"

"Now. Where were we?" Frida surveyed the now ruined landscape of the basin, looking surprisingly calm for how much of their surroundings had been destroyed. "Oh, right. You." Looking toward the edge of the cliff, she opened her bag. "Vien-no-ba." The buffalo skull lifted and swiftly flew into her bag. Closing it once more, she took a step forward, and her boot splashed thickly in the pool of green serpent's blood. A surprised little hum escaped her as she turned to find the severed head next. Raising her brow, she asked, "Did I miss something?"

"You could say that," Matik said with a chuckle.

"Well, I'm guessing it was entertaining, at the least," she replied. Frida peered closer at the venom still oozing from the dead serpent's fangs, then dug quickly in her bag for a jar and a delicate kerchief. Shielding herself from the stench with the silk hanky, she inspected the creature closer, leaning almost entirely inside the serpent's maw to do so. She placed the jar under the thing's fangs to collect a few drops of the venomous ichor. Dipping out from under the beast's jaws, she gazed in satisfaction at the neon-green liquid. "There, now. That may come in handy."

Percilla took a deep breath as she looked at the Eye of Rou in her palm; after what it had done for Frida, the gem's glowing essence had faded almost entirely. All that remained of the shimmering lights within the sky-blue gemstone was a faint glimmer, just enough to last until they could make it to Rou. "I can't believe I was still so unprepared."

"At least we're alive," Matik reassured her, placing his hand on her back. "And I could not have done for Frida what you did."

"Alive?" Frida whirled around to regard them both with wide eyes. "What happened?"

"That's a long story," Percilla replied. "Perhaps another time. All I will say is I have a feeling the Dignitaries were behind this attack too. And if they were, they must be flown out of their minds to summon these kinds of evils on us." She met Frida's gaze and frowned. "I think they came after you, too, Frida, and that's why you wouldn't wake. We need to get out of here before they can try anything else. Anyone have a suggestion for getting us up there?" She pointed to the mainland around the shattered basin, which remained about six feet above their heads now.

"Yep," Matik said. He swiftly and skillfully climbed his way up the jutting rise beside them, then reached back down to pull up first Percilla and then Frida.

"Thanks," Percilla said, finding her optimism much improved now that she was a better distance from the serpent's head. "We need to step a little livelier, I think."

"I've got just the thing!" Frida reached into her bag, plunged in a little deeper, and produced three glass vials of a dark, sparkling liquid. Percilla stared at what looked more like the night sky filled with blinking stars than any concoction. Frida carefully doled out the vials and said, "Drink up. We'll be in Rou in no time."

Together, the trio gulped down the mystery concoction. Percilla tasted sweet fruits of every kind, finely distilled and concentrated. The moment the liquid touched her tongue, she felt better than she ever had in her life—fully rejuvenated, her spirits at their peak of hope and confidence after such an infusion of flavor and energy packed into the tiny vial.

Matik let out a whoop and grinned. "What was *that?*"

"A little something special," Frida remarked with a coy smile. "Picked it off a mad alchemist who needed some shoes. But that's a story for another day."

"We have enough time while we walk," Percilla replied, eager to hear of something other than evils and Dignitaries and the journey still ahead of them.

Frida cleared her throat, and the trio turned together to continue their travels across the Barrens. "I was speaking with a witch who needed a cloak made," Frida began. "Then this barefooted man comes running into Fridanda, claiming to hear snake voices—"

"Hold on," Matik shouted, his eyes alight as he pointed at the desert horizon. "Do you two see that?"

The women stopped to study the distant horizon, and Percilla squinted, making out only a wavering outline of tall structures through the fuming haze of heat and the sun's glare. But then she realized she was actually looking at a city—a real city, finally within their reach.

Frida chuckled. "Well, I'll be."

"Is that Rou?" Matik asked, his mouth hanging open.

"I think it is," Percilla exclaimed, almost unable to believe they were this close. And to think, they'd almost been stopped by the Dignitaries again. She was more than ready to step through Rou's gates and be done with the lot of them.

Frida plunged a hand into her bag again and whipped out a flying carpet large enough for all three of them, its finely woven patterns brightening in the sun. "Care for a ride?" she asked.

"Of course," Percilla answered, then turned to shoot her great aunt a disbelieving glance. "Why didn't you pull this out before?"

"Still working out the kinks," Frida replied with a casual wave. Each of their party stepped carefully onto the floating carpet, and when they'd all taken their seats, Frida grinned. "Hold onto your hat!"

At her words, the carpet surprised them all and flipped upside down. Even more surprising was the fact that all of them remained seated upon it. Percilla clamped her hat down over her head as the flying carpet rose into the sky over the ruined basin and set off toward the distant city.

Atop the Sky Way, Shru held a spyglass to his eye and diligently watched the journeying trio. The trickster sat alone, his goggles strapped tightly to his face. Smiling, he returned his spyglass to his inner coat pocket and raised his hands. "Allow me ta give yas a welcoming committee," he muttered, and his fingers glowed with his readying magic.

Beside him, a white cloud puffed open to reveal a raven, which headed right for him with incredible speed. The bird grabbed the shoulders of Shru's jacket in its talons before he could complete his spell, then lifted him from the Sky Way and flew off with its catch.

"What's goin' on?" Shru asked, craning his neck up toward the raven's head. "I was just about to get the Eye of Rou!"

CHAPTER 26

Looks Can Be Deceiving

PERCILLA, FRIDA, AND Matik hid behind a lone spire of desert rock and gazed at the bent, broken gate of black metal. The jagged portcullis boasted thick bars barely held together around deep claw marks. The ground was unnaturally pale—a skeletal white plateau of shriveled, dying earth. Rattlesnakes slithered from underneath the gate, flicking their tongues and rattling harshly before slinking for cover again beneath nearby rocks. Atop the black gate, a one-eyed, molting vulture perched atop a row of sharp spikes beside a stone gargoyle with fierce eyes and saw-like teeth. On either side of the gate, tall walls of black stone rose from the earth, cloaked in a thick gray mist. Beyond those walls, the shrieks and roars of unseen beasts echoed within a city hidden from view.

"What is this place?" Matik swallowed thickly.

"This is the demon city of Viln," Frida replied with an uncharacteristic frown. "I've only ever heard of it in stories."

"What happened to it?" Matik asked, shaking his head.

"Here, there is only darkness. It is a gathering of all manner of evils."

"This can't be Rou," Percilla almost whispered, clinging to a thin strand of hope. "But the path ends here."

"If the Eye of Rou has led us to this place, Rou *must* lie within," Frida replied. "What does it look like when you open the Eye?" Frida's usual calm had not left her voice, but a tinge of fear lingered in it still.

"A skeleton tree," Percilla said.

"Why don't you open the Eye?" Matik asked, gazing down at the gem in the girl's hand.

"It's not safe here. And the Eye doesn't have enough energy. I don't want to use it until I'm certain we've found Rou."

Frida took a deep breath. "We'll just have to search it out." She dug through her bag and pulled out three long black robes with hoods, then handed two of them to Percilla and Matik. "When we step through those gates, we must not alert the denizens of Viln to our presence. If they discover us before we can find Rou, we will be truly lost."

Percilla and Matik nodded and donned their cloaks, concealing themselves entirely beneath the shadowy hoods and the thick black threads.

 "Stay close to me," Percilla said. She looked up to the sky one last time, searching for the golden star of Rou. A toxic haze churned over the city and all but hid the sun from view. Even still, a faint glimmer shone through the shroud of

darkness—a single star far overhead, visible even during the day. With that, Percilla knew their quest was finally close to its end, and she led the way through the black gates into the city.

From the moment the three stepped foot inside Viln, a wave of nauseous, inhuman stenches assaulted them, rising with the unhampered cries of beastly terrors echoing from every direction. The ground beneath their feet was damp and slick with unknown substances varying in shades of green, red, and black. All of it combined to form an oily ichor that coated everything it touched, including the soles of their shoes. Everywhere, ghastly, demonic beings prowled the streets, looking for life to feed upon, moving between disheveled shacks of splintered iron and burnt wood. Monstrous beasts with curved horns and thick hooves thundered through buildings, setting them ablaze with breaths of fire and casting the lesser creatures out into the streets while they hunted their prey. Only maddened humans openly walked the streets of Viln, twisted and lost with no reason left in their minds, some of whom were as wicked as the monsters in whose company they existed. In the most dangerous parts, demons wandered aimlessly, their only intent to steal the souls of the living and bind them to such a wretched place as this.

Centering herself, Percilla steeled her mind for this final, desperate push to the end of her journey. If she could brave the terrors of Viln, she could find Rou and free all the people she loved from the Dignitaries' villainous grasp. "You've come this far," she reminded herself in a barely audible whisper. "No sense in turning back now." She led them through the streets, keeping them as far away from the wicked beasts as she could. Only a vague sense of direction drove her, but Percilla knew the golden star and the Eye of Rou would surely guide their path.

Matik stood directly at Percilla's side, always with one hand on the hilt of his sword. Whenever they passed one of the depraved city's monstrosities, he pulled the edge of his hood farther around his face, but he did not once look away from any of these potential enemies.

On one street corner, a pack of feral dogs with bloodshot eyes and foaming mouths turned on one another, scrabbling on the slick ground and snapping their jaws in rabid hunger. Along another side street, neon-orange parasites oozed out of the living beings upon whom they fed as their hosts lumbered through Viln, seemingly unperturbed. Just ahead, massive, demonic figures with leathery wings and piercing horns fought among themselves, tearing at each other with claws and gnashing teeth. And everywhere, hordes of huge black scorpions crawled along the walls and over the ground.

Percilla felt her spirit strangled more and more with every step deeper into the bowels of Viln. Of all the dark and rotten places in the world, this was surely the worst of them. She wanted desperately to turn back, to leave Viln forever and never return. To take even just one step back would have been a blessing, but she pressed on. Though she was sure her companions felt very much the same, they followed her through it all.

Just when she felt her courage wavering, a rise of spectral light moved in her periphery, and Percilla turned her head just barely to look at it. What she found there was not of Viln but from a time before Percilla's journey had even begun. There, across the street, stood the spirit of Bianca, her great-grandmother. She looked upon Percilla with knowing eyes, locking gazes with her for only a moment before disappearing down the next street.

"Follow *her*," Percilla announced, rushing off in the ghost's direction.

"What? Who?" Frida asked, but she and Matik took off after the girl just the same.

Bianca's spirit moved rapidly through Viln's streets, leading them into the depths of the demon city. Each avenue grew darker and more violent than the last, but Percilla would not stop—not now that they were close to their goal. At last, Bianca led them into a large courtyard in the center of Viln hosting a circular gathering of the darkest creatures inhabiting the city. And then, just as the trio stepped foot into the courtyard, Bianca disappeared.

"No," Percilla whispered. "Where did she go?"

"This is bad," Matik whispered in reply, tugging at Percilla's cloak to bring her back to his side. "We must find another way."

A horrifying shriek rose from the shadows of the tall buildings behind them, and a clawed hand lunged forward to catch Matik in its grasp. Percilla whirled around to stare at the thing, half man and half bull with long horns and wickedly sharp teeth. Its clawed hands gripped Matik with an inhuman strength as it towered over the trio on two legs. The beast reared toward Matik and opened its mouth, sucking a hazy glow from its prey with each breath. Matik groaned and struggled within the demon's grasp, but the forces being drained away from his body left him weaker and more haggard-looking with every passing second.

Frida dug through her bag and removed an ornate golden jar with jewels affixed to its surface. She removed the lid and aimed the container at the demon, which nearly exploded into billions of black particles before filtering in an instant into the open mouth of Frida's enchanted vessel. With the jar sealed once more, Frida tucked it away again, and Matik's body crumpled to the slick, noxious ground.

Percilla fell to her knees and fortunately managed to cushion his fall when his head landed in her lap and not the stone of the courtyard. Matik's chest rose and fell just barely with shallow breath, but he was still alive.

All the commotion, though, had caught the attention of every other wicked being in the courtyard. Each demonic beast paused and turned toward the trio to see them now for what they were—fresh meat. The gathering of monstrosities closed in on them with all manner of foul limbs, crawling, slithering, stomping on two feet to make the ground tremble beneath them. Slavering maws hungered for human morsels, claws and teeth snapped and clicked with delight, and evil flowed into the courtyard from the darkest places of Viln.

Surrounded, they had no choice but to stand their ground and fight. Frida retrieved a small vial of purple liquid from her bag and hastily poured it into Matik's open mouth. He jerked awake with a violent cough and a wide-eyed, bewildered stare. "What did you do?" he asked.

"No time," Frida replied. "Ready your sword."

Only then did Matik notice the horrors closing in on them. Percilla held the Eye of Rou from its chain around her neck, ready to use it if she absolutely had to and willing to protect it with her life, if it came to that. Frida dug through her bag once more as Matik snapped back into action. He leapt to his feet and drew his sword as the trio pressed their backs together, readying for the next fight.

An earth-shattering growl erupted from deep within the city, followed quickly by the clamor of beastly footsteps rushing toward the courtyard. From every entrance to Viln's center, a legion of soldiers, part dragon and part human form, charged through the gathered beasts with lances and swords to surround the travelers. They boasted glistening, scaled skin of all colors, long tails ending in frills, and elevated brows jutting up into crowns of horns and plated bone. Their heavy armor bore the symbol of Rou on breastplates of silver, and each wielded a sword like Matik's. The dragons formed a protective circle around the trio, creating a thick line of defense against Viln's encroaching hordes.

At first, Percilla thought herself and her companions doomed, but when she recognized the symbol of Rou and the craftsmanship of the swords, she quickly realized the creatures had come to their aid. From within the defensive circle, the trio had to do very little but stand and watch the throng of demons assault the dragon line. Viln's worst creatures swung their heavy arms like clubs and breathed fire, but the dragons' armor and scaled skin served as more than enough protection. Swings that would crush a mortal man's bones merely glanced off Rou's defenders. And in retaliation, the dragons' blades fell upon the demons with a righteous fury, decimating the demonic ranks. But with each felled demon, it seemed the chaos of dark energy only attracted two more rushing into the fray to take up arms. The beasts of Viln surged in endless numbers, and although the dragon line held, they could do no more than that.

Frida produced a golden wand with a large, crystalline tip. "Ula-tama." Her spell sparked a radiant light on the wand's tip. "Lead the way, Percilla," she said with grave urgency.

"I..." Percilla remained completely unsure of herself in the midst of such carnage. Then Tibs took off from her hat and flew past the demonic horde, straight into the innermost depths of Viln. "That way!"

Frida aimed her wand in the very same direction, and the dragon line opened in response, clearing a path for the trio within their defensive formation. Taking their one and only chance, Percilla led her companions through it as quickly as she could. It was not fast enough to escape the lurking demons who launched themselves from rooftops and over the dragon legions to infiltrate the protective circle. One horror landed directly in front of Percilla, who froze as the tall beast loomed over her, its great shadow stretching over all three of the travelers. Matik flung himself in front of Percilla and cleaved the demon in two with one swift slash of his blade, roaring in triumph when his enemy fell. The dragons made quick work of other invading demons, keeping the path clear for Percilla to travel onward.

Frida forced her wand into Percilla's hand and clasped the girl's fingers over it, staring into her grandniece's eyes with pure conviction. "Keep going."

"What about you?" Percilla asked as Frida turned away from her to dig around her bag.

"Do not worry about me. Lady Frida knows how to handle herself in a fight." With those words, she produced her three musician figurines and set them on the ground. "Makrat-burato shay!"

The marching band burst to life, growing to their full size to play a delightful tune. From their instruments flowed a color-ful smoke, which drifted throughout the courtyard battlefield, silently working its way into the deepest ranks of the enemy. As the demons fought ravenously with piercing shrieks and fierce snarls, the smoke slipped into their mouths, noses, and ears. Their beastly forms stilled, twitched, then lurched into awkward, jerking steps infecting their movement. Within seconds, every demon the smoke had touched burst into dance, flinging their legs into the air and spinning around like fools who had lost all reason. Even as their brethren continued the bloody battle, the dancing demons careened into their allies, smacking them and throwing others aside with passionate motions fueled by Frida's music.

Percilla ran after Tibs, staying close to the bee with a retinue of dragons at her back and Frida's wand clutched tightly in her hand. They passed into the very center of the courtyard and Viln itself, where there stood the golden skeleton of a cherry tree. The sweet scent of its fruit's nectar still hung in the air, over-powering the filth of Viln's stench. Percilla could hardly believe her eyes; it was exactly as she had seen it in her vision of the portal. She was so close now, finally at the very end of her long journey. All that was left to do was use the Eye and open the Golden Gates to Rou. The dragons following her formed another protective circle around the girl, the screams and bestial roars of the battle in the courtyard filling the air around her.

"This is it," she said in a breathless whisper, then took a deep breath and prepared herself for what was to come next.

She tucked Frida's wand away, then clutched the Eye of Rou and tore the chain from around her neck. When she opened her hand, she let the last bit of the Eye's essence flow freely into the aura of the skeleton tree. A bright golden light shimmered within the husk of golden bark as Percilla opened her palms to the sky. With all the strength she could muster in her voice, she recited the words that would open the Golden Gate. "Al-bista trun-ona dimos-ka!"

CHAPTER 27

No Home for Evils

WHEN PERCILLA OPENED her eyes, she found herself in the portal dimension once more. The sacred, geometric shapes and surging energy flowed through everything and surrounded her. The kaleidoscopic tunnel stretched forward to the skeleton tree—the final landmark on her path. As the shapes turned, the tree transformed as well, becoming moment by moment something gleaming and radiant.

The beaming golden trunk grew, its branches extending until they touched the ground, and for a moment, the brightness enveloped Percilla's vision and blinded her from the rest of the change. When the light faded, she found herself standing before not a tree but the Golden Gates of Rou themselves. And a glowing hole shaped as the Eye of Rou beckoned her to those gates like a lock ready to be opened.

Percilla stared at the sight, amazed by the grandness and power of the gates keeping the purity of Rou safe amid the evils of Viln. She felt more than privileged to have been a part of it, to have lived up to her family's duty. Now she only had to open the way back to Rou. With a long step forward, she approached the gate, reaching toward it. Then a cold chill ran down her spine, and the presence of something entirely alien to this dimension entered the closed space. She spun around, only to find herself facing Vahn.

"Percilla." Vahn nearly laughed, his smile bursting wide. "You made it!"

He looked and sounded exactly as she remembered him, but something about this was wrong—terribly wrong. "Vahn, what are you doing here?"

"I told you I would help you find Rou," he said, stepping closer with the same glistening grin.

Percilla wanted to believe he was truly here, but a flutter in her chest told her not to rush toward him. The certainty that Vahn was not really Vahn could not be ignored; she just didn't know why. "How?" she asked. "How did you get here?"

"Give me the Eye. I can show you..." He studied her face, then paused when he saw her step away from him. "Why are you looking at me like that?"

Percilla had to be certain it was him. Gathering her courage, she stepped toward him again and held his gaze, which seemed to surprise him. She remembered the one trick Symon had taught her in Dawookrunk. A flash of light sparked from Percilla's eyes to Vahn's, connecting them in the Look Beyond.

"Are you the real Vahn Blunderworth from Gangleton?" she asked, fearing the answer she sensed was coming but having to ask regardless.

"Of course I am," Vahn said, his smile never wavering, even as his words twisted in on themselves.

Percilla felt it—the truth warped, the connection lost. The flash of light between them flickered out of existence. "You're lying."

Vahn's smile pinched into a grim, unnatural frown. Then his body dropped to the ground, flailing and jerking in unnatural ways; it bent and twisted, muscles clenched at crude, sickening angles. Then the head that looked like Vahn's lifted and glared at Percilla with black eyes. When the mouth dropped open, a pitch-black fog flew from the lifeless body and barreled toward her. As a dark wind howling with life, the shadows surrounded the girl, and there was no one to protect her. Percilla turned and sprinted for the gates as fast as she could, still clutching the Eye of Rou.

Even as the evil energies permeated the dimension, the gate remained standing, and the bright light emanating from the hole at its base pushed away the darkness. Percilla leapt toward it and pressed the Eye of Rou into the glowing keyhole. At once, the howling of the shadows behind her ceased entirely, as if time in this portal dimension had frozen. And then ... *nothing*.

Percilla blinked, standing in front of the skeleton tree just as it was before she'd opened the Eye of Rou. The clamor of battle raged on in the courtyard, but the magnitude of darkness that had loosed itself from Vahn's body charged through Viln. The winds barreled through the city streets, sending wave after frigid wave of ice-cold air over Percilla.

She caught sight of Frida and Matik running toward her. Thunder clapped overhead, the winds surged, and massive funnels descended from the sky, sending tornados raging around the city. A streak of lightning crackled overhead, and the filthy veil hanging over Viln darkened with ill omens.

"That gate is supposed to open," Percilla yelled over the blaring winds. "I don't know what to do." She dropped to her knees in front of the tree, gazing at the Eye of Rou nestled in its trunk and praying that by some miracle the Gates would open. But in her fear, she'd forgotten what rested upon her head. Another icy gust struck her, stealing her hat and whipping it away in the storm. Her ravens, now exposed to the wind and open sky, lifted their wings on the powerful breeze and took flight with desperate force. They lifted Percilla into the air, the discord of their cawing joining the shriek of the strengthening storm, as if they too meant to keep her from the Gates of Rou.

"Percilla!" Matik shouted over the winds. With his sword in hand, he leapt toward her and brought his blade cleanly through Percilla's long black hair, severing the connection between her and the Dignitaries' ravens forever.

Percilla fell to the ground as her ravens flew into the dark clouds hanging over Viln, vanishing inside the black. Matik spun to catch her in the air and landed on his feet, and when he smiled at her, she blinked quickly and smiled back. The star performer let her safely to the ground, and they returned their attention to the skeleton tree. A bright light burst from its center, and its many rays illuminated the despairing streets of Viln. Frida let out a whoop of joy as the tree shone with an overwhelming brightness before becoming once more the Golden Gates of Rou.

Without preamble, the gates swung open to release a full beam of overpowering, compassionate light, bursting through Viln, past its crumbling black gates, and out into the wasteland of the Barrens. Everything the light touched was cleansed by Rou's very essence. Viln's demons shuddered and dissipated into darkness. The murky veil above the city dispersed, revealing a clear blue sky and the mighty light of the sun.

The Golden Gates' light poured out endlessly, nearly blinding the group as they joined together, hand in hand. At last, their journey was over. The trio ran through the Gates of Rou, letting their golden light wash over their bright, smiling faces.

CHAPTER 28

Timeless Allegiance

T HEY STOOD TOGETHER on a tiny floating island in the sky, covered in lush green grass and tall, fully grown Bodhi trees reaching toward the horizon. All around them, hundreds of other floating islands drifted blissfully through the air, forming the picturesque landscape of mystical wonder. The sun beamed its brilliant afternoon light as it peaked above the field of clouds before them. The air was warm and pleasant, filled with the scents of fresh flowers and sweet cherries on the breeze.

A distant roar grew louder from above, and they looked up to see a golden dragon soar across the sky. Percilla's heart filled with warmth at the sight of this majestic being—the one who had protected her through the darkest times, now here in front of her. As the clouds parted over the valley below them, she now gazed down upon countless waterfalls cascading into a jungle utopia, where rivers stretched across the land for miles, spreading life with their glistening waters.

A single tear of joy fell from Frida's eyes as she gazed upon her people's homeland for the first time, taking in the sights and sounds as though they were the nectar of deities themselves. Percilla and Matik stood beside her as if spellbound. Everything the elders had written and told was true. Every word from Victoria's mouth was of perfect accuracy. Compared to this glory of nature and harmony, The Gold was truly just a pale imitation of the original utopia. Just as Victoria had promised her she would, Percilla had finally found Rou. Her family's sworn duty had been upheld, and at last, it was time to complete her quest and save her loved ones with the aid of Rou's guardians. Percilla's breath joined with the wind as she let out a long sigh of relief. Having done what she could never have imagined doing, she could finally relax and bask in the beauty around her.

A bright streak flashed toward them beneath the sun, quickly approaching the trio. Soon enough, Percilla found herself staring at a golden chariot flying through the sky, led by a beautiful black stallion with a fine coat shimmering in the light. The stallion neighed as the chariot approached, stopping at the edge of the floating island. Even more stunning up close, the black stallion lifted its head, studying them with deep, glimmering eyes as its smooth mane fluttered about its neck. The chariot was just as impressive; shields of glimmering metals hung from the finely carved wooden base, and the door engraved with the symbol of Rou opened, beckoning the trio inside. Admiring such a brilliant presentation, the travelers stepped into the chariot and sat together for a ride through the skies.

The stallion galloped over the valley below. Percilla marveled at the vibrant green canopies of the jungle and the exotic, colorful plants growing within. Trees and flowers of every variety bloomed between the spacious rivers of the valley, growing taller than any of these wary travelers had ever seen. Animals that couldn't survive in the Barrens thrived in Rou, feeding themselves from the bounty of pure nature. And in the skies, birds as colorful as the landscape fluttered among the faeries, whose wings sparkled with lunar resin decorating the sky. The stallion soared through long rainbows in the mists of the valley's waterfalls, refreshing and rejuvenating its passengers with the cool spray of Rou's pure waters. Everything here was the pinnacle of life itself—perfection filling their hearts with song and inspiring them to spread its paradise to all who would share it with them.

Eventually, they came to a temple of gold set on a levitating island. From every edge of this island, water poured down into the valley, sending sprays of mist surrounding the temple walls. Pillars of rune-inscribed history supported a smooth pyramid from which the purest golden lights shimmered. From within the temple rose a pleasant hum, filling Percilla with calm and belonging. She felt the aura emanating from the temple—the very essence of Rou itself.

Waiting for them at the temple's vine-covered entryway was a woman with enchanting purple eyes and long, braided white hair. She wore a full-length, pastel-aqua gown of silk, a delicate golden chain hanging from her neck, and a gemstone

headpiece. She smiled at Percilla and her companions as they arrived, nodding in approval when their eyes met.

"Who is that?" Percilla asked Frida as the stallion leading their chariot came to a stop at the temple's entrance.

"That is Valti," Frida replied with a respectful whisper. "She is one of the Timeless and Speaker for the Sages. Be on your best."

"What's a Timeless?" Percilla whispered, and the trio stepped from the chariot and onto the temple's island.

"Shh," Frida replied. "You shall learn soon enough. Come."

Percilla and Matik followed Frida toward the woman and found themselves entering a large, arched doorway. Inside the temple, the Council of Rou sat cross-legged on golden seats crafted in the shape of lotus flowers and decorated with jewels, each of these floating in a pool of crystal-clear water. True lotus flowers and lily pads dotted the water's surface. Vines and ivy draped over walls of shimmering gold, a combination of the beauty of creation and nature together as one.

Three other Sages awaited the travelers' arrival, all of whom wore golden gemstone headpieces. On the left sat a man with long white hair tied back by a length of gold twine. His aqua eyes were beautifully accented by his white and gray silk gown sparkling like starlight. Another captivating woman sat in the center, wearing a pastel-purple gown of silk, which hung like flowing water over her figure. Her eyes were aqua as well, her long white hair braided into the draping golden headpiece. The man on the left also had long white hair, swept back, and his purple eyes looked kindly upon the group. He wore a pure-white gown and a golden chain around his neck like Valti's.

"Reenz, Phadela, and Casmir," Frida whispered to Percilla, her voice barely audible in the pristine silence of the temple.

"Greetings," Valti said, her voice filled with an ancient wisdom. "And welcome home. Please, sit." She ushered the travelers into the temple and guided them to their lotus-flower seats in the pond, whereupon they all sat. Percilla found her own seat exceedingly comfortable, like a bed of warm water beneath her. "We understand why you have come, but there is not much we can do to aid you at this time. Too many have fallen slaves to evil." Although it clearly pained her to admit this truth, Valti spoke it plainly, as there was nothing in the world of greater importance.

"Communities once filled with compassion are now under the rule of such darkness," Phadela said.

Casmir nodded. "People have lost faith in their power to lead with love and so live in fear."

"The seven Eyes must return to Rou before aid can be offered," Valti finished.

Percilla was struck silent for a long moment by the Timeless Sages' words. She had believed only moments ago that her journey had come to an end. How could it be that not even the people of Rou could help her free Gangleton without all seven Eyes returned? She knew not what to say. She wanted to be outraged, but in such a perfect place, the emotion seemed impossible. When she looked to her two companions for guidance, she saw the same sentiments reflected on their faces, clear as day. None of them could have imagined that their journey would only lead them to the beginning of yet another quest—a quest that might very well be even more difficult than the last. But beyond that, Percilla also saw in them the unwavering bonds she shared with Matik and Frida, and they with each other, as well as the bravery they each held within themselves. She still did not know what to say, but in her heart, she knew what she must do.

"How will we find the Eyes?" she asked Valti.

The woman smiled and bowed to Percilla. "Have faith and lead with love."

Fairy Play

INSIDE THE GOLD, Shru paddled an old, worn-out canoe down a clear blue stream flowing through the imitated valley of lush ferns and vibrant flowers. Extraordinary fish of bright, exotic colors swam past Shru's paddles in small, tightly knit schools, heading upstream toward a short waterfall. Shru scoffed at it all, uninterested in anything he could not steal or use to steal something else. He kept on paddling.

"Savin' me," he mumbled, then barked out a laugh. "I never needed savin'."

A little faerie with bright blue wings and glowing eyes flew right in front of Shru's face, poking its head right up against his nose to fix him in its unwavering stare. Shru stopped paddling to get a better look at the tiny creature. As he locked eyes with the faerie, he felt himself softening, pulled into a gaze from which he could not turn away.

"Well, hello there, sweets," he said, blissfully unaware now of everything but the tiny creature; he did not have enough time to realize the creature now performed the same trick he himself was quite fond of using to take advantage of the lesser-minded.

"I need you to help my friend." The faerie spoke with a seriousness rather uncharacteristic of faeries.

"You got it, cupcake," Shru answered without as much as a second thought. "Where?"

The creature pointed to a young elephant standing beside a tree that had fallen across the river, desperately trying to lift it out of the water with its trunk. But the little elephant wasn't nearly strong enough, and it kept dropping the tree with a heavy splash.

"On it." Shru gave the faerie a quick wink.

He paddled toward the elephant, coming close enough to the shoreline to reach out and touch the fallen tree, trying to help prop it up against the riverbank. But as he leaned in to help, the young elephant's trunk spun around and shot a spray of water directly at him, completely drenching Shru from head to toe. The thief spat water out of his mouth as the elephant trumpeted and stomped in the river, splashing triumphantly. Three more little elephants emerged from the jungle before they too sprayed another watery attack at Shru, who now sat in a canoe sloshing with river water, which still trickled from his clothes and ran in rivulets down his face.

The little faerie whizzed in front of him yet again, locking an even more intense gaze upon the thief. "Remember your innocence," the faerie said without a hint of malice.

"Yes..." Shru replied, his eyes growing wide, and stepped out of the canoe. As if it were the most important and completely natural thing in the world, the man whooped and splashed in the stream beside the elephants with childlike enthusiasm, who in return doused him with more water.

The faerie left Shru with his new friends and took flight into the air, where it landed on one of The Gold's floating islands, away from prying eyes. As its feet touched the ground, the creature shimmered and grew, wings disappearing while clothes and every other physical feature transformed into someone else entirely. A man now stood alone on the floating island, looking out over the replicated valley of Rou and down at his unwitting student. Symon had a new plan.

Kaiva Rose is a Writer, Astrologer, Intuitive, Reiki Master, and Instructor. Her passion for writing fantasy began as a means to create eccentric characters, though it quickly turned into a means to mirror society in an alternate reality. Inspired by writers of antiquity, Kaiva creates pieces of writing which are meant to stand the test of time.

Join the "Rou Odyssey" Community!

Connect with us, write us a letter, check out the Rou Odyssey website!

We would love to hear from you!

www.RouOdyssey.com

Follow us on social media for the latest updates and offers!

Blessings and special thanks to these Magical people of the Rou Odyssey Community!

Chelsey Jameson
Laura Flynn
Hillary Preston
Rick Rea
Jamie Hartje
Lynette B.
Nicholas Harper
Kate McCanna
Cindy Mills
Carrie Markel
Annabelle Haeems
Anna Hanlon
Charlie Tétreault
Sarah Nather Jacobs
Pat Scanlon
Michelle Francis Vasicek
Julie Bladow-Anderson

And to all my lovely family and friends.

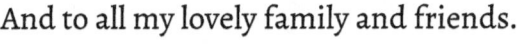

To Pluto & Back

Bridget L. Rose